APPOINTMENT

AT

AMEN CORNER

Appointment

at

Amen Corner

A Drew James Novel

By

Jay Macklin

JADE Press
Alexandria, Virginia

Copyright © 2016 by Jay Macklin

ISBN 978-0-9978177-0-6

Printed in the United States of America
by JADE Press

For my bride Anya, the love of my life
and my best friend.

Golf is not a life or death situation.

> Chi Chi Rodriguez
> PGA Professional

Correct me if I'm wrong Sandy, but if I kill all the golfers, they're gonna lock me up and throw away the key.

> Carl Spackler, *Caddyshack*

Anything can happen at Augusta, especially at Amen Corner.

> Lee Westwood
> PGA Professional

Prologue
BEIRUT, LEBANON – 1968

Glittering and shimmering like so many thousands of perfectly cut diamonds, the sea reflected the dazzle of the warm summer sun. Palm fronds clattered, stirred by fresh breezes blowing off the Mediterranean. It was a perfect day. The hot sand warmed his body, lulling him into a state of semi-consciousness. Idly he grasped a handful in his closed fist and let the granules slowly pour out, watching as the wind whisked them away like a shower of tan raindrops.

It had been a good day. Finally giving in to his mother's persistent urgings, his father had taken a break from the never-ending stream of business meetings and conferences and taken the three of them to the beach. On their first family outing since arriving in this strange land a month ago, he had gained some solace from the comfortable familiarity of a sandy beach and gently lapping waves. He reflected with a sense of teenage pride and a touch of homesickness that this beach wasn't nearly as white or clean or pretty as the one back home. The water wasn't as clear either. The picnic lunch his mother had packed had been another treat, filled with his favorite snacks and drinks from the Embassy commissary. His stomach full from the lunch and his body tired from swimming in the water, he had collapsed on the warm sand, dozing in the afternoon heat.

His father called his name, interrupting his momentary reverie with the unwelcome announcement that it was time to pack up and head back to the apartment. He watched his father through slitted eyelids, drowsy from the warmth of the sun and the soothing

1

sound of the waves. He saw him rise from his beach chair, turn towards the man waiting by the car, and yell something in the garbled language he still could not understand. Nodding, the driver in the black suit and cap started towards him and his parents to help with the packing.

With a suddenness that sucked the air from his lungs and drained the blood from his face, the air around him exploded. The shock of sound and pounding concussion of noise pressed him into the sand, immobilizing him and stunning him with its fury. As if pressed down by a giant unseen hand, he remained stretched on the sand, taking note of the horror before him like a pedestrian casually viewing a storefront television set but unable to change the channel. As if in a trance, he watched his father grab his mother's hand and run for the street and the seductive safety of the buildings and storefronts.

The blast of noise rose as small explosions blew holes in the walls of the buildings nearest the car. Turning his head slightly upwards towards the source of the noise, he saw a jet aircraft streak over him, puffs of fire and smoke appearing rhythmically from the guns on the underside of its wings. Other jets followed behind it. His mind flashed in recognition - they were Israeli fighter planes. At the same instant, the building and sidewalk to his front erupted in a searing flash of heat, thunderous noise, and flying chunks of concrete.

The concussive force of the blast lifted his body slightly then slammed him back into the sand, expelling his breath in a rush. Still unable to move or breathe, he looked in shock as the spot where his parents had been seconds before now appeared as a jagged crater of broken concrete, bent and twisted steel bars, and lumps of melted asphalt. Numbed from the physical assault on his body and senses, his mind recoiled into blackness as the lifeless bloodied body of his mother landed and rolled next to him.

Chapter 1
The Present

I gripped the shaft of my nine-iron firmly but not too tightly, as my golf instructor told me, and stood over the ball. I saw the flag waving gently in the distance, just beyond a small pond. About 130 yards, I guessed. "Visualize your shot," I heard his voice telling me. "Imagine each segment of your swing coming together and culminating in a perfect shot." So, trusting him, I closed my eyes and pictured the takeaway, started by the left shoulder, moving in an arc up and back. I saw my wrists cocked, pausing at the top of the swing and then, with a smooth arm swing and body turn, bringing the club head down, focusing on keeping the toe of the club angled towards the ground. I could feel the club head coming smoothly down and through, and then could hear that glorious sound of impact. I pictured the turn of the hips toward the target, and the smooth flight of the ball, high and arching - white ball spinning effortlessly in a brilliant blue sky over sparkling water. Then, with a satisfying "whop," I could see the ball hitting the green ten feet beyond the flag and back-spinning slowly to a stop pin high and three feet from the cup.

"I got this," I muttered. "I've visualized this shot a thousand times." So I began my address, waggled the club head, took a deep breath, let it out, left shoulder started the swing, hips turned, left knee pointed, a pause but no stop at the top, and down and through the waiting white target. But with an ugly clunking sound, the edge of the iron hit fat. As my hips carried through pointing to the green, I looked up just in time to see my ball take off in a flat curving line-drive slice towards the right edge of the pond, skip once off the surface, and take off into the trees, shearing a low hanging branch as it disappeared into oblivion.

Instantly my thoughts turned to my golf instructor and, with a warped sense of pleasure, I visualized him with a nine-iron wrapped around his skinny little neck, arms flailing through that lovely blue sky as I threw him high and arching into the center of the pond. With that sense of mental satisfaction floating through my head, I shoved the iron back into the bag and, turning towards the clubhouse, strolled slowly up the fairway.

It was one of those incredible summer twilights sometimes seen in the Northern Virginia suburbs of Washington, D.C. A cold front had passed through the night before, complete with gale winds, the rumble and clap of great thunderheads, and the sudden on-rush of fat drops of rain. The normally oppressive August steam bath had been temporarily pushed to the northeast leaving a day that had been warm, dry, and breezy. It had been a picture perfect day for golf - not that any day wasn't - and it was turning into a perfect evening for a cold beer with a pink and purple sunset coloring the sky. Settling into a lounge chair on the club veranda, I propped my feet on the railing, sighed, and took a long drink from a frosted mug.

God works in mysterious and amazing ways. It never ceased to amaze me how, after all that I'd been through while serving in the military in special operations and all that I had endured in my past, I would end up here and now as a golf journalist writing monthly columns in Golfer's Journal, a major national golf magazine. Golf, however poorly I played it, had always been my passion. In my years after college, I was rarely in any place that was nice enough to have a golf course. Later, during the gut-wrenching experience of watching my wife Marie slowly die after six months of debilitating cancer treatments, it had offered me an escape from my daily reality and ultimately led to my emotional recovery. Now, I could work for the magazine, interview the best golfers in the world, travel to the finest courses, test out new equipment, and turn my observations into monthly musings on the sport. My work life had become a fantasy come true.

To top it all off, I could even expense this fabulous Friday of golf because I'd been checking out the latest TaylorMade driver in preparation for a short review in next month's column. My short game, as evidenced by my last shot, was still miserable, but given the unusually better-than-average drives I'd had with the new driver, my review would be glowing.

Towards the West, narrow patches of clouds were lit up like strips of liquid fire as the sun slowly set. The trees appeared as black paper cutouts, their leaves shaking in the last breaths of the dying breeze. Turning and signaling the waitress for another cold one, I glanced through the window at the television, glowing brightly inside the clubhouse in the gradually darkening twilight.

The World Golf Championship at Firestone Country Club in Akron was winding down to the cut for the coming weekend. The scores scrolled through and the highlights showed Moshe Goldman making a clutch sand shot to save par and move up a spot. Moshe was not only going to make the cut, he was now on the leader board in ninth place. Because Firestone was tough, requiring the players to hit long iron after long iron approaches into the beautifully bunkered greens, it was a significant accomplishment for any player to make the cut, much less appear in the top ten.

Although Moshe was a relative newcomer to the U.S. tour, he was very popular overseas and known as the "Jewish Jack Nicklaus." I had already been planning on writing a monthly column leading up to the Masters next April. I'd write articles on some of the qualifying tournaments, on the history of the Masters, and on Augusta National Golf Course. I realized I'd never actually heard of a Jewish golfer on the pro tour before. Breaking into a smile, I thought this could be a great human interest story to include in the piece. I'd call my editor, tell her my intentions and then schedule Goldman for an interview.

"Here you go, Mr. James," said Julie, one of the regular waitresses at the club, as she interrupted my thoughts and handed me another mug with the seemingly obligatory, yet totally dysfunctional, four-inch square cocktail napkin. Julie was easy on the eyes. She was a tall slender blonde with long tanned legs rising practically to her armpits. We'd flirted on and off over the years. As good as her physical attributes were, and they were superb, she was even better at diagnosing my golf swing.

I'd often wondered about gorgeous bar waitresses. They had such an innate ability to smile and flirt right up to the edge of being asked out. They laughed at your jokes and nodded with approval at anything you said, when in reality, they'd heard it all and would lead you on only as long as they thought they had a chance at a decent tip. Cynical as it sounded, it seemed to me that most of them had plastic smiles and hearts of stone and were as impenetrable as the triple canopy jungles I'd run across in parts of El Salvador, Panama and Columbia. Sheltered by the total disdain so typical of their generation and emboldened by the total wisdom of body and instinct of their kind, they were more than a match for this thirty-something golf bum.

Truth be told, I recognized my cynicism for what it was – frustration at the difficulties of meeting another soul mate like my Marie.

"How'd you hit 'em today big guy?" she asked, brushing her taut hip against my shoulder. Her slight smirk signaled the fact that she'd probably witnessed my lovely iron shot on the last hole. Her brush against my shoulder caused the beer to splash out of my mug and into my lap. Pausing while looking down at the spreading wet spot on my trousers, I sighed and responded, "As usual, I had a fine day, Julie. I hit 'em long and hard and hit every green. I keep golfing this well and I may just need to join the tour."

Then looking up at her, I said, "you're looking your usual fabulous self, but man oh man, you think you could cut me a break and give those hips a rest? I'm wearing half my beer."

She smiled back at me and with wide innocent eyes said, "come on Drew, you know you like it. And I'm just a poor starving waitress trying to earn a living with these hips. And I suppose I do know a thing or two about golf having watched a busload of hackers work their way up the last hole."

She continued with a serious look in her eyes. "Really Drew, if you'd just listen to me for once, rather than always stare at my butt, you might not have to buy so many new golf balls. If I've told you once, I've told you a hundred times. Watching you on that last hole, I think you need to adjust your grip and close the clubface. You're what, about six-two and 225? For a guy your size, you just don't get the yardage you should out of your clubs. I'd say you're using your arms way too much and not that hunk of a body of yours. But that's just my opinion and I know you're not going to listen to me anyway."

She turned, winked back at me over her shoulder, and, knowing full well it would never happen, said with a tease, "you ever gonna ask me out?"

I watched her walk off and took another long swallow of beer. The sun speckled day had turned to full night. The first glint of the moon glowed on the dark horizon. I sighed, with contentment this time, and looked back at the television. Moshe was being interviewed in the clubhouse. Maybe I was on to something with an interview and article. After all, with the constant stream of different major winners on the tour, there was no reason Moshe couldn't be the next golf phenom. I recalled that he'd been on a fairly meteoric rise since he'd come out of nowhere, won big in the Caesarea Classic in Israel, come in third at the Algarve World Cup in Portugal, and then showed well at the AT&T National in Pennsylvania. And considering current world events in Lebanon, Egypt and Syria, and the continuing conflict all over the Middle and Near East, maybe a little positive coverage about someone from that region would be a welcome change.

I drained the last of my beer, rose, stretched, blew a kiss at Julie, and headed for the parking lot thinking that I'd give Goldman a call in the next couple weeks. If nothing else, maybe he could help me with my slice.

Chapter 2
1983

He could see the sailboat bobbing gently in the distance, the mast moving slightly from side to side in the swell. Sitting on a dock jutting out from the shoreline, he adjusted the mask on his face, put in the mouthpiece, and then slipped quietly into the dark water, pulling the buoyed bag of equipment behind him.

A trail of bubbles marked his progress from the shore out to the stern of the darkened boat. Reaching the dive platform at the stern, he tied off his equipment and pulled off his fins. He pulled a collapsible steel baton out of the bag, extended it to its full four-foot length, and climbed noiselessly onto the deck. At the rear cabin door, he shoved the baton from one side, through the handle, to the other side, effectively locking the door from the outside.

Movement sounded below his feet. "Hello? Who's up there?" a voice called out.

Ignoring the sounds, he moved casually on the deck, not worrying about any noise now. The door moved against the baton as the occupant tried to open it, followed by a banging of fists on the inside of the door.

"Who are you? What are you doing out there? Let me out," the voice yelled with a rising sound of panic.

Sitting again on the diving platform he calmly put his fins back on, whistling tunelessly in the night breeze. He eased back into the water. Drifting down eight feet below the surface under the boat, he opened the bag and pulled out the heavy duty underwater cordless

9

drill. He placed the tip of the four-inch drill bit just to the side of the keel and pulled the trigger, watching the bit dig into the wood hull, the sound muffled by the water. He repeated the process at three other places on the boat's bottom, watching with satisfaction as large bubbles of air escaped and floated up to the surface. Placing the drill back in his bag, he swam to shore leisurely, unable to hear the screams of terror as the boat slowly sank under the water.

Chapter 3
The Present

Wednesday of the following week dawned hot and hazy. Summer was back with a vengeance. The worthless weather forecasters called for sunny days but the humidity was so high the shadows of the hazy morning were indistinct and muted and you couldn't see that the sky was actually blue. It was like looking through the sides of an aquarium that hadn't been cleaned in weeks. The dog days of August were here. Hot, humid weather left everyone and everything damp, listless and limp. Kids moped around with the guillotine of the first day of school hanging over their heads, waiting for the blade to drop down in just a few short weeks. Commuters were disgorged from the subway system looking wilted, disheveled, and ill-tempered.

I'd spent the first part of the week writing up a review of the TaylorMade driver. It was a hell of a club. The first time out with it, I really blasted the ball. I was excited to see that I was reaching parts of the fairway I had never reached before, but disappointed to see that it hadn't completely cured my slice. I accepted it as a likely fact that no driver could.

I knew from my frequent interviews with the best golfers in the world that the only factor causing my slice was my inerrant ability to leave my clubface open at impact,

11

just as Julie had so kindly pointed out. Somehow, I needed to overwrite my natural impulses and find a way to make my hand, arm, and clubface rotate through when I swung through the ball. But if knowing were doing, I'd have invested in Apple long ago. My head knowledge didn't seem to help me at all on the driving range or the course and it didn't stop me from trying out every new driver I could lay my hands on to see if it would help. Or for that matter, seeking suggestions from every golf pro I met.

As I've done nearly every morning since my years when being in good shape was literally a matter of life or death, I headed out for a five-mile run. Going out my front door, I saw the door was open in the vacant condo across the stairwell hall from mine. I went down the flight of stairs to the front door of the building and stepped outside. A curtain of warm moist air slapped me in the face, causing beads of sweat to instantly pop out on my forehead. Wiping my brow with the back of my hand, I had to sidestep two men coming in the door with a large blue sofa. I grimaced as the two men, one pulling and one pushing, shoved the sofa through the doorframe, breaking off one of the sofa's wooden legs in the process. Oh the joys of moving, I thought.

Living in Old Town Alexandria just south of Washington, DC had its advantages, one of which was living close to the George Washington Parkway bike trail. I headed south on the sidewalk, passed Porto Vecchio, a strange looking condominium complex sitting practically on top of the low tide mudflats of the Potomac River, and set out on the smooth asphalt path that runs all the way from Teddy Roosevelt Island near Rosslyn to Washington's former home at Mount Vernon. South of Alexandria, it was a rare refuge, passing through the beautiful woods and tidal marshes that bordered the Potomac. White herons transformed themselves from still life statues to soaring gliders, skimming along the surface with powerful down thrusts of their wings. The water sat tea-colored and smooth, while the tree leaves hung limply in the heat. As I ran, I could see sail boats out on the river, a scene looking just like a still life painting by Renoir.

Every time I ran, I thought about life – the great friendships I'd formed on various covert operations, happy times before the cancer took Marie, current articles I was in the process of writing, the political mess in Washington between Republicans and Democrats or the White House and Capitol Hill, and any other matters that came to mind. Lately the political mess seemed worse than ever, with the approval ratings of both houses of Congress, as well as the President, at an all-time low. I had long been apolitical, a tradition of the professional military since 1800. So I didn't care who ran the country, as long as they got things done, let me keep my weapons, and didn't suck every last penny out of me in taxes.

On this run, the main focus of my thinking centered on how much Washington summers in general, and this morning in particular, sucked. It was like running in a sauna while wearing a swim mask and snorkel. Delightful, as long as you didn't need to breathe.

I thought about the quick passage of time since Marie had died and how fleeting the time we had actually been together. Marie had lost her valiant fight to cancer three years ago, and when she died, we'd only been married for four years. Life is such a vapor, a brief shimmer of time eclipsing into that golden sunset of eternity. Each of us coasting towards the same ending at precisely the same speed. The old and the young, the dull and the beautiful, the rich and poor alike. Time is the great equalizer, clicking one second at a time from now to forever, moving all of us straight toward the grave, until all the living are as dead and forgotten as if they had died in ancient Greece. The only unknown is how many days we'll spend here until we give it all up and meet our Creator. And after that? Guess it depends on your view of your Creator, although for me, God and His Son were personal realities. As they say, there aren't any atheists in combat. So I felt assured that when my time came, I would join Marie in heaven.

I finished the run mulling over the last few spots in my review about the driver. By the time I'd finished my run and the sit-ups, pushups and pull-ups that followed, I was drenched with sweat and sucking in air hard. But I'd succeeded in another day of staving off the specter of eventual physical slackness and shortness of breath, as well as coming up with the finishing touches to my article.

It was becoming harder and harder to stay in some semblance of shape. The early years had been much easier - the body was more limber, the mind was more willing, and the incentives much greater. But now, years removed from that rigorous lifestyle, my fondness for beer and warm Krispy Kreme doughnuts continued to take its daily toll, necessitating even more lengthy and strenuous workouts.

While I showered, I thought again about the feature on Goldman. Turns out he had finished in the top twenty at the Firestone so he was definitely moving up in the PGA rankings. My editor had approved my plans for the monthly column on the Masters, as well as my idea of covering Moshe and following him on his quest to qualify for the April tournament. Whether he ultimately made it or not, I hoped the story might add some color to the Masters column.

I turned the shower off and stepped out of the tub to dry off. While doing so, I noticed for the umpteenth time the small steady drip running from my bathtub spout.

And as I did every day, I tried tightening the faucet handles, hoping to continue putting off the inevitable time consuming washer repairs. I just had to fix the damn thing and stop procrastinating. So much for the home handyman.

After getting dressed, I sat down at my computer to begin an initial search for information about Moshe Goldman. Piecing together what I could, I learned that Moshe was born in a kibbutz on the West Bank and had lived a fairly normal Jewish childhood. That normal childhood diverted slightly when, during his high school years, he'd picked up a golf club and found he was a natural talent at the sport. He then left Israel to attend college in southern California. It was widely rumored that he had become particularly adept at placing wedge shots from his frat house roof onto the third-floor balconies of the Tri-Delta house across the street. From the frat house roof, it had been an easy jump to the local public golf courses and the discovery that somehow he had been gifted with an ability to swing a golf club.

There were a few reports on his gold medal success in the Macabbiah Games at the Caesarea Golf and Country Club and of his receiving support and admiration from the Jewish people. There were also a few minor comments on his fledgling success on the PGA Tour.

I next accessed Golfer's Journal's internal database to see what it had on Goldman, but it only contained a listing of his finishes and ranking for the year. Not much else there. It was definitely time to set up an interview. I looked up the number for Goldman's agent in the latest agent's directory and called him.

"Nick Rosenberg, you gotta hold," a voice said with a heavy Brooklyn accent, followed by the soft sounds of elevator music for the next three minutes.

Then finally he answered. "Yeah, Rosenberg here. What do you need?"

"What, they don't say 'Good Morning' in New York?" I said.

"Yeah, yeah, 'Have a great day,' what da you need?" he said.

"I need one of your clients, actually. This is Drew James from Golfer's Journal and I'm calling about Moshe. Moshe Goldman. I'm writing a series of articles leading up to the Masters and was thinking about covering him in some of them. Do you think he'd be interested and available to meet with me?"

His attention perked up. "Well now, I expect he would be," he said. "That Moshe. I tell you, he's a real good guy and a terrific golfer. I know he would be honored to meet with you and talk. I'm a friend of the family, as well as his agent."

"So how does next week look?"

"Hold on a sec and lemme check his schedule."

More elevator music and then more Nick Rosenberg.

"OK, looks like you're in luck," he said. "We're all set. He'll be in the city next week before he heads to his next tournament. I know he could meet with you over lunch, say maybe Tuesday? That work for you?" he asked.

"Fine, yeah that works great for me," I said. "I'll meet him next Tuesday at noon at Katz's Deli on East Houston."

"Great. Perfect place," he said. "He'll be there." And with that, the phone line went dead.

Chapter 4

Tuesday morning arrived gray and overcast, the air still heavy with humidity. I drove north up the parkway, across the 14th Street Bridge, and over to Union Station. I parked in the garage then boarded the Acela for the trip up to New York City.

Riding on trains always seemed to put me in a reflective and nostalgic mood, made more so by the gloomy day. As the train shook and swayed along the tracks, my view out the window was filled with a constant stream of graffiti, run down warehouses with broken windows, mounds of trash, and tangles of vines and lifeless bushes. The view differed little between DC and Philly, through Jersey, and the edge of the Palisades as the train began its descent under the Hudson for Manhattan.

I got out at Penn station feeling restless and ready to meet and interview Moshe. The sky in the City matched my mood, gray and dark with low hanging clouds carrying the threat of rain.

After a quick cab ride down to the Lower East Side, I hopped out and found Moshe waiting for me in front of the deli. He looked just like he did on TV. He wore his typical gray golf slacks and a black polo shirt. He was about five-ten with a slight build and thick dark curly hair. His face was round and intelligent looking with a large forehead and crinkle lines radiating from the corners of his eyes. The smile was the same brilliant one he showed on TV, but in person, the look in his eyes didn't quite match the smile.

We both ordered Reubens with fries and snacked on pickles from the jar set out on the table while we waited for the food. I had an Amstel Light and Moshe had a Diet Coke. The food was good, the conversation easy. I told Moshe my idea for the column on Augusta National, including tracking his progress leading up to the Masters and he was excited about helping me with the article. Despite his excitement, however, there seemed to be something else, some undercurrent of despair, behind his look of happiness. Perhaps it was the violent state of affairs back in Israel or the prolonged separation from his family and friends while he was on the tour. I ordered another beer for me and Diet Coke for Moshe and after they were delivered, pulled out a notepad and pen.

"So Moshe," I said, "Let me ask you a few questions. Why don't you start by telling me what it was like growing up in a Kibbutz in Israel?"

He smiled with genuine warmth and looked in the distance out the window as he returned in his mind's eye to his homeland.

"Not so bad, but not so easy either," he said with a slight Israeli accent and reflective flip of his hand. "Living there was like living in one big happy family. Lots of love and support from my family and close friends. We had a comfortable home and plenty to eat and always someone around to talk or play games with. But on the other hand, the work was hard and there were always concerns about rain, whether the seed would be right, and whether we could produce enough crops. On top of that there was the fear of violence. When we'd ride the bus into the city every other week we had to wonder whether that would be the day we would be the random choice for some suicide bomber. Still, it is my homeland and I miss it."

Drifting off in an obvious reverie of pleasant memory, he said, "I have never felt such love and support as I felt living there. You could share your dreams and nobody would laugh. It was a place of sharing hopes and a vision for the future that seemed at times to be impossible. It was very difficult to leave when I made the decision to go to California for my studies. I think that I will always have a piece of my heart missing until I return for good to my homeland."

In a flash, Moshe's words took me back to my own life, the tragedy with Marie and the chunk of my heart gone forever. The intensity of the feelings of loss caught me by surprise. And pulling back just as quickly, like one's reaction to touching a hot .50 cal machine gun barrel, I mentally shoved them back into their little box in the back of my mind, slammed the lid and locked it fast.

We continued back and forth in an easy rhythm, me asking and Moshe answering. He told me about his years on the golf team at USC, his success in the NCAA championships and a few amateur tournaments, his return to Israel, and the several years he'd spent on the European circuit. It was fun throwing out a question and sitting back listening to his animated responses, complete with quick hand gestures, while I took notes.

Two Amstel Lights had turned into three and, while I was content simply watching Moshe's expressions as he spoke, the light in his eyes, the sincerity of his speech, the movement of his hands, and the apparent vitality with which he lived his life, there seemed to be something else there, some hidden worry deep inside. Moshe continued talking, pointing out that after his success in Europe he'd set his sights on a return to the U.S. and a try at the PGA

Tour. Finally, with a determined look and a downward, almost shy, turn of his eyes, he whispered aloud his burning desire to fulfill his lifelong dream to qualify for, play in, and somehow win the Masters at Augusta National, even perhaps next April.

I continued making notes and we chatted amicably about golf in general and about my penchant for slicing in particular. Moshe offered me a few tips, including commenting instinctively on the way I gripped my driver, even though he'd never seen me play.

"You know that your grip on the golf club should be just enough to support the weight of the club throughout the swing," he said. "I would bet that you must be taking a tighter grip. It inhibits the club's release so the face is open at impact and produces a left to right ball flight. If you use a lighter grip, it will cause your forearms to rotate and square the clubface earlier. I think you should try that next time and see if that will help."

Amazing. One after another they could peg my slice. And Moshe had done it without even seeing me play. "Man, you make it sound so easy," I said. "But I'll give it a shot. I'm willing to try just about anything. My budget for new golf balls is killing me. Thanks for the tip, Moshe. I'll see if that'll work."

As the interview wound down, I told Moshe a little bit about myself, some of my exploits on past missions, and my job as a golf Journalist. Moshe quickly became interested in and began asking question after question about my special ops military training, abilities, and combat experiences. I just assumed it was because he had grown up in the midst of violence and weapons and his interest tended towards those things. Having had three beers to loosen my lips, and feeling that twinge of pride in telling others about my prior life, I answered far too many of them in way too much detail.

As we wound down our conversation, I called for the bill. Moshe suddenly leaned forward towards me and grabbed my arms with both of his hands, his eyes wide and shining with intensity. He blurted out in a rapid-fire whisper, "I need your help Mr. James." He leaned even closer, pulling me towards him, and said, "I have come to believe that I can trust you, and from what you've told me you are a man very capable for solving problems. I have to turn to someone for help with a big problem. I can't take it anymore. I'm always looking over my shoulder now and it's eating me up inside. You see, I believe someone is trying to kill me. Please help me."

<u>Chapter 5</u>

While we had been eating, the weather outside had worsened. The sky had grown darker with sharp gusts of wind slamming through the concrete canyons of the city, threatening a late summer thunderstorm. The change in the weather outside seemed to match the changed mood inside.

I pulled away from Moshe's hands and leaned back slightly from the table, questioning whether I'd heard him right. But the urgency in his voice and the look of near panic that had replaced the normal smile on his face convinced me. Leaning forward I asked in a low voice, "OK Moshe, why don't you tell me about it. What's going on? Why do you think someone's trying to kill you?"

He bit his lip and said hesitantly, "I'm just not sure. I don't know. I keep telling myself it must be nothing. But it has really started to bother me more and more and things seem to be getting worse and I did not know who I could go to who might believe me and listen to me and be able to do something about it. And what I tell you, you must promise, you must swear not to tell anyone because I do not want my family to hear about it and I do not want to involve the police."

"It's ok Moshe," I said. "I don't know why you wouldn't want to contact the police. I think that'd be a good thing to do. But whatever, we'll fix it. Now slow down, take it easy, and start from the beginning."

Moshe took a deep breath, looked around him, rubbed his face with both hands, and began. "Ever since I have come to America and begun to do well in tournaments, there have been questions to me about my country and our violence and how we are fighting with the Palestinians, the Syrians, the Hamas, and everyone else. Questions about how I will deal with the Islamic problem, my country's retaliation for suicide bombings, the walls we are building, and Israeli settlers living in Palestinian areas. As if, because I am a well-known golf player, I can solve any of those social and political problems, much less ones that have existed for thousands of years since the time of Isaac and Ishmael."

I nodded, encouraging him to continue.

"Sometimes, it seems like the questions try to make me out to be a bad guy and say that my country is wrong for wanting to exist and defend itself; for the way we are doing things. So if the news media should find out that I went to the police with a complaint and there are problems with me here, I think that it will make all these questions harder and make it seem like I am causing trouble here in America. And all that would be a bad thing for my family and my country."

He paused, looked intently at me and said, "You understand this, Mr. James?"

I'd seen the press in action and knew how they could be. Hell, for that matter I was sort of the press, and I knew how I was. Moshe was right. Rarely well-intentioned, always looking for edgy and sensational, the press invariably put a negative spin on any celebrity involvement with the police. I could see how it would play out. This would cause a real commotion in the national media. I remembered how I had done it myself in a column on another golfer's public meltdowns before he'd had his most recent upswing. If Moshe did go to the police, there would be a feeding frenzy like piranha after a floundering water buffalo. His concerns would certainly trigger stereotypical comments about Jewish paranoia, over-exaggeration, and self-preoccupation and somehow make it seem that Moshe, his family, and Israel were all at fault.

So I was all in. I really did want to help him, and try and find out what was going on and who was doing it.

"No worries, Moshe. I understand. I really do." I said. "You can trust me. I know all about the media and I can see why you're worried about them. I'll see what I can do and I promise I won't tell anyone. I can keep a secret. So tell me what's happened?"

Chapter 6

Glancing around the room again with quick nervous movements, he related in a tumbled rush a series of incidents that had happened within the past three months.

At first it was merely an annoyance. Calls to his cell phone with no response on the other end but just the sound of breathing. Then calls in a rough accent telling him he would die because he was a Jew playing golf in the U.S. The caller did not identify himself and there was nothing on the caller ID on his phone.

"Did you report it to anyone, like the phone company, so they could try and trace the calls?" I asked

"No," he said. "I just did not take it that seriously at the time. And after my pathetic performance in several of those tournaments, I was focusing more on myself and my rather inept golf game than on anything else."

"I should be so lucky to have your inept golf game," I said. "So keep going. What happened next?"

He continued. "I was playing at the tournament at Oakland Hills, just outside of Detroit. I had rented a small house near the course. On Friday I went into the garage to drive to the course and found a dead cat on the windshield. There was a note pinned to it that said I better leave the tour and return to Israel. I don't know how anyone got in and didn't hear a thing during the night."

"That was about two months ago," he said. "The next time was last month. I'd been away from my home in Florida for two weeks. I'd planned to return home a week earlier, but stayed over at my last tournament to get a driver repaired and refitted. While I was away, the first tropical storm of the year hit Florida. So when I finally returned to my home in Tampa, it was still raining and there was water everywhere. When I pulled into the drive, I noticed a package right by the front door. It was wrapped in heavy brown paper and tied up with string, but because of all the rain, it was soaked through and through. The postmark and the addresses were all smeared and stained. I took it in and set it in the laundry room sink while I showered and changed. I guess I got distracted because I forgot about it until the next day when I was packing for another tournament. I saw it there when I went to do a load of laundry. I grabbed a pair of scissors to cut the string and the box but as I picked it up to open it, the box literally fell apart in my hands."

"What you'd find? What was in the box?" I asked.

"I think it was a bomb, but it's not like I'm an expert in those things. At least it looked like one. There were wires wrapped around a block of ... what do you call it...like silly putty?"

"That sounds like C4 explosive," I said.

He continued. "And there was some electrical looking device on top of three batteries wrapped in tape and connected to the string that tied the package together. But because of all the water that came down on it, the whole thing had disintegrated into a water soaked mess."

"So what did you do with it? Is it still at your house?" I asked.

"Well I definitely took it seriously, but I just couldn't call the police. I can't bring them into this without feeling like I'm giving up on playing professional golf. It really was pretty easy though. I just clipped all the wires between the device and the putty, put it all in a trash bag weighted with some rocks, and then dumped it in the deep water channel running behind my house."

He looked weary and distraught. "With this new threat, I was more worried than ever and realized I would have to find help somewhere and find it soon. I didn't have any idea what to do or who could help me."

"I think you got really lucky on this one, Moshe. You really shouldn't have messed with the box but I guess it should be safe enough where you dumped it. Do you have any security cameras at your house or anywhere else in the development? Anything we could look at to see who came in the area, who didn't belong?" I asked.

"Nothing at my house, but it's a gated community and there should be a camera at the front gate. I think I can have access to the tapes."

"Alright," I said. "For starters, we'll have to get copies of those tapes so I can work my way through them. What else?"

"Well, the worst, actually." He continued with a tremor in his voice, his eyes showing the pain of his remembrance. Just last week after his success at Firestone, and while he was still trying to figure out what to do and who could help him, it got really ugly. He was awakened in the middle of the night by the sound of his dog growling downstairs. It sounded like someone was trying to get in the house through the patio door. As he heard the door open, the security alarm went off with a loud shriek and his dog started barking furiously. The community security guard responded to the alarm quickly but whomever had been there was gone, chased off by the noise. They found his dog in the back corner of the yard, its neck broken.

27

His voice faded as he finished this part of his story, head hanging down, seemingly defeated by these turns of event. But when he looked up at me, I could see in his gaze, besides the underlying trace of sadness and pain I'd noticed first off, a look of ageless defiance. A look that said he would survive whatever was going on here through to the end, and he would endure like his countrymen had for thousands of years.

"You know I won't." he whispered. And looking straight into my eyes, again "you know I won't quit the tour now. I've got to make it to the Masters."

I could feel the heat of his conviction blazing like the sands of the Sinai and in that instant, with that look and that attitude of determination, I knew that I would do all I could to help him.

Chapter 7
1996

The garage was quiet and dark in the still of the night. The raucous noise from dropped tools, pneumatic wrenches, and car lifts had ceased with the end of the work day and the departure of the mechanics. The last salesman had left the showroom floor, turning out the lights in the dealership before departing for home.

With a shriek, the chain stopped in the winch used for lifting car engines. The engine secured by the chain reached its stopping point, rotating slowly in the dim light. Drops of oil seeped from a hole on the bottom, spattering into a raindrop pattern where they hit the concrete floor below.

He was seated in a chair off to one side, his legs crossed casually and his hands clasped together in his lap. A smirk formed on his face. He watched the man in front of him let the electric control for the engine winch swing freely in the air then saw him turn and walk over to the body lying face down on the floor. The man used his foot to flip the body over. Bending low, and putting his ear to the chest, the man listened to the uneven but still present heartbeat. Rising up, the man looked over to him and nodded.

"He's good, boss. Still breathing," the man said.

"Good. Let's get it done, then," he said to the man.

The man readjusted the gloves on his hands and bent down, grabbing an ankle in each hand. With a grunt of effort, the man dragged the body to the area under the raised engine leaving an uneven trail of blood on the concrete floor from the wound on the body's head.

29

The man straightened and grasped the electric control, positioning it correctly in his hands.

"Hold it," he told the man in a loud and commanding voice. He rose slowly from the chair and walked over to stand next to the engine, now hovering in the air over the body. He knelt and gently stroked the side of the face, smiling and humming softly.

Standing up, he grinned and surveyed his handiwork, clearly enjoying the moment. This one was turning out very well, he thought with a real sense of satisfaction.

He held his hand out for the electric control and the man gave it to him. Taking a deep breath, his eyes reflecting the madness within, he studied the scene again for any errors. Then, convinced that all was in order, he pushed the lock release button on the control and the engine plummeted down crushing the body below.

Chapter 8
The Present

I paid the bill and we rose to leave. I told Moshe that I would do whatever I could to try and find out who was doing these things and, even though I'd been out of that business for many years, do what I could to stop them. I also told him I would do my best to keep it confidential, and, stepping out now into the dark gloomy afternoon, I warned him to be very careful.

"Keep your head about you and be aware of your surroundings," I said. "As I like to say, 'stay alert – stay alive.' Stay with other people and don't go off by yourself. Don't be predictable – don't stay in the same places you have before. There's enough normal security around the tour so you should be all right. When you're at home, use your security system and double check that it's always on. But keep my number with you and call me if you see or hear anything, ok?"

"Ok," he said.

"And when you get back home please see if you can get copies of the security tapes for your neighborhood so I can see what's on them."

I handed him my card with my cell phone number and address on it and said, "Let me know how you're doing. If you need me to, I'll come keep an eye on you."

"I will," he said. "And I thank you, Mr. James."

"It's Drew. And you're welcome Moshe. I only hope I can find out who's doing this and put a stop to it."

With a growing look of relief, he said, "You are a blessing that has fallen into my life, Drew James. I believe you can find out what this is all about and make these people stop. I believe you can help me to make it successfully to Augusta for the Masters tournament."

"Yeah, well, don't count on me for any advice on your golf game," I said. "I may be able to write a good game, and maybe I can find out what this is all about, but when it comes to qualifying for the Masters, you're on your own there, buddy."

We made arrangements to meet again after Moshe played at the Valero Texas Open in San Antonio in two weeks.

After leaving Goldman, I walked around the city some, the impact of Moshe's worries flooding my mind. Why would somebody pick him out of the pack? He wasn't a bad guy. He was actually pretty cool. Someone you'd want to hang out with and drink beer together. He didn't bother people, wasn't obnoxious, arrogant, or pretentious. And it wasn't as if he was embarrassing the rest of the field. So who would do these things and why? Just because of his family's heritage?

With my thoughts swirling around me, matching the wind that gusted and careened around the crowded corridors of steel and concrete whipping up scraps of paper and debris, I walked and walked. As a result, it was close to seven when I finally arrived by foot back at Penn Station, windblown and slightly damp from the occasional rain burst, to grab the next available train. The return trip to DC was uneventful except for my dark and brooding thoughts about the nature of humanity, the state of the world, and the type of person or persons who would do such things to a guy like Moshe.

Back at Union Station, I took the series of escalators up to my car, a four-year old dark blue Land Rover, parked on the third level of the parking garage. It was close to eleven and quite dark except for the splashes of light thrown out by the overhead garage lighting.

Despite my admonitions to Goldman to keep his head about him, my head was anywhere but in that parking garage as I headed for my car. Just as I'd told Moshe to do, in my past the mantra "stay alert, stay alive" had been driven into my head by various special ops instructors. But I suppose I was too far removed from that type of action now and too caught up in Moshe's circumstances to remember the admonition. As I walked up to my car at the driver's door, right hand fumbling in my pocket for my keys, a hand clamped on my left arm and spun me around against the door. A 6-inch switchblade knife held casually in front of my face distracted me from the boy speaking in broken English and demanding my money.

Two others were fanned out just behind him. They wore oversized baggy blue jeans that hung down below their hips, unbuttoned flannel shirts, and unlaced tan suede work boots. Three Asian teenagers looking for an easy mark and a quick ripoff. The moment seemed frozen in time, like a tableau in Madame Tussauds' wax museum. I towered over all of them, but it made no difference to how they reacted. These kids were the cold hard ones, living their lives in a constant struggle for existence and an eternal game of tag with all authority. They were the sort who looked at and through all adults with the same sense of concern or emotion they would show when staring at a traffic light waiting for it to turn. They had no conscience, no feelings, and no regard for anyone. I knew immediately that, if it served their purpose, they would slit my throat as calmly as they might brush some spilled food off the front of their Tommy Hilfiger shirts.

The one holding my arm reached up and stuck the tip of his knife into my cheek. In broken English, he hissed "you understand what I say, man? You give me your money or you die." I felt a small droplet of blood form and roll slowly down the side of my face and neck.

It's one thing to ask me for money. Most times, I even oblige. It's another though to think you can stick me with a puny 6-inch knife, and I'll roll over, show my stomach, and stick my arms and legs in the air. I'd had enough and it was clearly now or never. The old instincts kicked in as the words from an old Ranger instructor teaching me about knife fights went flashing through my mind, "Just say to yourself, 'self, you're gonna get cut.'" Perhaps it was the pain of the knife stick in my cheek, my anger over what was happening in Moshe's life, or maybe just a result of my general disgust with the state of this world. It was probably a combination of all three that got the better of me and caused me to overreact with perhaps a tad more force than necessary.

Without any pause or hesitation, I grabbed the wrist holding the knife with an outward flick of my left hand, and at the same instant my right hand came out of my pocket with the keys pointed up, slamming them into the soft underside of the teen's jaw. My right knee drove up sharply into his groin and, as he sank to the ground with a foreign expletive and a groan, I twisted his arm up behind and between his shoulder blades, feeling the ligaments in his shoulder tear, and pulled the knife from his grasp. In one motion, I switched the knife to my right hand, and spun towards the one slightly to the left and behind my downed attacker. Before he could react, I roundhouse kicked him in the side of his head, and then, with knuckles extended and locked, shot a left jab into and through his solar plexus, just below his breastbone. He dropped without a sound gasping and choking for air, the breath knocked completely out of him. I dropped into a crouch, held the knife low against my right thigh, knife-edge facing back and out ready for use, and faced the remaining teen.

At the very least, I expected some reaction from him. Some movement, whether out of loyalty to his fellow gang bangers or a greedy desire not to lose a mark. But he just stared impassively, realizing they'd picked the wrong target this time, turned slowly and walked casually away, hands in his low slung back pockets, never glancing back. At my feet, his partners in crime writhed and moved their mouths in soundless expressions of pain, one clutching his stomach and gulping for air, the other holding his crotch with his good left hand, while his ruined right arm hung useless and still and a thin trickle of blood ran down the front of his neck from his chin. I opened the door, climbed in, started it and put it in gear. "Have a lovely evening," I muttered and, hands shaking like dry oak leaves in a sharp autumn wind from the adrenaline rush and my anger at my lack of self-control, I took off for home with dark ugly thoughts about wasted youth and mindless violence.

Chapter 9

My sleep was restless and fitful. I woke up wet with sweat and the sheets twisted around me. Acts of physical confrontation and violence sometimes prompted such nights. I remembered after waking that it always seemed to be the same dream I've dreamt many times with just slightly different variations, though in sleep it always seemed new and unique.

I was back in Afghanistan in that run-down goat herder's stone hut with its partially collapsed wood beam roof. Silvery shards of light from a full moon streamed through the jagged openings and, try as I might, I couldn't seem to squirm my way completely into the shadows in the corners. I was on a pine-covered ridgeline just northeast of the small drop zone in a valley in northeast Afghanistan. The frigid night air, blown by a sharp wind, was like a honed razor blade, a living, pulsating cold that sliced through clothing into one's very bones. The wind had carried me past the drop zone and, as I landed in a large pile of rocks, I felt my leg snap. After crawling out from under the parachute canopy and into the shed I'd spotted a hundred yards away, I was lying on my side, the bone protruding through the skin on the snapped leg. I held my M4 assault rifle, quickly blinking my eyes, trying to clear my vision and push the shock induced illusions out of my mind so I wouldn't imagine seeing things in the patterns of moonlight, fire at hallucinations, and give the Al-Qaeda soldiers combing the slopes around me the chance to find and kill me.

I crawled out from the tangle of sheets and took a long hot shower, trying to wash away the realities of the parking garage scuffle and the remnants of the dream. My cheek hurt in the spray of the water. I followed the shower with several mugs of hot coffee and a toasted bagel. Feeling a little more human, I sat down to try and chart out my next course of action. I took out my previous research on Goldman; my notes from our interview; and material I already had on the Masters series, including drafts of columns on the history of the course, its past champions, and the likely pack of contenders for next year's tournament. I then reread my notes from Moshe, thinking about how I could integrate him into the column on Augusta National and what I could start to do to find out who was messing with him.

Reading through my interview notes, I jotted down a list of things I needed to do first. Buying fresh Krispy Kreme doughnuts was at the top, followed by calls to Moshe's cell phone provider and neighbors. I made a list of potential groups that could conceivably be targeting him, including a lot of Middle Eastern terrorist groups I knew to be antagonistic towards Israel. Then I made a list of any friends or old sources I still had who might be able to give me information on terrorist cells operating in the U.S.

Reluctantly putting off the Krispy Kremes until later, I called Moshe's cell phone company and gave them his cell number, home address, birth date, and other identifying information he had given me. They gave me the numbers covering a two-week period around the dates of the phone calls Moshe had received. I then matched them with known numbers Moshe had given me, but couldn't come up with anything unusual. I could account for the phone numbers of each of the calls. There seemed to be no record of any unidentified or unknown caller.

Similarly, in quick order, I struck out after calling each of the neighbors who lived near him. No one had even noticed the package that had been left at his door and no one had seen or heard anything unusual the night his dog was killed. They hadn't even heard the alarm or the dog barking. Typical. Most people closed themselves into their homes at night, not aware of anything going on around them besides the latest reality show on television. Seemed like soon enough there'd be nothing left to do but take that doughnut run.

I turned to my list of old sources and called the first one, an old academy classmate who was now a national security attorney in Homeland Security, but his assigned area was South America and he had no information that could help me. Next on the list was a Foreign Service Officer who lived in the old neighborhood where Marie and I used to live, but the message stated that she was out of the country on an extended overseas assignment. I struck out in rapid succession on the next three names.

Last on the list was an old friend who used to work in the State Department's national security section. I figured he wouldn't be able to help me, but being one of my last shots, I thought I'd give it a try. I was hoping that he would remember a favor I'd once done for him. Ben Cooper and I had started our careers together in the Infantry at Fort Benning, Georgia, out in the woods beyond Harmony Church. There was something about Ranger training that causes men to bond together in a way that survives the passing of years and the eventual divergence down different paths of life. Then again, keeping another man's smelly dirty feet from getting frostbite while lying out at an observation post on a frigid night by putting them against your warm, bare stomach had a way of creating that tie that binds. At least, as the foot warmer, that's what I was counting on.

I called the old number I had for him, but the voicemail informed me that he had left and moved on to another government agency. I got a forwarding phone number and gave it a shot. The phone rang a dozen times and just when I was expecting voicemail to kick in, a voice answered, repeating back to me the phone number I'd just dialed.

Chapter 10

Trying to sound as earnest as I could I told the voice I wanted Ben Cooper. I was told to stand by. And then a minute later, a voice answered, "hello?"

"Ben Cooper?" I asked. "Hey Coop, it's me Drew James. Your old Ranger buddy. How the hell are you?"

A brief pause and that familiar voice dripping with a North Florida accent hollered back, "Hey there Drew! Man it's been a long time. It's so great to hear your voice. I can't remember when we last saw each other. Maybe at our ten year West Point reunion?"

"Yeah, I think so," I said. "Sounds about right. A lot's happened since then, though."

"So I heard. Really, really sorry to hear about Marie," he said. "Something like that sucks royally. You holding up ok?"

"As well as you'd expect," I said. "Good days and bad. Mostly good these days, thankfully. How about you? How's the family?"

We shared the typical catching up small talk. My ears perked up when he told me that five years ago, he had moved from State to the national security section of one of the intelligence agencies. I told him briefly what I'd been doing and where, following our last assignment together jumping out of airplanes with the 82nd Airborne Division. I gave him more details about Marie and the struggle for her life, which evoked more sympathies from him. But, as it invariably does, when I got to the part about working for Golfer's Journal, it prompted comments that mixed various profanities with the word "lucky." Lucky was certainly not how I felt in light of Marie's odyssey, but I guess all things considered, I could understand why they always said it.

Trying to refocus the conversation, I jumped right to the punch. "Listen Coop," I said. "I need a favor. If it helps any, this one isn't for me. I'm trying to find some information for a friend who's getting seriously threatened." I gave him the complete rundown of what Moshe had told me.

"They're getting to his head Ben, and he's a decent guy, so I'd really like to help him if I can," I said. "Oh, and by the way, he's an Israeli national."

Silence on the other end.

I continued. "I don't know exactly what you do, but I'm hoping you work near enough to the guys who do electronic surveillance and counterterrorism intel for the mid-East. I'm hoping you might be able to at least run a name through their systems and see if you get any hits. Like I said, he's an Israeli and if his name's been mentioned by any terrorist groups in that part of the world, your system should pick it up."

More silence.

I tried harder. "They killed his dog, Ben," I said.

I was getting warmer.

"Man, Drew, you know I could lose my job for this," Ben said.

"Come on Coop," I said. "This is me. I've got no personal angle on this. And I promise I won't ever mention who got the info for me."

Still more silence.

Then my trump card. "Shoot, Ben, you think if I was willing to put your nasty stinky feet against my stomach and save you from walking around on stumps the rest of your life I'd ever reveal where I got my info from?" I said.

The ensuing whispered expletive signaled that I'd hit my mark.

"Alright Drew," he said. "Give me his name. I'll run it and let you know if anything comes up. But it probably won't be till next week. As you can pretty much figure, things have been pretty busy around here and I really shouldn't be taking time out for something this crazy."

He paused. "And one more thing, Drew."

"Yeah, Ben?" I said.

"You're one of my best friends, but please don't pull this feet thing on me again. I tell you, that's just plain used up. After this, as far as I'm concerned, we're pretty much even. Know what I mean?" he said.

"Yeah Coop," I said. "I do. Just do this one thing for me. I promise I'll even try and get you a pair of tickets to the Tour Championship this year."

His voice softened. "You know, that'd be great, Drew, but I'm happy to do it anyway. Thanks. Listen, it was great catching up again with you. I'm happy to see what I can do and I'm really sorry for Marie and sorry for your friend. I'll give you a shout if I hear anything."

I gave him Moshe's name and my cell number and we parted with pleasant words and the unspoken understanding that we would always be friends. That is, I figured, as long as I didn't print his name next to any info he gave me, or bring up the feet warming again.

I got up and stretched, and looked out my living room window. A cold front was coming in and a strong wind was pushing clumps of dirty clouds across the slate blue sky. The dog days of August were coming to an end and the glorious days of autumn in Virginia were just around the corner.

Near the bottom of my list now, it was time to get more background on the Masters from the official press office for Augusta National. I grabbed a Diet Coke from the fridge, put on some Paul Desmond jazz, and sat down again at my desk to place the call. A woman with a strong Southern voice announced that she was "Sara Grace," and asked if she could help me. Since I knew that, for whatever reason, most women in the South seemed to have two names for their first, I probably had the right place. I identified myself and told her that I was writing a column concerning the Masters and needed as much background information on Augusta National as she could give me. She was quite pleasant and expressed her happiness to provide me with their standard press package, as well as press releases on the current board of directors and the changes being made to the course. Thanking her effusively, I gave her my address and, with typical Southern graciousness, she promised to mail out all that she had as soon as she could.

Finally I called Moshe to check in with him and see how he was doing. I was relieved to find nothing new. His new cell phone number would be effective the next day, he had already arranged to have copies of the surveillance tapes from his neighborhood sent to me, and he was preparing for his trip to Connecticut for the Buick Championship. He told me he was being careful.

With the phone calls finished, I remembered it was high time for Krispy Kreme. I also remembered that I did have a job and a real office and that it might actually behoove me to make an occasional appearance there so that my boss wouldn't forget either of those two crucial facts. I grabbed my brief case with my notes stuffed into it and a large bottled water, and, arms full, yanked open my front door and walked briskly out, into, and over five feet, four inches of soft and sweet smelling new neighbor who was just then walking past my door on the way to hers.

She was slim and tanned with light brown hair framed softly around a pretty face with auburn lashes and brows accentuating sparkling green eyes. At that moment, however, looking up at me from her current sitting position against the far wall, amid the remnants of her groceries scattered about her, those sparkling green eyes were not looking at me with the kind of open attitude of acceptance and friendship I would've expected when meeting a new neighbor.

On the other hand, all I could do was stand there and stare with my mouth open.

"Crap! That really hurt!" she said. "Why don't you watch where you're going!"

Even though I thought that wasn't a very original or creative rebuke or much of an introductory greeting, given the circumstances I also recognized that this wasn't a particularly opportune time for me to share that thought with her. And while I was pondering these things, she got up, opened the door across the hall and went in, slamming it shut behind her. I was left with a hallway full of slowly rolling cans and bruised fruit, wondering just what the hell happened.

Chapter 11

Several weeks had passed. The hint of cool weather was gone for now, pushed out by a brief period of Indian Summer. Moshe was back in Florida gearing up for the PGA Championship. The sky was deep blue filled with towering white cloud masses fringed with gray. The temporary return of the heat and humidity made everything look dry, brown, and lifeless. I'd finally received the security tapes from the gatehouse at Moshe's gated neighborhood, as well as the packet of information from Sara Grace on Augusta National. I started reading about the golf course, including information about the history of the course, the changes of the hole layouts, the leading contenders for the next Masters, and the current board members.

I read that the masterpiece that is now the Augusta National Golf Club was the brainchild of golfer extraordinaire Bobby Jones and Wall Street tycoon Clifford Roberts. In the 1920's they met at Knollwood Country Club in Westchester, New York, intent on building a great golf course that would challenge the pros but still appeal to the average golfer. They settled on Augusta, Georgia, because of its mild climate and lack of big city crowds. Finding a 365-acre parcel that was once an indigo plantation and former commercial nursery, they started construction of the course in 1931. The next year, the club opened with 59 members paying the required membership fee of $350.

As Jones was quoted to say, "no good golf course exists that does not afford a proper and convenient solution to the average golfer and the short player, as well as to the more powerful and accurate expert." With large forgiving fairways and few bunkers, yet greens that always challenged every player, the course was a great success.

In 1933, Jones and Roberts came up with a scheme to bring attention and publicity to the course. They approached the U.S. Golf Association about having an Open tournament at the course, but the Association refused. So they decided to hold their own tournament, inviting the best golfers at the time and calling it the Augusta National Invitational Tournament. By 1938, Roberts' nickname for the tournament became what it is today, just "the Masters."

The crown jewel of Augusta National was Amen Corner, the name given to the 11th, 12th, and 13th holes tucked away in the back corner of the course. They were spectacular sights. Smooth and perfect greens were backed by flowering azaleas and surrounded by towering pines. Rae's Creek flowed down from the 13th, in front of the 12th and under the Hogan Bridge, and then past the 11th, sparkling in the sunlight as it broadened slightly and exited Augusta National. As demonstrated by Greg Norman and Jordan Spieth, many a golfer leading in the final round at the Masters was overcome by disaster trying to navigate the three holes. Amen Corner was so christened following the 1958 Masters in a *Sports Illustrated* article written by Herbert Warren Wind about that year's tournament.

Needing a break from the Masters info, I picked up the security tapes Moshe had arranged to have sent to me. There were five tapes covering the week before Moshe had returned to find the package on his doorstep, and two for the day before and the day after his dog had been killed by the intruder. The tapes just showed the entrance road leading past the gatehouse. I was not expecting much from them.

I put each one in my laptop and fast forwarded through them to each vehicle that entered the gated community, making a note of the make and color of the vehicle and seeing if there was a repeat entrance for any of them. I paid particular attention to any service vehicles. There were a number of cars that entered. Using the zoom feature, I zoomed in on each of them, and eliminated those with women driving or children in the car.

There were ten service vehicles. Eight of them had writing on the side announcing they were plumbers, electricians, and utility companies. I figured that whichever group was after Moshe, they wouldn't have the time or resources, or even need, to steal some company's vehicle, or copy a logo. Two of the service vehicles were plain white vans. I focused on those as closely as I could, looking at the grainy images on the tape.

The first video of interest showed a white van with the windows up, driven by someone wearing a tee shirt and a baseball cap. The lights reflected off of the windows, making it very difficult to see inside. I thought I could see movement from someone on the passenger side of the van but couldn't make out any other details of the inside.

Focusing on the rear license plate as the van passed through, I could barely make out that it was a Florida plate. Out of seven numbers, I could only read the last four numbers which were closer to the camera. I wrote them down.

The second van was driven by a heavy looking guy with a pony tail. His left arm was cocked, the elbow hanging outside the open window as he drove. He looked like any other service man I'd ever seen.

Again focusing on the license plate, I saw it was bent from some past contact with a curb and I couldn't make out the state or any other detail. By the end of the first week, I could see that neither of the two vehicles had entered the development a second time.

With little to show for the first five tapes, I went through the other two in the same fashion, excluding the same cars with women and kids and vans with obvious commercial markings. The tapes were recorded three weeks after the first five. As the daylight faded, I could tell from the tapes when the lights around the entrance came on, casting a brighter illumination and deeper shadows away from the gatehouse. The contrast between the lighted area and the dark background became more pronounced as the night got darker, making it harder to see inside the vehicles. I sat up and came to attention as I saw a plain white van come through. It was about 11 p.m.

Zooming in and looking as carefully as I could, I saw a vague shape at the wheel, the face hidden under what looked to be a hooded sweatshirt. It was too dark in the interior of the van to spot anything else inside it. The van came through the gate at a slight angle so when I focused on the license plate, all I could see was the last number. It was the same last number as I'd seen on the van with the driver wearing the baseball cap. I sent Ben Cooper a text asking him if he could run the last four numbers through the Florida DMV and send me a list of possible matches. Minutes later I got a text back from Ben saying he would.

That was a start to trying to figure out this mess, but I still had no real idea what I was doing. With nothing better to do than fix my leaky tub, I decided I might as well go play some golf.

Chapter 12

I ignored the hot weather and headed out for the course. I knew that Moshe would be playing at the PGA Championship that weekend and hoped to catch glimpses of his play on TV later in the day. So I drove south down the GW Parkway, around the Mount Vernon circle, and down to the clubhouse. I waved at Julie, busy serving beer. I got no response whatsoever, grabbed my bag, and joined a threesome heading out.

As we walked towards the first tee, we exchanged the usual information about our current occupations and chatted about the weather. As is usually the case after I share my line of work, they insisted I share one of my learned nuggets of truth that would elevate their game to a higher level. Not wanting to disappoint, since we were going to spend the next eighteen holes together, I shared with them my favorite tidbit from Ben Hogan. Fifty years ago, Ben had written "when you grip a golf club to take your first swing at a golf ball, every natural instinct you employ to accomplish that objective is wrong, absolutely wrong." He advised that, in order to be a good golfer, "you must reverse every natural instinct you have and do just the opposite of what you are inclined to do, and you will probably come very close to having a perfect golf swing." Oh, that it could be so easy to beat one's natural instincts.

I went on to say that most pros would tell them that for normal shots, their grip on the golf club should be just enough to support the weight of the club throughout the swing. A tighter grip would inhibit the club's release so the face would be open at impact producing a left to right ball flight. Boy, what I knew about left to right ball flight. Instead, a lighter grip would cause the forearms to rotate, squaring the clubface earlier and inducing a draw from right to left.

The funny thing was, I knew dozens and dozens of such tidbits, but it never seemed to help my own golf game. My newfound golfing buddies were certainly impressed, though. So we each moved to the first tee and went through our pre-swing rituals. The good news was that I proceeded to hit my ball straight and true down the middle of the fairway. The bad news was that it went straight up in the air like a mortar round and landed about a hundred yards beyond the ladies tee. At least I didn't have to buy them a round of drinks....yet.

Fortunately, the rest of the round went better than normal. As I played the course, my mind wandered to the articles I was writing about the Masters and on Moshe. It struck me that I'd never known of, or even heard about, any other Tour players who were from Israel. I could think of half a dozen who identified themselves as being Jewish. But none of those were like Moshe who had grown up in Israel and were Israeli citizens. I couldn't think of a single golfer from Israel who had ever played at Augusta. I made a note to look into that.

As the round came to an end, I finished with one of my best scores. This time, I even managed to put my final approach shot in the middle of the eighteenth green for a birdie putt, but when I got to the clubhouse and ordered my beer, preparing to gloat, there was no sign of Julie. Go figure.

I spent the rest of the afternoon in the clubhouse drinking beer and watching Moshe on TV at the PGA Championship. Going into the final round he had been in twelfth place, but throughout the day he had failed to capitalize on openings. With each par, he lost ground to the birdie makers and moved steadily lower on the leader board. I watched with great interest, especially on the few occasions when they showed close-ups of his face. The smile was still there, but it was empty and clearly over-shadowed by the worry lines. This thing was certainly taking its toll on him. And there wasn't much I'd done so far to help him out.

Outside, the heat and humidity from the day had built up into a humdinger of a thunderstorm. Probably the last of the summer season, I thought. As I drove home in the gathering gloom, the flash and bang of lightning went with me, great sheets of water washed over the Land Rover, and the severe gusts of wind rocked it from side to side.

When I got home, I tried calling Ben. It had been over three weeks and I'd heard nothing from him. Then again, I'd heard nothing from anybody. I was no further along in helping Moshe than I'd been the day I'd met him. When I heard Ben's voice on his voicemail, I hung up without leaving a message.

It is good to hear the thunder of night rain, to feel the muscle soreness of a good round of golf when you move, to have a chill glass in your hand, to know the beginnings of ravenous hunger, and to realize that in a few hours even a bed made of cobblestones will feel deep and soft and inviting.

I cooked a steak, potatoes and vegetables and wolfed them down. Then turning out the lights, I put in a

Sinatra CD, arguably the greatest one ever - *Sinatra and Jobim* - and poured myself a tumbler of bourbon. As I sipped that first sip, the liquid warmth rolling down my throat and caressing my stomach, it hit me suddenly that this was Marie's birthday.

In hindsight, I should have remembered this date and seen this coming. My emotions were still too fragile and raw, the memories too vivid, running through my mind in high definition flashes of Marie's eyes, her smile, her face in quiet repose. I poured more of the clear amber liquid into my glass, swirling it in my hand and watching the different colors in the flash of lightning outside.

Reflecting on life, it struck me that a significant emotional event such as Marie's birthday becomes like a milepost that you see from the window of a speeding car. If you forget to look at the proper moment, it's gone and nobody in the wide world cares whether you happen to notice that milepost or not. If you miss your chance there's no going back, and the guilt of that failure can haunt you forever. So I studied those mileposts with care - meeting my lovely Marie at a party with old friends, hiking with her on a beautiful fall day in the Blue Ridge Mountains, and dining together in some of the country's finest restaurants. Then, thinking of our marriage and the wonderful years we shared together as husband and wife. Finally, watching my lovely Marie take that long, slow, painful slide to oblivion, her body fighting every inch of the way, while I sat by, holding her hand, and praying that God might show His mercy and miraculously heal her.

I rationalized that a man owes himself a few drinks on such an occasion and, afterward, feeling that pleasant numbness where he can sit and eat with slower gestures than usual and think long somber thoughts of time and life and how very dead you will eventually be when at last there are no mileposts and no windows in moving cars to see them from.

The thoughts and memories of my forever-lost Marie were alive with sounds and textures that exploded in my consciousness with the crack and sizzle of each bolt of lightning outside. With my eyes closed, it was as if she were there with me, talking softly, touching my arm, and pulling me into the vortex of her eyes with their look of love. When Frank's "Once I Loved" came on, the combination of the remembrance of her birthday on a dark lonely Saturday night, too much Bourbon, and the bittersweet slow motion highlight reel of my lost love, struck me full force with the same devastating effect as taking a direct hit by a rocket propelled grenade. I spiraled downward into a devastating whirlpool of self-pity, nostalgia, emptiness and blinding grief as the night turned slowly from stormy blackness into the faint pink glow of dawn.

Chapter 13

I awoke totally drained and with a blinding headache, recognizing last night for what it was - yet another stop on the long and bitter road from grief to recovery and healing that comes after the death of the love of one's life. "I gotta get a grip," I said, while sitting on the side of the bed, elbows on knees and hands holding my head.

Determined to make some effort at moving forward with the day, I consumed a pot of coffee, cheese omelet, and half a dozen strips of bacon. Feeling slightly revived, I set my sights on finishing the large box of glossy brochures and information papers Sara Grace had sent me. I read through pages of biographies and pictures of the board of directors, viewed architectural landscape drawings of hole changes, and perused Augusta National's riveting versions of past Masters tournaments that read like suspense novels.

As for the board of directors, there was a list of five. Conner Thompson, Parker Toomey, Clive Perkins, Carter Robbins, and the Chairman, J. J. Gann. Their biographies described in colorless detail their careers, companies and philanthropic activities. I figured most of the articles included in the materials weren't exactly accurate. Filled with fluff and positive public relations viewpoints, they painted a picture of a very exclusive and very private group, solely concerned for keeping the same continuity of tradition and excellence at the course that had existed from its early days.

I read through every bio. Thompson was the CEO of a national investment company based in Chicago. Parker Toomey was a real estate developer whose company had built resort properties all over the U.S. Perkins was the head of a national chain of restaurants, Perkins' Southern Grill. Robbins was head of American Flight Technologies, a defense contractor company that produced navigational systems for military airplanes. Finally, J. J. Gann was the CEO of SCC, a national construction company that had built roads and bridges all around the country.

As Sam Snead once said, "when you go to the Champions Dinner and look around at everyone in their green coats, you realize you're a member of one of the most exclusive groups of people in the world." That was certainly true. But the exclusivity of the Augusta National board of directors rivaled even that of being a Masters Champion.

Moving to my computer, I logged on and started searching to see what I could find about Augusta National and the board. There was an interesting story about a certain former member, who owned a national home building company, and who had been asked to construct several more cabins like those that started at the tenth tee and extended down the left side of the tenth fairway. He'd been instructed to build them in the pines farther down the tenth fairway. The story went that he questioned the wisdom of the plan, refused to build them where he was told, and suggested a different location for the new cabins. The next day he received a Fedex overnight box with the notice that he was no longer a member and containing all of the contents of his member's locker at the clubhouse.

True or not, the tale certainly left the impression that the board of directors was exceedingly powerful, especially when dealing with matters involving Augusta National Golf Club. I pulled up whatever I could find on each of the directors, trying to separate reality from fiction.

Chapter 14

I started with Connor Thompson. Everything I read about him made him look like a boy wonder. With an Ivy League education and a Rhodes Scholar, I imagined most of the financial decisions for the course were at the very least made by him, if not approved by him. He was described as brilliant and analytical and a man who never slept. The son of a long line of professional politicians, he'd gone to Princeton and then gotten an MBA at Harvard. He'd worked his way up from one financial investment company to another. Fresh out of business school, he'd started out with APS Funding, a California company engaged in the business of offering short-term, high-interest loans for business and real estate development businesses. He made his first million at APS by the time he was 30 and then moved back to the east coast, joining Bernie Madoff's investment securities firm. Two years after he left California, the founder of APS was convicted for mail, wire, and securities fraud. There was no mention of Thompson's role in the investment fraud conspiracy. Three years after joining Madoff Investment Securities, he'd earned close to half a billion dollars, and then left to form his own investment company based in Chicago. Three years after that, Bernie Madoff pled guilty to eleven federal felonies. Again, Thompson escaped any involvement with the scheme. So he might look like the

Golden Boy of the group, but the trail of corrupt companies left behind him gave a different impression.

Next on the list was Parker Toomey. The bio had a picture of him sitting in a chair overlooking the Pacific, with a pair of young buxom assistants on either side. Toomey was born and raised in Mississippi and started his first real estate development company in Gulf Shores on the Mississippi coast in the early 80s. I read that in the 1990s, he'd begun development of a resort on one of the barrier islands just off the coast, paying up front for storm insurance. A short time later, the hurricane season had hit with a vengeance, the storm surge inundating the island and wiping out all the work that had begun. The insurance company balked at paying out what Toomey claimed he was due for the value of the developed property. They doubted the extent of the development, but unfortunately hadn't been on the island to record the progress before the hurricane hit. Toomey took them to court and scored big, the court awarding him a cool three million. Rumors abounded that Toomey had paid off the attorney who had represented the insurance company. With that haul, he'd expanded to a national scale earning a reputation as a tough businessman with a weakness for the finest food, drink, and women. Recently, he'd put his profits into the best NASCAR cars and drivers he could buy and his teams were tearing up the NASCAR Sprint Cup circuit.

Clive Perkins was the quintessential good-ole-boy. He'd grown up in Southern Alabama and learned how to cook at a very young age from the granddaughter of a former slave. He'd never graduated from college but instead, in his early twenties he bought a used food truck and sold home cooked southern delicacies out of the back at different construction sites around the state. In 1987, he opened his first restaurant in Montgomery, Alabama, calling it Perkins' Southern Grill and over the next 20 years, turned it into a national icon for greasy food, putting a Perkins' Southern Grill at just about every interstate intersection throughout the South. There was a picture of Perkins outside one of his restaurants and he looked just as he was described, as being pure country, quick with a joke and a slap to the back.

Carter Robbins was the Chief Executive Officer for American Flight Technologies. He grew up in New Hampshire and joined General Electric in the eighties. He served there 20 years, progressing through a series of leadership positions until he became a corporate senior vice president and CEO of one of GE's subsidiaries in 1996. In 2006, he announced he was leaving GE and heading for AFT, one of GE's main competitors. Apparently the news surprised employees and executives who learned of his departure hours before the announcement. I thought of his reputation for exacting standards and failure free performance. Then I thought of the planes that his company made that I'd flown in and jumped out of countless times, including one jump where the plane's navigation system deposited my planeload of jumpers across five miles of Georgia pine forest. I just hoped he ran Augusta National better than it seemed his company made airplane navigational systems.

Last on the list was J. J. Gann, the CEO of Shelley Construction Company or SCC. Growing up in Alabama, he had started out with a used bulldozer and worked his way to success clearing land and working on road building projects. The SCC name certainly caught my eye. I saw that his company had not only made many of the recent changes to Augusta National, it had also been responsible for the huge Wilson Bridge construction project right where I lived. Wilson Bridge spanned the Potomac River connecting Virginia and Maryland just south of Alexandria and carried I-95 on its journey around D.C. I thought of the countless hours I'd spent driving bumper to bumper moving at five miles an hour through the bewildering maze of construction around the interchange of I-495 and Route 1, just west of the Wilson Bridge.

From the material I read, Gann had evidently been a huge success in the actions he had taken as chairman. One of the articles discussed Gann's uncanny ability to submit winning bids, starting with his early years, and now to major construction contracts all around the country, including the $667 million dollar Wilson Bridge construction project.

After my quick review, it looked like each of the board members had an interesting issue or two that I could try and dig into. On a whim, I sent another text to Ben asking him to pull the National Criminal Information Center data on each of the directors to see if anything interesting came up. As I got more information, I'd do my best to write on each of them, but with the connection between Gann's company and me, I'd start off seeing what I could find out about SCC and him.

SCC was a large national construction corporation that had developed a specialty over the years in major interstate and bridge construction. While they seemed to have concentrated their work in the South, they had gotten contracts all around the country. Interestingly, it seemed SCC had a connection with Clive Perkins and his Southern Grill. I read that they had some agreement that resulted in a Perkins' Southern Grill being placed at every major interstate interchange that SCC developed. Recalling the number of Southern Grills I'd seen around, SCC must have gotten a lot of road work contracts.

A few blogs mentioned SCC and the Wilson Bridge, but they were mostly scathing complaints of the traffic congestion caused by the company's construction activities. Nearing the end of the available information on SCC, one of the blogs claimed that Gann had pulled strings at the highest level in the Commonwealth of Virginia, allowing SCC to win the Wilson Bridge contract. The blogger hinted, without coming right out and saying it, that SCC had bribed officials in the Virginia Commonwealth.

As I started to wrap it up, I remembered my thoughts on the golf course the previous day about the lack of any other Tour professionals from Israel. I did a search on Google and in the Golfer's Journal database and saw that there had indeed been one Tour golfer from Israel. His name was Nathan Levin and he'd played for a brief period twenty years ago. He'd actually qualified for the Masters but had withdrawn for unknown reasons. With no further explanations, he'd left the tour and disappeared from sight. There was no other information on him or where he was now. I made a note to ask Moshe if he knew anything about Levin.

With nothing left to do on a late Sunday afternoon, I considered going next door and trying to start things over with my new neighbor, but as I stood up the phone rang. The caller-ID told me it was Ben Cooper. I quickly picked it up.

Chapter 15

"Hey Coop, I was wondering when you'd call," I said.

"Well, it isn't exactly real helpful news," he replied.

"What's up? What'd you find so far? Did you get any hits on the license plate numbers? Any info from the NCIC on the Directors?"

"No, not yet. I'm doing my best here Drew. I'll send it if and when I get it," he said. "But, first things first. You need to remember where it's coming from and keep it real close. Otherwise, you'll get my ass thrown in jail."

"My lips are sealed. You know that," I said.

"Yeah, well then, here it is. As I you probably know, we've been doing our best to monitor wires in and around known terror cells all over the globe, especially in the mid-East. I've been keeping my ears open for any mention of an ongoing operation against any Israeli nationals in the States. At first, I figured there must be some connection with ISIS, but tell you the truth, while they may try and blow themselves up in a shopping mall, we don't think they're sophisticated enough to come to the States and pull off a major operation like this would be. So I did a computer search of our archives data and came up with some info. Hezbollah may be overshadowed lately by ISIS, but they're not completely out of the picture. It seems we got an old splinter cell of Hezbollah operating in the border area between Lebanon and Syria and it looks like they've got something in the works. We've seen a number of intercepts that mention an op coming up in the U.S., but we have no real details. We've got nothing specific yet and nothing that mentions the name of Moshe Goldman. I don't know if you're on to something there with that friend of yours, buddy. But just to be safe until we get anything more substantive, you just might want to shadow him and keep your eyes open. I also strongly recommend that you consider bringing Israeli intelligence and FBI into this as well. You hear what I'm saying, Drew?"

"Yeah, I hear you Ben," I said. "I know what you're saying and I appreciate your help and your concern. But I can't bring them into this, at least not yet. Moshe really wants to keep this thing quiet and if Mossad or FBI get wind of this, they'll likely yank him back to Israel and kill any chance he might have of getting to Augusta for next year's Masters. That'll only play into the hands of these scumbags."

"Jeez, you're killing me Drew," he said. "You're making this harder every time we talk. As it is I'm going out on a limb telling you this stuff. You know that's our standard procedure when we have concerns about a foreign national, especially an Israeli national. Now you're asking me to break protocol again by not telling anybody about this. If I don't mention it to Mossad and your friend gets whacked, I better have a pretty good explanation or I'm done. My ass will be out on the street."

"Think about it Ben," I said. "This guy has a shot at playing in the Masters. You don't think that's worth something? How do you think you'd feel if you gave it all up?"

He paused for several seconds. "OK," he said finally. "But I really don't like it. I guess I see your point, so I'll see what I can do. See if I can delay sending it up the line for awhile. Just remember though, you're putting me so far out on that limb you better make sure you've got my back and don't end up cutting that limb off with the chain saw you're holding. And just in case there's anything to this new terrorist cell, you can help by keeping a close watch on your friend so he doesn't take a bullet in the forehead and I lose my job, alright?"

"Yeah, I hear you," I said. "You don't know how much I appreciate this. I know you're sticking your neck out for me on this, but I think this guy's worth helping. He's a great guy and somebody's really messing with him. I'll keep an eye on him."

"I know you will," he said. "You watch your back too," he said.

"Thanks, Ben. I will." I said. "Please give me a call if you hear anything else."

"You got it."

I hung up. I got a Michelob out of the fridge and sat down at my desk. This next weekend Moshe would be playing at the Michelob Championship at Kings Mill Golf Course near Williamsburg. With this latest info from Ben, even though non-specific, it was time to start following Moshe more closely. I'd get a press pass for the tournament and then arrange to follow him around the course. The crowds at even your average PGA event had swelled so much in recent years it would be no easy matter to screen any likely attackers, even if they were of Middle Eastern descent. Then again, it would be just as difficult for someone to make a getaway in those crowds, probably necessitating an attack before or after the actual tournament play. Regardless, I'd be there and do the best I could. Besides, who could turn down a glorious fall weekend in Williamsburg?

I called Kings Mill and after speaking with a desk manager was finally able to pick up a room that had just been cancelled. I then called Moshe's cell and left a message that I'd meet him Wednesday in the clubhouse after the practice round. Next, I dashed off a quick request to the Virginia Commonwealth Office of Information asking them for copies of all the VDOT contracting files for the Wilson Bridge Project. Maybe I could find something in the files about SCC and Gann.

Finally, I wrote the finishing touches to my draft for the next column, writing about the changes on the seventeenth hole after the loss of the Eisenhower tree, the background I'd developed on Moshe and his quest to go to the Masters, and the information I'd read about Parker Toomey and the questionable barrier island insurance award. I emailed it to my editor, then grabbed another beer and lay down on my couch to think about what I'd heard from Ben.

What was the deal with the situation in the Middle East? It was true the Israelis had gone there thousands of years ago and killed or displaced the people living there. But those people were hardly a uniform group, much less a group you could call "the Palestinians." Instead, they were a myriad bunch of various tribes, with names like the Amelikites, the Amorites, the Hittites, and the Jebbuzites. Now, it seemed to be another case of the Hatfields and McCoys, one group of people who hated the other, taking pleasure in killing off each other in the greatest numbers. Blow up a bus here, strafe a village there. Fire a rocket on this city, launch an attack on that one, tit for tat. It was hard at this point to figure out which acts were retaliatory, and for Moshe Goldman, it had apparently become personal. I wondered if this particular Hezbollah faction really would try and get the greatest amount of publicity possible out of taking out a rising PGA Tour player. If they did, I'd do my best to get in their way.

Chapter 16
2011

The desk looked as massive as an aircraft carrier. He sat behind it looking like the President in the Oval Office, puffing on a cigar and taking an occasional sip of Scotch from the heavy highball glass placed on a coaster on the leather desktop. With each movement of the glass, the ice tinkled lightly in the amber liquid. The smoke rose above his head and hovered by the ceiling, dimming the sunlight that streamed through the window behind him.

He looked at the men gathered in the room, some standing and leaning against the bookshelf covered walls, others sitting in chairs.

"I hear that it's your collective judgment that Crawford might prove to be pretty useful to us. Billy and Kurt, you both personally vouched for his reliability and loyalty. As you all know well, I hold those two qualities to be of utmost importance to this organization," he said, calmly glancing around the room as he spoke.

"And you know what happens, what I require, if there's a betrayal of either of those qualities," he said, looking directly at Billy and Kurt. "So I believe it is now time to hear about our Mr. Crawford's abilities and how he handled the test given him. Kurt?"

One of the men who had been leaning against a wall, arms crossed casually in front of him, straightened and stood, facing him. "Piece of cake, really," he said. "Crawford went with the idea you came up with. He waited outside the courthouse and watched that Jew Silverstein do his press conference after the jury verdict. Silverstein was full of crap talking about how the verdict made it clear his client was innocent. Said the usual stuff about this being a typical case of anti-Semitism and he wouldn't let that happen. He was talking big as you've seen him do a hundred times. Well, this was the last time, for damn straight. Crawford had it all worked out. He'd tailed Silverstein for weeks, following him from his office to his home and seeing him take the same route every time, just like the moron he is. So Crawford lifted the delivery van from that lot near LaGuardia. He got Smithson to drive for him. They picked Silverstein up leaving the garage on 45th, followed him up the Westside parkway, and when they reached that dark stretch around west 158th, Smithson pulled in front of him, Crawford opened the rear doors letting them swing wide, and opened up with his AK-47. Shredded the fool's windshield and chest to ribbons. Watched him veer his shiny Mercedes into the retaining wall, then over into the southbound lane, where some lucky Joe hit him broadside. Last thing they saw was the flash bang of the collision. They dumped the van in Highbridge Park, where they'd parked another stolen car, took 95 out of the city to Newark and flew home. Just like I said, boss. Piece of cake."

He leaned back in the desk chair, exhaled a fresh cloud of smoke towards the ceiling, then smiled broadly. "Outstanding job. Music to my ears, boys. Another one sent to his Jehovah."

He laughed, seeing in his mind the fireball from the collision and the impact on Silverstein's body, then looked at Kurt and then Billy. "Please let Crawford know that I'm impressed with his abilities. So long as he maintains his loyalty to us, he's got himself a very promising future. Kurt, Billy, you all let him know I welcome him with open arms into our brotherhood.

Chapter 17
The Present

I looked out the window as I got dressed on Wednesday, thinking of the drive down to Williamsburg. The day was bright and beautiful, with a light breeze blowing. The maple outside my window had a tinge of red on its leaves. There was a bit of nip in the morning chill and it was clear from the look of the trees that the annual splash of color in the leaves had begun. Fall was in the air and you could sense the rise in spirits of my fellow Alexandrians.

Before I left I put the finishing touches on a small piece for the column on the distinctive green jacket awarded to a Masters champion. At the awards ceremony early Sunday evening of the Masters, the just-crowned champion is helped into his jacket by the previous year's winner. I wrote how the green jacket had a fairly humble beginning. The first versions were worn by club members at the 1937 Masters to allow patrons to be able to easily find out information about the course. Apparently, no one could recall who had the original idea of awarding a green coat to the Masters champion, and with it honorary membership in Augusta National Golf Club. But in 1949, Sam Snead became the first recipient when he won the tournament.

It was late morning when I finished the piece and prepared to leave. I packed a small bag and at the last minute pulled out my old reliable .45 caliber service automatic, a belt clip holster, and a couple magazines from the chest I kept them in. Several years ago, I'd gotten a permit to carry it concealed, but it'd certainly been a while since I felt even a slight need to do so. I figured, however, that it wouldn't do much good to protect Moshe from a Hamas hit team if all I could do was wave at them with a golf umbrella. I pulled back the slide and released it several times to check its action; since I kept it cleaned, oiled, and sighted, it was ready to go. Hello Williamsburg – John Wayne meets Jack Nicklaus.

The drive down was spectacular with the glorious fall weather, but otherwise uneventful. I was amazed at the spread of suburbs all the way down the I-95 corridor. From the looks of it, people were now commuting into DC all the way from Fredericksburg. A lovely hour and a half drive at 10 mph in stop-and-go traffic with 20,000 of your closest friends. Sign me up for some of that fun.

I pulled off of I-64 onto the exit for Busch Gardens. Kings Mill was right next door so within minutes I was pulling into the circle in front of the hotel. I checked in at the front desk, got my keys, and then drove around to the back of the pool area to my building.

As I was walking to my room, my phone buzzed with an email from Ben. Opening it up, I saw that he'd sent a list of possible matches for the license plate. There were 136 of them. Thankfully only thirteen were even reasonably near where Moshe lived. I noticed with interest that of those thirteen, one of them had been reported as stolen.

My room was on the backside of the building, looking out onto the broad expanse of the James. What a magnificent view. The sky was so clear I could see all the way down the river to the ghost fleet, the grouping of dozens of odd and assorted merchant marine vessels anchored and awaiting the nation's call in time of war. Looking to the west, past Jamestown Island, the sun hung in the sky, its trail of light glittering on the slowly moving surface of the river like molten gold. Pulling myself away from the view, I called Moshe on his new cell number.

"Hey there Moshe, how you doing? I just arrived. Is everything OK?" I asked.

"So far, so good, Drew," he said. "I'm set to head out for a practice round in about twenty minutes. I must say, it is good to hear your voice and know you are here."

"No problem at all," I said. "I was planning on taking a look around the course and the clubhouse and then maybe we could meet for dinner after your round. That sound good to you?"

"Yes, that would be great," he said. "I am at the driving range now, trying to work out a little problem with my three-iron. I'm not hitting it well and my shot is not fading quite like it should. But I should have it figured out shortly."

My, oh my, I thought, he's probably only hitting it around 275. And probably just hitting the side of the green instead of dead center. Guess it sucks to be him. He'd better get to work on that quick. But just when I thought to myself how I wished I had his problems, I remembered my real reason for being there and felt ashamed of my thoughts. Everyone had talents and gifts, and just because Moshe's involved hitting amazing golf shots and mine weren't, I shouldn't be envious of him, particularly when some terrorist group was out there trying to kill him.

"By the way, I meant to ask you. Ever heard of a golfer from Israel named Nathan Levin? He was on the tour years ago and then dropped out of sight. Do you know him?" I asked.

"Nathan Levin? Yes, of course I know him. Or at least know of him. He was an amazing golfer. I was a child when he played on the tour so I was never able to see him play. But I've heard stories about his great game by people who did. They said he had the smoothest swing around since Sam Snead. I have no idea though what happened to him or where he is. There was a story floating around that he had some family issues and had to quit the tour because of that. But I don't think he ever returned to Israel. I don't know where he lives now, but my country's embassy should. It's near you in Washington, D.C."

"Well that's helpful. I'll have to check it out when I get back home. Maybe they'll be able to tell me where he is now."

"Yes, they should," he said. "Use my name when you call them. That might help you to get the information easier."

"Perfect," I said. "I'll do that. And don't forget. I'll meet you at the restaurant in the clubhouse, at seven. And I hope you can work that three-iron out."

"Thank you Drew. And thank you very much for being here with me," he said. "I cannot thank you enough."

"No problem, Moshe. Just keep helping me with my slice and we'll call it even." Between the two of us, it was a sure bet that he had the harder task.

Chapter 18

I hung up and walked down to the clubhouse. I checked out the locker room and the club storage room and strolled around the perimeter of the building. I had no idea what I was looking for, but figured as with most things, if something didn't quite look like it fit, it probably didn't. Particularly if it was a group of middle-eastern looking men in head coverings and robes lurking around and holding AK-47s.

Everything looked like it fit, and there were no groups of men with that general description, so I moved out onto the course. A new three-man group was heading out on the River course for a practice round. I watched them tee off and then took off for the backside of the course, holes 4, 5, and 6, and where 12 joined 13. I figured if it were me trying to take someone out, I'd set up on the perimeter of the course in the wood line, with a sniper rifle and scope. That way, it'd be much easier to make a hit and get away quickly. So I walked down the main road that led back to the clubhouse and main hotel building and then went backwards from green to tee along the tree line moving down the side of the holes and into the woods on the out of bounds side.

I love walking through woods, particularly on a day as glorious as this one. There's a certain quiet in the bush, broken only by the intermittent calls and whistles of birds, the movement of small animals, and the muted rustle of the leaves high in the trees. The sun shone through in shifting dapples of light that highlighted the changing colors of some trees and bushes, while casting others into deep shadow. As I always did when moving through the woods, I moved as quietly as I could, lifting my feet high when I walked and placing them carefully to avoid piles of leaves and deadfall, looking from side to side constantly. From long practice, I knew that the sound of sticks breaking in the woods carried a good distance.

I moved quickly and easily around the perimeter of the course, looking for any signs of obvious recent entry through, or tampering with, the surrounding high chain link fence. I found one place where the fence had been cut and bent in to allow entry, but on closer inspection, saw that the cut ends were rusted from long years of exposure to rain.

I was crossing a small ridgeline at the back corner of the course, moving from the 6th hole to the 5th, when I saw movement ahead of me. I stopped and eased behind a large oak, careful to avoid the ropes of poison ivy climbing up its trunk. Sinking lower to the ground, I eased to my left moving carefully and slowly down a shallow ravine. I could see a figure in the distance ahead of me, bending down and working on something with his hands next to the trunk of a fallen tree. He wore dark jeans and a dark shirt, and on the ground next to his feet were a backpack and a metal object about the size of a small rifle.

Glancing over my left shoulder, I had a clear view of the fifth green. Yes sir. This is just about where I'd set up well in advance, and wait for Moshe to come to me. Looks like I'd found that thing that didn't fit.

I eased the loaded .45 out of my holster and flicked it off safe. I estimated roughly 60 meters separated us. Probably not too far a shot with a handgun for Jason

Bourne or James Bond, but it was too far for me. I had to get closer before confronting him. I continued very slowly down the ravine until it leveled out and then moved in a low crouch in his general direction, hidden by a low growing tangle of wild blackberry and laurel bushes.

The bushes came to an end and I knew it was now or never. In one quick movement, I jumped up, .45 held in front of me in both hands, and moved to within 10 meters of him, standing still in a crouched firing position.

"Freeze and stand up where you are, hands above your head," I shouted.

The effect was like poking him with an electrically charged cattle prod. He started violently, whirled around, and while attempting to throw his hands in the air, proceeded to catch his feet in the straps of his backpack and then fall over backwards with a loud cry.

I quickly covered the remaining distance and looked down at him, .45 aimed directly at his forehead.

He looked to be about fourteen years old, wide-eyed and fearful, with one iPod ear bud remaining in one ear, the other dangling down his chest and emitting the sounds of some rock band blasting with guitar and drums. "What...what do you want, mister? Please don't shoot me," he stuttered loudly.

Still covering him, I reached down and grabbed the backpack and metal object and then took several steps back.

"Don't move," I said.

Still watching him, I put my left hand into the opening of the backpack and reached carefully inside. I felt golf balls. A lot of golf balls. I looked down at the metal object. It was a collapsible pole for retrieving golf balls from water hazards. With chagrin I discovered that I had very expertly immobilized a teenager looking for lost golf balls. Not to mention one who wouldn't have heard me if I'd traipsed right up to him through the deadfall.

"Sorry to frighten you," I said, putting the .45 back on safe and into my belt holster. "One of the pros here for the tournament is having some issues with some tour stalkers and I thought you were one of them."

Slowly collecting himself he said, "Yeah, well I'm not. You scared the crap out of me, man. I'm just looking for lost golf balls that I clean up and sell to hackers. You coulda killed me."

"Not even close," I said. "I might've shot off your arm or leg, maybe taken out a lung, but I definitely wouldn't have killed you. So tell me, how many golf balls you got in that bag?" I asked.

"I don't know. Probably around 40," he said.

I pulled out my wallet and handed him 40 bucks. "I could use 40 golf balls. A buck a ball seems reasonable, you think?"

"Well, yeah, that works for me," he said a grin slowly spreading across his face.

"Get outta here, go clean up the balls, and drop them off at the front desk at the clubhouse. They'll have another $20 waiting for you. Make all this nonsense worth your while."

"That's awesome, mister. Thanks a lot. I'll bring them there later today, promise."

There's nothing like a budding entrepreneur living the American dream, I thought. And with that, I thanked him, turned and continued on my way.

Chapter 19

Finally making my way around the far side of the course, I headed back towards the clubhouse, moving easily through the pines and hardwoods that paralleled each hole as the sun moved closer to the horizon and the shadows lengthened. Other than the kid in the woods looking for golf balls, everything still looked like it fit.

In the gathering dusk, I walked towards the press tent situated near the 18th green across from the large Kings Mill symbol on the pond bank. Even though I was there to watch Moshe, there was no reason why I couldn't do my job and work on my column at the same time.

Flashing my press pass as I entered the tent I walked along the different tables to see what they had to offer. The first table described the most recent PGA rules on clubs and balls. A blue and white placard with pictures of various golf balls explained that golf balls that weighed more than 1.62 ounces, were smaller than 1.68 inches in diameter, or looked clearly like they didn't meet the spherical symmetry standard were illegal. So that ruled out a ball designed to self-correct in flight, or a "hot ball" with too high an initial velocity standard. I was happy to see that the Titleist I used was on the current list of conforming golf balls. So perhaps I could find comfort in the fact that even though my game sucked, I had conforming equipment. Small consolation.

As I stood looking at the table, I overheard someone several tables down addressing someone else as "Mr. Gann." I casually moved in that direction and discovered, much to my surprise and delight, none other than J. J. Gann himself in close conversation with three PGA officials talking about how they had set up the Michelob Championship at Kings Mill and asking questions about the PGA's role in setting up for the next Masters.

As I listened, it was clear that Gann was the authority figure, apparently well known by the officials, who didn't miss a chance to compliment him or agree with one of his points. I turned and walked up to the group.

"Mr. Gann? J. J. Gann?"

Gann turned to look at me. He was about 5' 9" and somewhat heavy around the middle. His black hair had a gleam like an old polished persimmon wood driver, slicked back with hair product. His face was smooth and expressionless and his eyelids were so heavy that they gave him a slightly sinister appearance with hooded watchful eyes that looked through people and spoke of money and access and privilege. Altogether, it was a pretty unpleasant face. But faces really mean nothing and looks can be very deceiving. I found that out once when we brought in an Iraqi commander, a favorite of Saddam's. He had just executed three Kuwaiti children with a machete, just for laughs. Yet, he was the nearest thing to Bob Hope I ever saw. When he smiled his eyes danced, and he had a deep warm laugh. But in reality, he was Evil personified. So, Gann could well turn out to be my new favorite drinking buddy.

"Yes, my name is Gann. Who are you and how may I help you," he said in a low voice with a slight Alabama drawl.

"My name is Drew James. I'm a writer for Golfer's Journal here to cover the Michelob Championship," I said.

"Pleased to meet you," he said. "I believe I've already read a few of your pieces in your column about Augusta National and our beloved Masters. Not entirely factually correct, I might add, but they seem entertaining enough for a golf magazine." He paused, looking straight at me, and added, "and how may I assist you?"

"As part of the series, I wanted to cover one of the club's directors, and since I live in Alexandria and have to deal with the mess around the Wilson Bridge construction every day, I thought I'd write about you and Shelley Construction Company. Any chance we could set up an interview?" I explained.

His eyes looked directly in mine and he held the gaze for several seconds. Then he said in a measured and clipped tone, "Mr. James, I appreciate that you are just trying to do your job, but at this particular moment you are unfortunately keeping me from doing mine. It may sound rude, but anything you need to know about my construction company and our current project at the Wilson Bridge can be obtained on the Commonwealth of Virginia's website dealing with the project. Put simply, I just do not have any time for any interview. Now if you'll excuse me, I really do have urgent business to attend to."

He started to turn away, then paused, looked back over his shoulder at me, and added, "If my response seems discourteous, I apologize. I am a very busy man. But please do feel free to call my company's Press Relations Officer. Her number is on this card. I'm certain she'll be happy to meet with you." He reached into his coat pocket, handed me a business card, then turned and walked away. And that was that. So much for a new drinking buddy.

I glanced down at the card. It was your typical business card, heavy stock in off-white embossed with the initials SCC in large print. In the middle were the name Michelle Gann, her title of Press Relations Officer, and a phone number. I placed the card in my pocket and then realized it was already past seven and I was late for my meeting with Moshe.

Chapter 20

I walked into the clubhouse and turned towards Eagles restaurant. Moshe wasn't waiting for me so I figured he'd already grabbed a table. I moved past the hostess stand and into the dining room, glancing quickly at all the tables to spot Moshe. But he wasn't there.

I turned back towards the hostess stand. Standing behind it was a slight brunette, deeply tanned, with a nametag that read "Kathy." I had the impression that she didn't have enough skin to fit her comfortably, so that it stretched tight over every inch of her, giving a slight tilt to her eyes, shortening her upper lip, and leading to an overall impression that said, "May I help you?" Perhaps she could.

"Hi Kathy, I'm looking for a friend of mine. He was supposed to meet me here for dinner twenty minutes ago. He's one of the tour pros, black curly hair, shorter than me. Maybe you know him, Moshe Goldman."

"I know who Mr. Goldman is, sir," she said somewhat breathlessly, as if talking about a secret lover, "but I haven't seen him here this evening. I did see him earlier when I came into work. He was walking across the parking lot and getting into his car. It was about five-thirty."

I thanked her and walked outside. This was odd. Moshe hadn't mentioned anything to me about going anywhere other than the restaurant after he was done. An

81

alarm gong started sounding softly inside my head. I tried his cell phone but it immediately went to voicemail. I left a message asking him to call me as soon as he could.

With nothing else to do, I strolled up to the main building to grab a drink and wait to hear from Moshe. One drink turned into several, and I was as nervous as a PGA rookie putting to make his first professional cut when my cell phone buzzed with an unfamiliar number.

"Drew, it's me," Moshe blurted out quickly. "Something just happened, but I'm alright. I need you to come get me."

"What happened? Are you sure you're OK?" I asked.

"Yes, I'm fine, but a bit shaken up," he said.

I thought back to Ben Cooper's warning about the Hezbollah splinter cell and a chill went up my spine, causing me to shudder. What could I have missed?

"What happened?" I said.

"I was frustrated with my three-iron. I just could not get it to work. I thought I could use some fresh air and a nice drive around this pretty countryside. So I drove over to the Colonial Parkway near Jamestown and headed towards Yorktown. I'd crossed under the interstate as the sun began to go down. I had planned on turning around at Yorktown and coming back to join you for dinner. I didn't think there was any harm in that.

"All of a sudden a pair of lights showed up fast behind me. I thought someone wanted to get past me, so I moved a little to the right and slowed to let them pass me. But they stayed right up behind me. Their lights were on bright, and I could barely see where I was going."

"Could you see what type of vehicle it was?" I said.

"No, not then," he said. "I thought I would try and go faster ahead of them but as I started to do that, the road ahead curved to the left, and as we entered the turn, they swung out and came even with me to the left of my car. I looked over and saw the passenger window coming down and a gun being aimed at me. I was terrified."

"What happened next?"

"I pulled to the right as we went into the curve and my right wheels slipped on the grassy slope. The car went over the bank and down into a small pond. Thankfully, my window was already down. I don't know what I would've done if it hadn't been. The car filled with water so quickly. Holding my breath, I pulled at my seat belt until it finally came off. I pushed myself out through the window and swam underwater as far away from my car as I could go before I went up. When I broke the surface, I knew enough to be as quiet as I could. I saw a dark colored large SUV stopped on the side and several men looking down into the water where my car had gone in. They were shining flashlights into the water. It was quite dark under the overhanging trees, so I couldn't see what they looked like. Their faces were dark in the shadows. The good news was they couldn't see me either. I waited in the water at the far edge of the pond near a clump of cattails."

"Did they try and come after you?"

"No, but good thing I had swum underwater away from the car. They had an automatic weapon that looked like an Uzi. They shot in the water all around the car. After about a minute of firing, they got into the van and drove away. I was still afraid to move, thinking they might have left someone there to check that I wasn't still alive."

"And then what?"

"I heard and saw nothing so I slowly climbed out of the water and walked around the pond back to the road."

"So where are you now and how are you calling me?"

"I was shivering from the water and the cold so I had to move. I had no choice but to start walking back towards Williamsburg. There's nothing out there along that stretch. I'd been walking about 15 minutes when I heard a car coming up the road from behind me. I was very scared but it wasn't the SUV so I took a chance. It turned out to be two fishermen headed home from fishing on the York River. They were very nice to me. I told them I had simply lost control of my car and gone off the edge. They took me back to where the car was and let me use their phone. They're waiting here with me."

"I'm glad you called me first instead of the police," I said. "I'll call a tow truck and be right there. Don't call the police, and stay there with those two until I get there. You sure you're alright, Moshe?"

"Yes I am sure, Drew. But please get here as fast as you can" he said.

"I'm on my way," I said.

I drove as quickly as I could down the Colonial Parkway until I found them. Moshe got in my car, while I thanked the two fishermen profusely and gave them each fifty bucks for their trouble. They took off and with Moshe sitting safely in my car I grabbed a flashlight from the trunk and looked quickly around the area. I found a pile of shells scattered down the bank in the weeds by the edge of the pond. I collected all that I could find and saw that they were .45 ACPs so Moshe could have been right about the Uzi.

There were tire tracks in the dirt on the side of the road, but it was impossible to tell if they were from the SUV or Moshe's car. Bracing myself for the chill, I waded down chest deep into the water and shined the light down on the side of his car. There was a streak of dark blue paint but nothing else that could identify the other vehicle. As I climbed back up the bank to the road, a tow truck with a couple guys arrived from the rental car company. It was hard work getting them to accept Moshe's story about losing control without calling the police, but my offer of cash for dinner on me satisfied them.

After the car was pulled out and taken away, Moshe and I drove back to Kings Mill, both of us wet, cold, and hungry. By the time I got him back to his room, it was past midnight. I waited until room service arrived, then after we ate, I ordered him to bolt his door and stay put until the morning when I would wake him in time to hit the practice range before his start time. Despite his aches and pains and overall tiredness, he was determined to play. With that decided, I headed for bed.

Chapter 21

He was sitting in the curve of the padded leather booth, savoring the perfectly grilled dry-aged filet and the bottle of Insignia wine. The wait staff came and went quietly, fulfilling their duties to perfection. The murmur of noise from the crowded room was muted and barely discernible in the luxurious surroundings of the restaurant. In between bites, he conversed in quiet tones with the man sitting across the table from him.

A soft chirping noise interrupted their conversation and he watched with concentrated interest as the man set down his fork and picked up the cell phone from the table top. "Yes?" the man asked, and then, after listening to the caller's voice, the man handed the phone to him.

His face grew dark as he listened. "Who was in charge?" he demanded, and then after a pause asked "what steps did you all take to ensure it was finished?" He listened further and then, in a barely controlled voice said, "This is flat unacceptable. We planned this for the perfect time and place and you were supposed to make it happen. I hope this doesn't give me cause to question your reliability."

He listened again, as the sounds of protestations could be heard coming from the phone. "Shut up," he said, ending the conversation abruptly. "Get it done right next time."

Handing the phone back, he looked over at the man and shook his head, saying in a low voice, "They can't confirm. They didn't try and find the body and since there's nothing on the news we can only assume they missed. Tomorrow we'll have a definite answer, *but it looks like they screwed this one up. This was Jerry's again. The timing was perfect. Not another soul around. There's no excuse."*

He looked intently at the man and said, "As you of all people know, we have got to get this done. We are running out of time and I simply can't afford failure. I won't stand for it. Regrettably, there's not enough time to set something up for the remaining events this year, so we'll have to aim for early spring. I want you to set up the planning and have one of your best bring it off. Can you do that for me?"

"Yes, Sir," the man said. "I assure you we'll get it done. And I'll see to it personally that we set the proper example for failure with Jerry."

He smiled and nodded to the man. "Good," then he picked up his fork and knife and resumed eating.

Chapter 22

I woke up a little sore and tired. I could only imagine how Moshe must have felt. Here it was, Thursday, and he had a tournament to play. The guy had more guts than Wyatt Earp staring down a gang of outlaw cowboys. I woke him up and after we had breakfast we were ready to roll. I left him at the driving range to try and bring back some semblance of normalcy to his day.

With a little time on my hands, and the image of J. J. Gann fresh in my mind, I called my brother-in-law, John Hewlett, an investment banker in Atlanta, to see what, if anything, he could tell me about SCC and Gann, as well as the other board members. If he didn't know anything, I hoped he'd have some connections. But after getting his voicemail, I had to leave a message.

I then pulled out the business card Gann had given me. Michelle had to be some relation to him - a sister, daughter, or perhaps his mother. No way of knowing yet. I dialed the number. I was asked to please hold and, being the obedient sort, did so.

A voice came on the phone, cool and polished.

"Shelley Gann. How may I help you, Mister James," she said. She had a nice way of drawing out "James" when she said it.

"Thanks for taking my call Ms. Gann," I said. "I work for Golfer's Journal and I'm writing a series of articles on Augusta National leading up to the Masters next April. I'd like to do some bios on each of the Directors for the Club and was hoping to start with a piece on Mr. Gann and SCC. I'm here at the Michelob Championship and yesterday he gave me your card and told me I should call you to set up an interview with him. Any chance I could do that?"

"Oh do please call me Shelley, Mr. James," she said. "Daddy told me you might call. I'd be happy to arrange to meet with you to talk about him and the company. As you can well imagine, he's quite a busy man, so I'm hopeful you'd be gracious enough to accept meeting with me instead."

"Of course, that's fine. I've got no problem with meeting with you Shelley, and I understand he's a busy guy, but isn't there any way you can arrange a meeting for me with your father? It would be most helpful to actually meet with the Chair of the board." I said.

"Now, Mr. James," she said, "I'm afraid that's just not going to be possible. Perhaps you'll be able to arrange something with the other members of the board, but not with my father. He's always on the road visiting his different projects. If you'd like to get information about SCC or my father or his work with Augusta National you'll just have to meet with me. Wouldn't you prefer that anyway?" she asked somewhat flirtatiously.

Having no other choice at that point, I made arrangements to meet with her. I told her an abbreviated version of the story I would be writing and we agreed to meet in five days, when she would be in D.C. We arranged to meet for lunch downtown at Old Ebbitt Grill and I thanked her for agreeing to meet me.

"Oh thank you, Mr. James. The pleasure is all mine."

"And you're certain that I can't slip in a visit with Mr. Gann sometime?" I asked.

"Yes, Mr. James. I'm quite certain. But I do believe you'll be satisfied enough meeting with me. Goodbye."

With that, she hung up. I got off the phone, somewhat intrigued by Shelley Gann's charms, and looked for Moshe. I found him practicing his chip shots from just off the green. Watching him, you'd never have been able to tell what he'd been through the night before. He was amazing. I watched him chip with a 6-iron, rolling the ball up a slight bank. Then use a 3-wood to hit a bump-and-run shot. Next, he went to an area of four- to six-inch rough, took his sand wedge and, rotating the club around his body with an open face, played a number of simply gorgeous flop shots. Every pitch he tried ended up just a few feet from the pin.

My normal course for chips and pitches was to skull them or hit them fat. I knew why that happened, but as with most weaknesses in my golf game, I couldn't seem to do much about it. For me the reasons were obvious. I'd forget and lift my head or shift my weight back. Mostly though, I invariably got anxious and tried to help the ball up in the air, especially in thick rough or in the bunker, instead of just swinging my arms and letting the loft of the club do the dirty work.

It was finally Moshe's turn to tee off to start the tournament. He hit a beautiful drive to the left side of the fairway leaving him with only a short iron approach into the green. After putting for par, he relaxed visibly and settled into a smooth and easy rhythm. The remainder of the tournament proceeded uneventfully with nary a sign of rogue lost ball seekers, or Middle Eastern terrorists.

Moshe ended up in fifteenth place for the tournament. Not bad at all considering the start he'd had to the week. With the tour winding down, he had decided to take a bit of a break and head back to Israel for a month or so to visit his family and friends. Given the most recent attack, we both thought it might do him some good, not to mention keep him out of the spotlight in the U.S. We agreed to meet again in November when he would return to close out the tour season. He'd been invited to be one of the three players from the PGA to compete in the Wendy's 3-Tour Challenge in Henderson, Nevada, just outside of Vegas.

I made Moshe promise to call me frequently so I could know what was happening with him, and he promised he would. And with that, I took off for the trip back to D.C. with visions of Hezbollah, D.C. construction sites, Alabama belles, and 300-yard drives dancing around inside my head.

Chapter 23

Back in Alexandria I got up, ran, showered and ate breakfast. The sky was covered with solid gray clouds and a cool wind brought an early season chill to the air. Left-over puddles from the rain the night before shimmered like mirrors in the coolness.

Anticipating meeting the face behind the voice of Shelley Gann, I dressed for success, slipping on a pair of light wool grey slacks, a black cashmere sweater, and some black driving mocs. The perfect outfit to impress a Southern Belle, or at least I hoped. Carrying a fresh cup of Starbucks, I looked cautiously out my front door before venturing into the apartment hallway. It was a good thing too. Coming out of the door across the hall at the same time was my new neighbor, looking polished and dressed for success in a slim fitting navy blue dress, and carrying a briefcase.

I gave her my biggest smile and said, "Hi there, I'm Drew James and it looks like we're neighbors."

Then holding out my hand to her, I said, "Why don't we meet the right way? I'm really sorry about our first meeting a while back. Not a great way to welcome you to the building. Guess I kinda blew out of here pretty quick."

"You can say that again," she said, looking up at me with those gorgeous green eyes. "What an unexpected surprise. Walk up the stairs and get my breath knocked out of me. Is that the way everyone moves around this town?"

"Well, I guess life is pretty fast paced here. So little time, so many traffic jams to drive through. I suppose you eventually get used to it. So what brought you to Alexandria?"

"I just got transferred here by my Company. I was working in their headquarters in Wisconsin and they decided to move me here. I'd never been to D.C. before so it seemed like a good idea at the time. But now I'm not so sure if this is a reward for a good job or some kind of punishment."

She smiled as she spoke, using her hand to brush her auburn hair behind one ear. Her emerald eyes looked directly at me and she spoke with confidence and grace. Altogether a lovely lady and a nice addition to the neighborhood, I thought.

"It's really not such a bad place to live if you can get used to the summer humidity," I said. "Maybe the hardest part is getting used to the traffic. That and meeting new folks. But I've lived here for a few years and the longer you're here, the more it grows on you."

"Well, I'll see about that," she said. "Nice meeting you officially, Drew. I've gotta run to work. By the way, ever thought of looking out your door's peephole before you blast out of there?"

Without thinking, the words blurted out of my mouth, "Well, truth be told, the fault wasn't all mine. I didn't expect someone to be standing right outside my front door."

Just like that, with a disbelieving look she stared at me, mouth slightly open, like I had a huge single eye in the middle of my forehead, then she grimaced, shook her head, gave me a "whatever" look, and went out the door. Not so much as a goodbye. I didn't even get her name, I realized as I stared at the now vacant stairwell.

With a sigh and a shake of my head at the wonder of what just happened, I got in my Land Rover and headed into town. Sure hoped this wasn't going to be typical of my morning's interaction with women.

Chapter 24

Since it was later in the morning, the traffic snarl had died down and I made pretty good time into the city. Avoiding the traffic was a good thing. Aside from the summer humidity, like I'd told my new neighbor, the traffic was one of the worst things to have to put up with in the area. It could change dull, mild-mannered federal bureaucrats into frothing, raging maniacs, quick to change lanes abruptly in front of you and flip you off at the same time.

The wind had picked up and as I crossed the 14th Street Bridge the surface of the Potomac was ruffled and choppy. It was slate gray like the dull finish of a Glock. Lines of froth blown by the wind extended eastward beneath the bridge. The sky was mostly gray with a brief glimpse of blue sky and sun occasionally breaking through.

The city still looked beautiful in the gloom, the changing fall leaves looking like a mosaic of red, gold and brown surrounding the white marble monuments. I stayed on 14th Street until I was even with the Washington Monument, turned left, then right onto 15th. Another block and I was past the Treasury Building with Old Ebbitt Grill on the right. I pulled into a space at the curb, fished some quarters out of the console, and got out to feed the meter. I was a little bit early for my meeting with Ms. Gann, but that was a good thing. I figured I'd go in, scout out a good table and be waiting for her when she showed up. I figured wrong.

As I walked up to the maitre d', I looked straight ahead at a booth and saw a set of cool expressionless eyes sizing me up. I moved to the table and looked down at her. Her eyes were the improbable sea blue of contact lenses, made more improbable by just enough eye makeup to make them look bigger than they were. And they were generous to start with. The secretive lashes half veiled the vivid plastic blue.

Her skin texture was like a new grainless plastic. The small mouth did not really pout. It was just that both upper and under lip were so heavy it was the only choice it had. They were artfully covered with pink frost, and a secret half-smile curved the corners slightly.

Looking cool and unflappable, her face was framed by a perfect arc of blonde hair on either side. The light of early afternoon came through the windows, highlighting the lustrous blonde fall of each arc. She was twenty-something and gorgeous, and vitally aware of her effect on every man in the place.

The sight of her completely fulfilled the imaginary vision I'd gotten earlier from the sound of her voice. She was wearing a cream colored suit over a white silk blouse. The top three buttons of her blouse were unbuttoned, exposing a tease of deep cleavage and an occasional glimpse of lacy bra. And the look of challenge in her eyes was unmistakable.

Most of the twenty-something girls I'd run across were full of fun and good times. They moved through life in a shining, laughing, clothes-centered, self-important immortality, existing for sun and fun and drink, always aware of being looked at and saying to any male with the courage to approach, "Let's see what you've got!"

But this was something entirely different. She was aware of everything around her, confident, thinking, scheming, planning, and always with a fixed smile. She appeared to be always one step ahead of the competition, playing by a set of rules of which most males weren't even aware. I looked into those eyes and behind the façade of loveliness, apparent good breeding, and gentility, saw a coldness that belied her intriguing voice and a firmness of resolve that got her whatever it was she wanted.

Usually I could sense a connection with most people I met through a smile or a look or a pleasant word. But looking into Shelley Gann's eyes was like looking into a pool of blue ice water on the surface of a glacier lit up by the sunshine - beautiful, sparkling, and cold as ice. She stayed seated and put out her hand for me to grasp. Not surprisingly, her grip was firm and dry.

"Ms. Gann, I'm Drew James. Very nice to meet you. I appreciate you being willing to meet with me."

"Pleased to meet you, Mr. James. As I told you on the phone, call me Shelley. Old Ebbitt is one of my favorites. I've taken the liberty to order for us. I didn't think you'd mind. The oysters here are wonderful. I've always believed they have a very positive effect on one's libido. Do you like them? And I ordered a bottle of Domaine Louis Moreau, my favorite French Chablis. I hope you don't mind my forwardness in ordering before you even got here."

And with that she'd proceeded to take complete control of my interview. With her perfect hair shining and her lip gloss gleaming, she'd picked the table and her seat, ordered the food and wine, and initiated the conversation. Before I knew it, she'd taken the conversation from the aphrodisiac qualities of oysters all the way to discussing the impact of Potomac River pollution on the indigenous

Chesapeake Bay oyster beds and how her company had worked diligently to prevent any pollution from the Wilson Bridge construction. And I was following meekly along just as if I'd had a ring in my nose attached to a chain she held in her hand. I'd had enough.

Chapter 25

"Damn Shelley, you are really good. The oysters were great and the wine was an excellent choice," I said, trying to get back on track, "but what I'd still really like to know for my column is how your father formed SCC, how he got involved in Augusta National, how he got the Route 1/I-495 interchange project in Virginia, and a description of the work SCC has done on the project. I know there's not a chance in hell of ever being able to meet with your father, but do you think you could at least give me some info about SCC?"

She looked at me, smiling, and said, "That would be correct, Drew. No chance in hell. That answer is not going to change. But as my father and I have told you, I'm more than capable of answering your questions about my father and SCC, and very happy to do so."

And with that she went on for an hour telling me everything about her father and SCC that I'd read about on-line and in the information received from Augusta National. After dropping out of college, he'd started off with nothing but a used bulldozer, pulling in any road job or land clearing contract he could get. He poured everything he had into the company, going from one dozer, to five, to a fleet of road building equipment, and over the course of ten years, he'd built SCC from nothing to a company that could compete for projects all across the nation.

I continued to ask questions about Gann, his duties and responsibilities on the Augusta National Board, and how SCC got such a sweet deal on the huge Wilson Bridge contract. Every question I could come up with was met with a rehearsed and polished answer, a cool denial, or a lengthy detailed description of some irrelevant aspect of Shelley Construction.

Throughout our conversation, her demeanor and poise were as unflappable as a polished politician running for office. As our discussions wound down, I threw out one final question. Ok, call it a cheap shot, since I'd never actually heard such a rumor.

"So Shelley, I'd just like your response to one last question. I'd like you to confirm or deny a simple rumor I saw on line. Just tell me straight up. Is there any truth to the rumor that your father was able to pull strings by greasing some palms at the highest level in Virginia to win the Wilson Bridge contract? You know what I'm saying. A good ole fashion bribe?" Maybe it was a bit of a stretch but I wanted to see if I could shake her at all.

But she didn't miss a beat. She responded evenly, "Quite simply Mr. James, no. There is no truth to that rumor. We bid on that project just like everyone else, putting together the winning package as we have for projects all over the country. My father didn't get to be in the successful position he is now by handing out money to corrupt state officials."

And then suddenly her eyes changed as she looked through me. One moment she was looking me straight in the eye, and the next, she stared unfocused as if she was watching a television that was on just beyond my head. Her eyes became moist and she whispered with lips quivering with emotion, "My father is a good man. He is a good and fine man. He would never do anything wrong. After Mother died, it was just him and me. He's all I have left. All his life he has had to deal with people trying to destroy him and I will do all that I can to protect him."

When they're really from the South, they have a funny way of making me feel a little self-conscious and guilty about being a "nor-thurn-ure." As if I had sharp edges. As if they all came from the same small town where they talk to each other in those soft lovely voices, and they have a code of acting superficially that is so deep and so much a part of the way they act and behave that they don't ever have to think about it as such.

She had lifted the edge of the code just enough so I could see in - see trouble and tears, and letting me look in was, in itself, a violation of the code.

Then her eyes refocused. She looked at me, smiled softly, and leaned towards me as if to share some lover's secret. And between pressed lips she said, "Mr. James, you of course know the rules concerning libel as it applies to journalists. If you do not, you should endeavor to learn them immediately. My father is an upstanding man of honor and integrity, a credit to his company and this great nation. He would never choose on his own to do something unethical or criminal. Please know that if you choose to smear his name, or that of SCC, with some crazy internet rumor you may rest assured that we will take any and all actions permitted under law to rectify the situation."

Then, in a remarkable display of self-control, she flicked an internal switch, smiled with dazzling white teeth, and continued in a normal volume, "I've very much enjoyed our lunch, Mr. James. It was a pleasure meeting you. I trust that our conversation has benefited you and will assist you in writing your article. My Daddy and I always stand ready to contribute information and assist in any pieces on Augusta National or SCC." She reached over and dropped a business card in front of me. It had only her name and personal cell phone number on it. "Should you desire more information, please do not hesitate to call me, Mr. James. I'd be delighted to talk with you again."

I sat stunned at the reversal in her voice and demeanor. With an apparent act of iron will, she had changed from sadness on the verge of tears, to outright defiance and hostility, to charm and flirtation. She rose, scooped up a matching cream-colored coat, shook my hand, and with the perfect amount of controlled hip sway, strolled out the door into a waiting limousine.

And with that, Shelley Gann was gone and I was left with a $300 lunch tab. Like looking for unbroken cherished family heirlooms in the aftermath of a tornado, I was left to pick through the remnants of our conversation and salvage any usable information. There wasn't much. I knew that SCC and Shelley Gann were both named for Gann's mother, that SCC had started small in Mobile, Alabama, and grown into a national company, that Gann had served on the board of Augusta National for the last 10 years, and that any mention of improper contractual dealings with the Virginia government had hit a soft spot and caused an instantaneous reaction, like the old paper mache volcanoes with vinegar and baking soda we made when we were kids.

Chapter 26

I walked out onto the sidewalk, feeling the wind hit me as it blew out of the North down 15th street. The old Treasury building was directly across the street, its white marble walls gleaming like an old Greek temple in the few patches of sunlight that emerged through the fast moving cover of clouds. The trees up 15th street had started to change to red or yellow, with flurries of falling leaves cascading through the cool air and skittering into piles against the curb.

I smelled deeply of the fresh air. Since I was this far into the city, it seemed like a perfect time to try and swing by the Israeli embassy in Northwest DC and try and get a lead on Nathan Levin, the former Israeli tour player. As I drove up Connecticut Avenue, the commercial part of the city faded away and the street was lined with large apartment buildings and embassies from around the world. Crossing over the bridge above Rock Creek Park, I could see the creek sparkling far below as it meandered through the trees.

Pulling off of Connecticut, I found a parking spot not far from the Embassy. It was a tall elegant four-story Brownstone, with a large groomed landscaped lawn surrounded by a 6-foot high iron railing fence. The lower floors all had filigreed steel bars covering the windows. There were large concrete planters full of an assortment of fall flowers lining the circular driveway, acting as an effective barrier for any vehicles allowed through the main gates. I could see the round smoky globes containing security cameras hanging from the eves of the house at every corner. There was little doubt that someone inside was watching me even as I walked through the open pedestrian gate and up to the door. Holding my notebook, in my left hand, I walked up and rang the doorbell, having no idea what to expect.

The door opened almost immediately. Standing in front of me was a tall, heavy-set Israeli security guard holding a Tavor TAR-21 automatic assault rifle in one hand. "Yes Sir, may I help you?" he said.

"I hope so," I said. I explained to him who I was and about the articles I was writing on the Masters and on Moshe. I told him I was trying to locate Nathan Levin and see if he was still in the U.S.

"So you actually know Moshe Goldman?" he asked.

"Yes, I actually do. Like I said, I'm featuring his efforts to get to the Masters next year. He's a friend of mine."

"That is very good. Before I became a soldier for Israel, I worked as a security guard at the Caesarea Golf and Country Club. Years ago I watched him win the Macabbiah Games there. I am a big fan of his. He is very good for our country."

"Yeah, I agree with you. Moshe's an awesome guy," I said. "So, is there any chance I can actually talk to anyone inside about Nathan Levin?"

He waved me in and I saw I was in a small entryway, at the end of which was a metal detector I had to pass through. I made it through and found myself face to face with a receptionist. She was a strong-looking chunky woman with round shoulders. She was middle-aged and had dusky skin, a weathered face, thin lips and no makeup. Her eyes were dark, with a look of challenge. She was clearly not a woman to be trifled with. The sign on her desk said simply, "Mrs. Frisch."

"How may I help you?" she asked with a tone that said she very much doubted she would and a look in the dark eyes that held no expression whatsoever.

I went through my same spiel, explaining that I was trying to find the address or phone number for Nathan Levin.

"Are you an Israeli citizen?" she asked, a frown furrowing her forehead.

"No. No, I'm not," I said. "Does that matter?"

"It matters if you want to get information on other Israeli citizens."

"Well how does one locate friends or business acquaintances who are Israelis and happen to be in the U.S.?"

"If you are an Israeli citizen, you come and ask at the Israeli embassy."

I had to find my way past that armor of suspicion. Funny how it used to be easier when suspicion was only based on individual circumstances. Now each one of us, Jew, Muslim or Christian; black, brown or white, is a symbol. The war is out in the open and the skin color, nationality and religion are a uniform. All the deep and basic similarities of the human condition are forgotten so that we can exaggerate the few differences that exist.

I tried again. "But what if one isn't an Israeli citizen, say like me? Someone who's a big fan of Israel?"

"You could check the telephone white pages," she said, a slight smirk forming on her thin lips.

"That's a great idea," I said "but I don't even know if he's in the U.S. or even which city's white pages to look in. How about a Freedom of Information Act request? Can I send in one of those and get the information?"

"You are confusing us with Americans, Mr. James. We don't have a Freedom of Information Act. We are Israelis with enemies on every side of our country. So we like to protect our citizens by not giving out their personal information to whomever asks for it."

"Wow. I've really met my match here," I said with a grimace. "I'm not trying to bother Mr. Levin, I promise. I'm really just trying to do my best to help out one of your own, Moshe Goldman. He's a friend of mine. Perhaps I could give you my cell phone and you can call him yourself?"

"But I have no need to call Mr. Goldman. I know already that he is one of our national heroes."

I looked down at her, sitting behind the desk with her hands clasped together on top. She looked up at me. I took in a deep breath and smiled as charmingly as I knew how. "Ms. Frisch, can you at least tell me if Mr. Levin is living in the United States? Can you at least help me that much?"

She smiled back at me, wearing the power of her position like a cloak. Then turning to the computer at her side, she typed a few words, waited several seconds, then looked at me and said, "Yes. He is living in the U.S. Now, will that be all Mr. James?"

"Yes, Ms. Frisch, I think that's about all I can handle," I said, "but thanks for the information and for your time. Have a nice afternoon."

Chapter 27

I drove home from the city just a tad frustrated from my interactions with Shelley and the formidable Mrs. Frisch and frustrated I wasn't able to get any solid information on SCC or Nathan Levin. As I walked into my apartment stairwell, I spotted a new nametag on the mailbox for my new yet-to-be-named neighbor. I walked over to the bank of mailboxes and bent down to read it, only to find to my chagrin that she was walking in the door right behind me. Straightening up, I looked at her and gave her my best smile.

"Hi there," I said. "With all of our comings and goings I realized I hadn't even gotten your name. I figured as long as I keep bumping into you and insulting you, I should know who you are."

She smiled cautiously, apparently accepting my somewhat vague acceptance of responsibility for our prior meetings, and said, "You're right. It's about time we met properly. I'm Anne. Anne Pomeroy."

"Nice to finally formally meet. I'm sorry we seem to have gotten off on the wrong foot with each other," I said. "Maybe we could grab a cup of coffee some time."

"Well," she said. "I'm in and out all the time so it could be tough to arrange, but maybe we could one of these next few weekends. Thanks Drew."

Saying that, she turned, walked up the stairs and went into her apartment, leaving me with a vague feeling of being left behind like seeing the C-141 aircraft I just jumped out of fly away from me as I drifted in the prop blast waiting for my parachute to open. The contrast between Anne and Shelley Gann was stark, yet even with Shelley's overpowering sensuality and my previous negative run-ins with Anne, I had felt a slight fluttering in my stomach when I had turned and seen her coming in the door behind me.

I went in to my apartment, grabbed a Michelob from the fridge, dropped onto the couch, and checked my voicemails. There were a couple messages from equipment distributors wanting me to review their stuff; one from my office telling me my trip voucher to Williamsburg had been paid; another from Moshe, made from an overseas number telling me that he was fine and enjoying being back home; and lastly, a message from my brother-in-law, John Hewlett, calling me back.

Making myself comfortable, I called him. "Hey John, it's Drew. Thanks for calling me back. Were you able to find anything?" I said.

"Well, yeah, possibly," he said. "But nothing that points directly at Gann," he said.

"I called around to several people to speak with them about Gann but only got one response. I have a classmate from business school who's President of the Builder's Association in Birmingham, Alabama. I asked him if he knew, or had heard, anything about Gann. Here's the word on the street that he told me.

"In the early eighties, Gann showed up in Gulf Shores, Alabama. First thing anyone recalls hearing about him he had a fairly small construction company, doing a lot of local work in and around Gulf Shores. Eventually he moved up to building roadways and bridges.

"Anyway, there was a guy about 60 years old named Harry Michaels who lived in Mobile, about 45 miles west of Gulf Shores. Mobile was booming at the time and spreading rapidly towards Gulf Shores. Harry owned a small company named Michaels Paving that advertised as specializing in site development and roadwork. He was tough and worked hard, but he was always on the fringes, just missing the big contracts. He mostly did a number of small jobs patching stretches of county roads or paving residential driveways.

"At some point, having watched the spread of development from Mobile towards Gulf Shores, Harry got wind that they were going to build a major interchange where Route 90, the Old Spanish Trail, intersects with 27 at Malbis. There was a tract of land there, about sixty acres on the southwest corner, owned by the Hackett family. They had been holding on to it with the idea that someday they could get at least five thousand dollars an acre for it. That's nothing compared to what it runs for today. Harry got there first and struck a deal with them. He'd give Hackett five thousand dollars non-refundable as option money that bought him the right to pay fifty-six hundred dollars an acre, cash money, or three hundred and thirty-six thousand total for the whole parcel. He got there a split second before a number of other builders. The value of that land once the interchange was built was obvious."

"How obvious?" I asked.

"Everybody expected it would easily clear five times the price once it was developed," he said.

"Well," he continued, "Harry had some friends in the local county government and they told him he wouldn't have a bit of trouble getting the zoning changed so that he could put up a top-end outlet shopping mall spanning one side of 90, and a hotel and restaurant on the other side. So he took the gamble and went ahead. He sold everything he owned, his shop and all of his equipment, and came up finally with the three hundred and thirty-six thousand dollars. Then he went to the Bank of Mobile and borrowed two hundred thousand, with the sixty acres as collateral. Then of course, all he needed was the zoning change and he applied for it.

"And then he waited and waited. He pestered the planning and zoning commission, but couldn't get anything going. He began to suspect somebody had set up a roadblock and used any connections he had but couldn't find out who was blocking him. The interest on his loan came to about twelve hundred a month, which isn't too much now, but it was enough to eat Harry up, because he had sold his income-producing equipment to raise the three hundred and thirty-six. When he saw what was happening and what probably would happen, he tried to get out of it as best he could. He made up a little package. At first he tried to get his whole three hundred and thirty-six back on a sale to somebody who'd assume the loan. The trouble was there was no alternate use for the land under the zoning they had on it, and he couldn't continue to handle that much debt.

"If he tried to wait it out, the bank would grab the sixty acres and he'd have nothing left. So he kept dropping the price, spreading the word. And finally when it got down to fifty thousand, a young lawyer showed up and said he represented Gemini Associates, and he paid the fifty thousand and Gemini took over the loan and the title. Six months later, the zoning change was granted and the bulldozers showed up. The sign said that this was the future site of the Kingsdowne Premium Outlet Mall, a

Holiday Inn, and a Perkins Southern Grill restaurant, all projects of Gemini Associates. Then, when the construction actually began, it was all SCC construction equipment. It was never proven, but always assumed that somehow Gann must've paid off the county commissioners. I tried to find out something about Gemini but couldn't ever find any connection with Gann or SCC. As for Harry, after he lost that title, he tried to come back, but his heart wasn't in it. He died three years later almost broke."

"What do you think, John," I asked, "is there any truth to the rumors about the bribe to the commissioners, the pay off? Anything to tie it to Gann?"

"I don't know Drew," he said. "I really thought so, but without any connection at all between Gemini and Gann, I don't see how it could happen. But one thing is certain. In that part of the country Gann's a home grown king."

"Well. This seems to fit what I've seen of him and his company so far," I said. I told him about the blog I'd read on Gann and the alleged payoff to get the Wilson Bridge deal.

"That certainly sounds similar," he said. "By the way, Drew, I know this seems like a good story for your column, but be careful. I have no doubts you can handle yourself, but watch out where you poke that stick. You never know if there's a snake hiding in that hole."

"Thanks John. I'll be careful," I said. "I just think it'll make a good story."

"OK. Call me if you need anything else Drew," he said and hung up.

I drank the rest of my beer and pondered what life and apparently J. J. Gann had given Harry Michaels, and then started laying out in my mind how the next column would look with this latest information.

Chapter 28

The next day the man in brown delivered a dozen boxes from the Virginia Department of Information that contained the contract files for the Wilson Bridge Project. It'd cost me a good bit of change for searching and copying costs. I hoped it was worth it.

I spent the next four hours reading the contract proposal packages that had been submitted for the Wilson Bridge contract and the evaluation packets prepared by the state for each of them. I'd have been out of luck if they had followed their normal competitive sealed bid process, but for this project, the Commonwealth had decided to fill the contract using a competitive negotiated Best Value process.

The autumn day outside was beautiful with the trees in full color against a deep blue sky. I'd rather have been waterboarded than have to spend four hours on a beautiful day reading contract proposals, but my next column was due soon and I had to see if I could find anything that substantiated the rumors of Gann's pay-off scheme for the project.

The best value approach allowed the Commonwealth to select a company that was not the lowest-priced or the highest technically-ranked, but the company that was subjectively determined to be the best value for the Commonwealth. It seemed just the sort of procurement action that could be influenced by a bribe.

Each proposal package was filled with all the required information, including the offeror's past performance, past experience, management approach, technical capabilities, project team qualifications, and the method they would use for subcontracting. I compared each of the proposals with the one submitted by SCC and from what I could tell, SCC was certainly competitive in the required areas.

At the back of the contract files, was information about the technical evaluation panel. From what I could tell, the head of the panel had been replaced somewhere during the process. There was no indication why, but it seemed to me that replacing the head of the panel in the middle of a procurement action could certainly raise suspicions about the process.

I read the report from the panel, which was supposed to explain how the panel had evaluated the different offers and why they felt that SCC had the overall best value. But the report gave no real explanation other than it was the judgment of the new panel head that SCC's offer demonstrated the best value for the project. Looked like the only thing I could do now was to try and talk to one or more of the individuals on the technical evaluation panel to see what they could tell me about picking SCC for the job.

Near the back of the contract files was a letter from an employee named Clifford Maybree, who worked in the acquisitions office and was one of the five members of the panel. The letter had been sent to Mark Girard, the new head of the technical evaluation panel, and was essentially a complaint about his handling of the panel since he'd taken it over.

I knew from the files that each of the five members of the panel was responsible for rating each of the submitted bids according to a specific factor which they then fed into the overall best value determination. Maybree was handling the factor that dealt with Management Approach and Technical Capabilities. In his letter, he stated to Girard that he had taken explicit notes and documented strengths and weaknesses for his assigned factor to ensure that his documentation supported the assigned score and acceptability determination. In Maybree's opinion, because SCC was involved in several other very large projects at the same time as the Wilson Bridge project, they would have an insufficient number of managers and not enough equipment nor operators available to work such a massive project. So he had given them negative ratings for that factor. And since the scores for the bidders were all very close, his negative rating for SCC would have resulted in The George Hyman Company, another national construction company, winning the project. In the memo, he questioned Girard on the final reported scores and, apparently referring to a conversation they'd had, asked him why it appeared that he had changed the score benefitting SCC. There was no response to Maybree's letter in the files and no further mention of his name.

If I could find Maybree, he might be the one to give me information about the actions of the evaluation panel, or point me to someone else who could. So I called the Commonwealth's Personnel Department and asked the woman who answered if I could get the number for a Clifford Maybree who worked in the VDOT Wilson Bridge Project Office. She said he no longer worked for the Commonwealth. When I told her that I had some very important information I needed to give him, she snorted and referred me to the VDOT legal department.

So I turned to my computer and searched Maybree's name in Google. Nothing came up. I went to People Finder and put his name in for Virginia and came up with listings for twenty Maybrees in Richmond. With a heavy sigh, I picked up the phone and started calling.

I got to number twelve and when I asked to speak to Clifford Maybree who used to work for the Commonwealth, the woman on the other end answered softly, "who gave you this number?"

"Ma'am, I got it in the phone listings for Clifford Maybree," I said. "I'm not selling anything, I'm just trying to find out if he's there by any chance."

"No sir, he's not here. I'm his sister. But I don't think he wants to talk to anyone about his former job with the government," she said.

"Well Ma'am, I'm sorry to bother you with this. It's just that I need to speak with him about something very important," I said.

"Well," she stammered. "I don't know. What do you need to speak with him about?"

"It's kind of a long story," I said. "I'm writing an article for a national golf magazine. I'm tracking a golfer on his way to the Masters Tournament in Augusta and, well, my column also involves the board members, one of whom owns the construction company that worked on the Wilson Bridge Project. I really think your brother may have some information that will help me."

She sighed heavily. "I'm just not very good at making important decisions. I hope he doesn't get upset at me." She paused for several seconds then continued. "He left his job with the government a few years ago and moved out to the west end of Richmond. He lives by himself in Short Pump."

She gave me the phone number where she thought I might reach him.

"Please be kind to my brother," she said. "He's been through so much. And he has been so kind to me. I'll call him now and tell him you may be calling." And she hung up.

Chapter 29

The call left a bad taste in my mouth. Maybree's sister sounded like she was a little off and it felt like I'd really disrupted her. It made me wonder even more what I was getting myself into. This was going pretty far removed from my normal articles on golfing.

With that thought, I took a deep breath, steeled myself and picked up the phone to call Maybree. The phone rang and rang. I was preparing to leave a voice mail message, when the phone picked up, and a man said hello in a very tired voice.

I introduced myself, explained that I worked for Golfer's Journal, and told him that I was writing a column on Augusta National. There was no response, but I could still hear someone breathing on the other end. So I told him about my column on the members of the board of Augusta National and Gann in particular. As the silence continued, I kept going. I told him I was looking into SCC's selection for the Wilson Bridge project and how it didn't make sense to me, given what I'd seen of the other proposals that were submitted.

Finally, I said into the phone that I'd seen his letter to the head of the technical evaluation panel and that based on all I'd seen, I couldn't figure out how SCC had been awarded the contract. Having nothing more to say, I shut up.

After a long pause, with no sound other than a deep breathing, Maybree spoke.

"My sister told me you might call. So what do you want from me? How do I know you're not out to get me? I did nothing wrong. All of my actions were done properly. I think it best for both of us if you just leave me alone," he said.

"I'm not concerned with your actions. I've got nothing against you," I said.

"So why call me? What are you planning on writing about in the column?" he said.

"Well, initially it was just going to be on the board members, but now I've learned more and seen the rumors about Gann and SCC paying off certain people on the evaluation panel to get the Wilson Bridge Project. I saw your letter in the file and thought I could get your thoughts on how the project was awarded to SCC," I said.

"Listen," he said, "I've really been through enough already. I'd rather not have anything to do with this."

"I understand," I said. "I just need some information. I'll do my best to leave you out of it," I said.

He sounded reluctant when he spoke, but finally relented when I asked to meet him in Short Pump. With a great deal of hesitation, he agreed to meet me in two days and gave me the address for his house. I thanked him profusely and hung up. The whole ordeal had caused beads of sweat to break out on my forehead.

I went into the kitchen and threw stuff together in a soup pot, then made a Manhattan. While the soup cooked, I sipped the drink and looked up on google maps where I'd find Clifford Maybree in Short Pump, Virginia. I hoped he would give me the information I needed about J. J. Gann, SCC, and his enchanting daughter.

As I sat down to eat, the phone rang.

"Mr. James?" a voice said.

"Yes, speaking," I said.

"Mr. James, this is Mrs. Frisch, from the Israeli Embassy. We spoke several days ago?"

"Yes, of course. I remember. How are you Mrs. Frisch?"

"Very well, thank you. I wanted to let you know that I got a call from Moshe Goldman. He told me you are a close friend of his and you're writing about his journey to the Masters. Oh, and you're helping him out with some things, as well. I spoke with my supervisor and told him and we'd like to show our appreciation by giving you the information you were seeking. You understand this is not our normal protocol?"

"Of course. Glad you called me back," I said.

"Mr. James, I can tell you that Mr. Levin is in the United States. He lives in Phoenix, Arizona," she said.

"That's great," I said. "I really appreciate that information, although an actual street address would be really helpful."

"I'm sure it would, Mr. James, but that's all that I'm permitted to give you," she said.

"Ok, I'll take that much. I appreciate it Mrs. Frisch. Trust me. I'll do all I can to help Moshe."

"I know you will, Mr. James," and she hung up.

Chapter 30

I pulled up in front of Maybree's house in Short Pump, cranky and tired from the ugly drive down I-95 from DC. Normally the trip took a couple of hours, but an accident near Ladysmith had caused three lanes to merge to one and the stop-and-go trip had taken twice as long.

I got out, stretched, and strolled up to the front door. The house was an old brick colonial. The front lawn was rutted and bare in spots and there were curly tendrils of vine that had climbed up one of the corner gutter down spouts almost to the roof. The gutters themselves had small seedlings growing up out of them. Parked in the driveway in front was an old Ford F150 pickup truck, the tires looking soft and worn and the door panels spotted with rust.

I double checked the address and then knocked on the door. I heard some footsteps in side and the door slowly opened. He was tall and stooped, with a gray gaunt face. I'd never seen a more defeated looking man.

"Mr. Maybree? I'm Drew James. How are you?" I said.

He squinted down at me with rheumy eyes. "'Bout as good as you'd expect under the circumstances. Come in," he said, as he moved to the side and let me in, then closed the door.

My eyes slowly adjusted to the gloominess of the house. The curtains were all closed so there was little natural light coming in through the windows. We were in a small hallway next to the living room. He motioned me to a straight back chair, moving ahead to take off a stack of papers that had been placed there. As I looked around I could see similar stacks throughout the room, on the furniture and on the floor in the corners of the room. Other than a couch, a stuffed wing chair, the chair I had, and two bookshelves filled with books, there was nothing else in the room. I could smell dust, mildew, and a strange scent like food that had been left out too long and had spoiled.

"Mr. Maybree," I said with a smile, giving him my hand to shake. "I appreciate you being willing to see me."

Maybree was close to six and a half feet. He had cowlicky hair around a long lumpy face with a lantern jaw. He had a nervous cough. He wore a light blue sports jacket. His big hand was warm, dry and utterly slack.

"Can I get you anything to drink?" he asked.

"Actually a can of soda would be great," I said, thinking it best to avoid any glassware or water from his tap.

He left me in the living room and walked into the adjacent kitchen, returning with two cans of warm Coke.

Speaking slowly as if each word took a concerted effort, he said, "Mr. James, I'm about at the end of my tether. I got unjustly fired from my job for pointing out what I thought was a legitimate problem with the Wilson Bridge technical evaluation panel. My sister needs a lot of my help with even the normal things of life. I love her dearly and have given her just about everything I have. And now, they tell me this thing inside me will kill me before the end of the year. So all that said, I'll tell you what I know about the Wilson Bridge Project."

He paused as if out of breath and sat on the couch, pushing a stack of papers to one side. Seeing him reach for a folder and collect his thoughts before speaking, I was hopeful that I'd finally learn something about J. J. Gann, SCC, and their dealings concerning the Wilson Bridge project in Virginia.

Chapter 31

"You know, Mr. Maybree…,"

"Please call me Clifford," he interrupted.

"You know, Clifford, I've lived in the DC area for many years," I said. "Almost every day I drive by the SCC project at Wilson Bridge and the Route 1 interchange. We're talking one massive project. I'm guessing whoever got that job made out very, very well at the end of the day. Just so you know, I got all of the proposals that were submitted on the project and looked through each of the technical evaluations. I'm not a contract expert, but it seems to me that under normal circumstances, SCC's proposal should never have been selected as the best value. What can you tell me about that?"

He nodded as I spoke and looked at me with a slight glaze in his eyes. "Exactly. Exactly what I thought. I worked in the Comptroller's office in Richmond for nigh on to twenty years. I was assigned to the technical evaluation panel for the Wilson Bridge Project. The head of the panel was Casey Brady, a fine man and a friend of mine. We'd worked together on multiple contracts. For this one, I was responsible for reviewing all the proposals sent in and analyzing them from the perspective of the bidder's management approach, how they explained they would run the project and what management teams they would use, and their technical capabilities, did they have the equipment that would be needed and the ability to operate it. I would give each of them a rating based on my review and enter it into a spreadsheet for Casey."

"Who's Mark Girard? I saw his name listed as the head of the panel in the materials I'd received from the Commonwealth," I said. "When did he replace Casey and why'd that happen?"

He looked down and away for a moment and became very emotional. In a low voice he said, "They say that Casey shot himself in his office while we were working the contract selection. They claim he put a shotgun against his chin, reached down, and pulled the trigger. They say it was a suicide." Then he looked up and into my eyes, and said calmly and emphatically, "I don't believe it for a minute. Casey was happier than I'd ever seen him. He'd just gotten married. And I know for a fact he was afraid of guns - any guns. There's no way he killed himself. No way. And then Mark Girard shows up to head the panel and he was something else. He's no Casey Brady, that's for sure. From that point on, the whole selection process was completely under his tight control."

"What about a police investigation? Did they look into the possibility of any foul play?"

"No. Much to my amazement, they didn't. They said there was no indication of any foul play. That it was a suicide all the way and they didn't want to waste scarce investigative resources. What a crock."

"Sorry about that Clifford," I said. "I really am. But, so what about your piece of the process?" I asked. "Based on the way the numbers came out, what was your conclusion?"

"Conclusion?" he said, leaning forward towards my face. "Well, just what you would think. It was clear as day to me that SCC was overextended. They had huge projects going on in New Jersey, near Atlantic City, and Georgia, around Atlanta. They had nowhere near the management structure needed on the ground to run this type of operation. Not to mention, the equipment it would take. They just weren't in a position to take this on. And from what I can see of their delay in finishing the project, my analysis was spot on. Just comparing SCC to the other bidders, I thought Hyman was the clear winner. So when Girard announced that SCC was the best value winner as determined by the panel, I was shocked. I looked at the spreadsheet with the rating I'd entered for SCC for management and technical, and it was not the same number. It had been changed in a way that made SCC look like a better value."

He then went on to tell me about the letter he'd sent to Girard to which he'd gotten no response. He pursed his lips and studied his thumbnail for what seemed a long time, then said softly, "and then I caught him cold."

"What was that?" I said. "What did you say?"

He looked at me steadily. "It happened like this. I'd gone out to eat lunch, by myself as I usually did. It was the Cracker Barrel just off the interstate. I was seated in a room right next to a cross-hatched partition you could kind of see through. Lo and behold, who should sit down on the other side of the partition but Girard with some guy who looked pretty tough, definitely not someone from work. I could see them through the partition, but they were placed in a way they couldn't see me. I saw Girard reach into his pocket, take out a piece of paper, and slip it in the plastic covering for the center section of the menu. All I could see on the slip was the number $500,000. He closed the menu and handed it to the other man who opened the menu, read it for a bit, then took the note out, looked at Girard, and nodded."

"I could probably fill in the blanks," I said. "It was the final sealing of the deal. Girard was all in on the bribe. And I'm betting that was some guy from SCC. What happened next?"

"Nothing," he said, shaking his head. "They ordered, ate their food, and then left. Didn't say a whole lot more."

"Did you tell anybody what you'd seen?"

"I called Girard. Probably not the smartest thing I've done. I told him what I'd seen, that I knew that's why he had changed the numbers and awarded SCC the contract, and that I'd have to let the Comptroller know."

"Did you really do that?" I asked.

"Yeah, I did," he said with a grimace.

"What'd he say?" I asked.

"Well, his voice sounded strained and upset and he told me he had no idea what I was talking about. He demanded to know if I'd called the Comptroller. I told him I planned to do it the next day," he said, with another nervous cough, staring at me with an earnest look in his eyes. "I guess I didn't realize how much trouble I was in until after the visit."

"What visit?" I said.

"It was pretty slick. The next day, Girard came to see me. He came into my office demanding to know what I'd done on the Wilson Bridge Project, acting like we'd never had the conversation the day before. He said he had solid evidence that I'd tried to steer the project to Hyman. He handed me a copy of a cancelled check written out to me for thirty grand from the Hyman Construction Company. Can you believe it? What a total frame job. He claimed I'd purposely entered wrong information on the spreadsheet so that Hyman would be rated higher and get the job, and then gotten paid for it. He told me I'd been caught and had two choices, be fired or sign a release and accept an early retirement from the state."

"So what did you do?"

"I told him he'd have to fire me," he said. "I told him that I'd never done anything like that and that if anyone had been paid off, it was him."

"How'd he react to that," I said.

"He just shook his head and looked at me. Then he did something that really scared me. He smiled, told me no one would believe me over him, asked if my sister was ok, and asked me how she would fare if I was fired."

"He knew about your sister?" I asked.

"Yes, he did. I have no idea how," he said. "But I certainly got the hint. I realized I had no choice. I had to do it for my sister. My God, does anyone really believe I'd be that stupid?"

The knobbly face colored a little and the mouth stiffened then relaxed as the color faded. "I checked my bank account and there was a deposit for all that money sitting there and then an immediate payout of all my money to another account. With that scam being held over me, I had no choice but to sign a release, taking the early retirement."

He glanced around the house with a grimace crossing his long face. "Between an early retirement and no money in my bank account, I'm now stuck in this hell hole to live the last few months of my life. Home sweet home," he said sarcastically.

"Mr. Maybree, I really don't know what to say. I'm sorry it worked out that way. You think the guy in the restaurant with Girard was from SCC?" I said.

"He had to be," he said. "Who else would've done something like that? And they ended up winning the project. Besides, you're talking about SCC and J. J. Gann.

That's a big powerful company run by a big powerful man. SCC obviously paid off Girard. And guess what he did three weeks after I left?"

"Tell me," I said.

"He bought himself a top of the line Mercedes. Just how do you suppose he did that?" he asked sarcastically, the pain showing on his face.

He was absolutely immobile for long seconds, his eyes staring sightlessly at the floor. I think he even stopped breathing. He got up and peered down at me. "I don't even want to venture a guess what really happened to Casey. Somehow, someone found him working late, killed him, and set it up to look like a suicide. But it sure worked out well for SCC that he could be replaced by Girard. So it's like this Mr. James. Sometimes the world sucks, and then you die. You just deal with what you get."

At that point, all I could do was try to stage an exit. I stood up and moved to the door. "I'm sorry Mr. Maybree," I said, as I stepped out. "Seems like you really got screwed. I'm happy to help however I can. As I explained on the phone, I'm doing an article on Augusta National and its members, and I've been focusing on J. J. Gann. So if you can come up with anything on his direct involvement in this thing, please let me know. I'd be happy to write about it."

As I drove back to Alexandria, my thoughts swirled with Maybree's information. Maybe there was some truth to what he'd said. If there was, SCC hadn't just bribed its way onto the Wilson Bridge Contract. They'd killed for it.

Chapter 32

The phone chirped in his pocket and the man picked it up. It was him. "Yes, sir," the man said.

"Got a little job for you," he said. "I'm reading stuff by that idiot writer that I don't like at all and it's pissing me off. We can take a break for now from our other project, so you need to get on it now and make this little problem go away. I don't figure this guy will be expecting anything. Find out where he lives, what he does, where he goes, and make it quick and easy, even if it's not clean. Fix it so there's no way it'll ever come back to us."

The man listened intently, keeping track of all that he said and writing down all the details. "No sweat at all, boss. The guy won't see it coming. I'll fly tomorrow, check him out, and have it done at the first opportunity," the man said, with a ring of conviction in his voice.

"Good," he said. "Take care of this and don't screw it up. Then we can focus on our real problem."

"Roger that, sir" the man said, and hung up as a slight smile spread on his face.

Chapter 33

It was late-October and the windmills of my mind were churning with all of the facts, names, and faces that I'd come across in my research on the other Directors and on Gann and SCC. I thought about the info I'd gotten from Maybree and the story of Casey Brady.

I had no idea how to figure out if the Brady suicide was real, but it was definitely convenient for SCC that it happened. I thought Maybree's description of the bribe in action was clear enough, but I had no real proof of that. Eye witnesses were notoriously unreliable and that seemed to be all Maybree had, besides of course the forged check to him from Hyman. Assuming it was forged.

And it was really interesting that the head of the evaluation panel should take a sudden interest in expensive German sedans. But even so, Maybree didn't have anything so far that directly implicated Gann or SCC. At least it didn't seem so. In any event, in next month's article I'd discuss the rumors and stories I'd heard about Michaels, Maybree, and the Bridge contract but indicate that they were, as yet, unconfirmed.

The previous week, I'd gotten a long voicemail from Ben Cooper. He'd run the NCIC check and nothing had turned up on Gann or any of the other directors. I noticed though that he'd said Clyde Perkins and not Clive

Perkins, so I made a note to follow back up with him with the right name.

As for the license plate number, turns out that the van with the stolen plates that I'd seen on the security tapes from Moshe's neighborhood had been found parked outside a rundown house in a rundown neighborhood about ten miles from Moshe's community. The police raided the house and found inside a veritable treasure trove of stolen electronics and jewelry, along with four juvenile delinquents who had been either too slow or too cautious to fence it all. The police had been aware of a rash of home break-ins and robberies in the area, and on the night captured on the tape, there had been a break-in reported in a house in Moshe's neighborhood. So it was clear to me that while the tape might help the District Attorney with their prosecution, it didn't help me figure out who'd planted the bomb and later killed Moshe's dog.

Finally, regarding the Hezbollah terror cell and the attack on Moshe in Williamsburg, Ben said that he hadn't seen or heard anything that mentioned a botched attempt, but then again, he figured they might have been a bit too busy to make any mention of it. Coop explained that an Israeli anti-terrorist strike squad had staged a helicopter assault on the suspected Hezbollah training camp, but found it empty when they got there. So the group was still alive and still possibly targeting Moshe with assassins who had already infiltrated into the U.S. Ben repeated his warnings and I repeated my assurances.

I felt guilty that I'd found nothing conclusive about the Hezbollah thugs going after Moshe. Try as I might, I could find no specific group that claimed responsibility, so there was no one I could try and go after to fix this situation. Moshe had been attacked in Williamsburg and it seemed to me that it had to be connected to the threat revealed by Ben.

Meanwhile, Moshe had been away in relative safety, but now he was coming back for the 3-Tour Challenge in Nevada, his last tournament before he took some time off until the spring. I figured I'd better be there with him and hopefully this time I could actually keep him from any harm.

I'd done my research. Hezbollah, literally the "Party of God" in Arabic is an Islamic paramilitary group and political party based in Lebanon. And what a difference perspective makes. The U.S., U.K., Israel, and other countries regard it as a terrorist organization, but many countries throughout much of the Arab and Muslim world regard it as a resistance movement against Israel and the West.

Hezbollah first emerged in response to the invasion of Lebanon by Israel in 1982, during the Lebanese civil war. Their inspiration was the infamous Ayatollah Khomeini who led the Iranian Revolutionary Guards, held 52 Americans hostage for 444 days, and took down the presidency of Jimmy Carter.

As a sign of their level of hatred against Israel and the Jewish Nation, Hezbollah's 1985 manifesto listed one of its four main goals as "Israel's final departure from Lebanon as a prelude to its final obliteration" and since then, Hezbollah leaders had made numerous statements calling for the destruction of Israel. It was no small wonder that they'd be looking for any opportunity to kill an Israeli citizen, especially one as well known around the world as Moshe. I took Ben's warnings as seriously as I took the prospect of a Hezbollah hit squad aiming for Moshe.

I closed my computer and looked out the window. Dull colored clouds were pushed across the golden sky by a sharp breeze that carried with it the hint of impending winter chill. The autumn leaves had lived out their glory earlier in the month and most had fallen, turning a lifeless dull brown in the process. The leaves skittered across the ground and were whipped into tiny random whirlwinds like so many miniature Kansas tornadoes.

I needed to clear my mind and try to let the images unwind to see just what I had for my column on Augusta National. My last column had just come out and I was pretty sure that Gann and the rest of his board of directors wouldn't be too happy about it. Besides writing about the upcoming 3-Tour Challenge and dissecting Moshe's chances to win it and eventually qualify for the Masters, I had described the different personalities on the Board and shared some of the stories I'd read about each of them. In sheer defiance of Shelley Gann, I'd included some rumored dirt on her Father. Thankfully I'd written the article in a way that pretty much foreclosed a libel lawsuit.

So, needing some fresh air, I did what I always did when I felt cooped up. I grabbed my clubs, threw on a wind shirt, and headed to the course to, as John Daly loved to say, grip it and rip it.

Chapter 34

The clocks had just turned back with the end of daylight savings time and I'd forgotten how quickly the days darkened now. I was putting out on the 6th hole when I thought I heard a cart back towards the 6th tee. Thinking that it might be the beverage cart, and hoping to snag a beer, I squinted back through the lengthening shadows towards the sound. The sun was low in the sky and, while the tops of the trees were bright with its reflected light, the edge of the fairway where it kissed the wood line was in ever-deepening shadow. I thought I saw the dark bulk of a cart but couldn't see anything more.

With a shrug, I picked my ball up out of the cup, collected my bag, walked down the slope, and headed towards the 7th hole tee box on the asphalt cart path. As I walked the path through the woods, the leaves still stubbornly gathered on the branches of several oak trees clattered and shook in the brisk wind. Again, I thought I heard the sound of a cart moving but with the sound of the leaves and the deepening gloom, I couldn't be certain. This would have to be my last hole or I'd be out here all night looking for my wayward shots.

I set my bag down on its legs and pulled out my Big Bertha. It had such a great feel to it and looking at the size of the club head with its enormous sweet spot, I wondered with amazement at my sheer inability to hit a ball consistently down the middle of the fairway. Ah well, practice makes perfect, or at least tolerable.

I'd worked hard on developing good aim as part of my pre-shot routine, figuring that if I aimed properly I'd at least know where my slice would be going. I knew that I needed to aim my clubface and align my body precisely and make a habit of doing it before every swing. So I would walk into my stance on a line parallel to the target line, tracking my eyes from the target back to the ball.

I teed the ball up, went through my aiming routine, and began my address, standing behind the ball and looking up the fairway in the direction I hoped the ball would go. I gripped my driver, holding it out in front of me. In the quietness, somewhere off to my right and back towards the 6th green, I heard the snick of a bolt on an automatic pistol as it slid forward pushing a round into the chamber.

As I dove and rolled towards the partial cover of my bag standing next to the tee box, a small flash of flame flared in the wood line, followed immediately by the spitting sound of a silencer. A round hit my bag, glanced off of one of the clubs inside, and just creased the outside of my left thigh with the white hot sting of a fire ant bite.

I rolled to my left, leaving a smear of blood on the ground, came up on my feet and hobbled off of the tee box and down the cart path limping hard down the left side of the fairway. Somehow, I was still gripping my driver with my left hand.

I could hear the cart start up and move. Glancing back over my shoulder in the darkening twilight, I saw the faint beam of the cart's headlights pause while highlighting my bag, which still stood on the tee box, and then continue bouncing and weaving behind me as the cart came across the 7th tee box towards the cart path. The driver had to see the blood stain and know that I was hit.

I considered running into the woods, but it's hard to move both quickly and quietly in the dark, especially with a bad leg. And the driver behind me was taking his time, knowing I was hit. He'd drive ten yards, then pause and shine a flashlight ahead and into the trees. I stumbled along, trying to think of something when I came upon a spot where the cart path took a sharp curve to the left around several large trees grouped together. I went around the curve and fell back against the large oak closest to the path, my back pressed against the rough texture of the trunk. It was going to be now or never.

My breathing was fast and ragged and I was starting to feel a little lightheaded from the blood loss. I tried to calm myself, taking in several large breaths of air. Gripping my club tightly, against Hogan's good advice, I raised it like a left-handed batter waiting in the batter's box for the next pitch, cocking my wrists and wagging the club head slightly. "Come on," I mouthed silently, "bring it home, baby."

The cart drew closer, then suddenly stopped at the beginning of the curve on the opposite side of the trees from where I stood. I held my breath as the driver listened and flashed his light to the left and right of the tree behind which I waited. I felt a rivulet of sweat roll down between my shoulder blades and my leg throbbed and pulsed with sparks of pain. The world seemed to stand still, poised at a literal "do or die" moment in time.

Then, with a clatter of sudden sound, the world moved to normal time again and the cart moved around the curve. I sucked in my breath and as the headlights swung around the tree, stepped out with my right leg while swinging the club towards the cart, doing my best to imitate Barry Bonds' alleged steroid-fueled classic home run swing.

The club shaft hit the left front roof post of the cart, breaking the shaft in two and spinning the broken club head into the driver's face. The driver grunted in surprise and pain, dropping the flashlight and sending it flipping and rolling off into the grass. A gun clacked onto the cart path and skidded into the brush.

Then, I stabbed the jagged end of the broken handle still in my hands towards the driver's neck, gashing the skin in a rip of flesh. He jammed his foot on the gas pedal and the cart lurched away from me careening back onto the fairway and heading off towards the 7th green. But in the instant of time when the broken end of the handle had pierced the surface of his neck and opened the skin up, I spotted a small tattoo at the base of his neck where it joined the top of his shoulder.

Collecting myself, I found the dropped flashlight and gun and then moved as quietly and quickly as I could back to the tee box. I tied my golf towel tightly around my leg, picked up my bag and made my way slowly back up the first six holes to the clubhouse, stopping and listening carefully with every few steps. Whatever was going on with this whole mess, things had suddenly turned south, and I hadn't a clue where it would end up.

Chapter 35

Two days later, I was at home sitting in my leather chair with my leg propped up. The bullet had grazed the outside of my thigh and, while it hurt like hell, it hadn't done any real damage. Just a flesh wound. Looking on the bright side, maybe it would cause me to put more weight on my right leg and actually help my golf swing. It was bandaged and really sore, but getting progressively better.

Outside, the day was cool and windy with a steady rain falling. Individual drops formed into rivulets on my windows and flowed in random patterns down the panes. The few people brave enough to venture out walked quickly down the sidewalks, hunched over under umbrellas that quivered and bucked against the wind. While I healed and watched the rain cascade down, I thought about what I'd seen.

I closed my eyes and tried to picture the tattoo on my assailant's neck. I started doodling to see if I could recreate it and ended up with something that came pretty close. It was a black circle with something red inside of it. Like a cross, filling up much of the circle. And there were two slashes of a lighter color forming an offset X on top of the cross. I played with the drawing, trying to make it resemble at least a little bit what I'd seen. I didn't recall any letters or numbers on it. With my computer on my lap I searched the net for tattoo parlors and tattoos they offered.

I saw a number of versions of the old Nazi Iron Cross and thought that the cross in the middle of the tattoo looked somewhat like that. And although I couldn't be sure, the bolts of lightning in the old Nazi SS symbols seemed to be what I had seen as the X on top of the Iron Cross. Was I dealing with some neo-Nazi group now operating in Northern Virginia? Had I cut off one of them on his motorcycle during rush hour? What could this possibly be about?

I googled tattoo parlors in the DC area and found one in Woodbridge, Virginia that looked promising. It seemed to cater to bikers and neo-Nazi types. As I placed a call to one of them, it struck me that I was getting as far afield from my normal column on golf as I usually was from the fairway in a typical round of golf. It would be interesting to see where all this would take me.

"Tattoos by Warren," the voice said.

"Hi, are you Warren?" I said.

"No, I'm Dez. Warren's busy. What do ya want?" he said.

"Well, I saw a tattoo that intrigued me and I'm trying to find out about it. I was thinking I might want to get it myself," I said.

"What'd it look like," he said.

I described the tattoo as best I could over the phone. There was quiet while he thought about it.

"No. Don't figure I've ever seen that one. We don't got nothing like that in our books here. Hold on," he said.

I waited. After several minutes Dez returned.

"I asked Warren. He ain't seen it either, but if you can draw it, he can tat it on you," he said.

"Great. Glad to hear it," I said. "But I'd really like to find out about it first. He know anybody in the business I could ask?"

"What do you mean find out about it," he said, a note of suspicion in his voice. "You a cop?"

"No," I said. "I'm researching a story and I need to find out if any particular group wears that mark."

After a moment's pause, he said, "Well, Warren's brother's got a shop in Macon, Georgia. Name's Mike. He might know, specially if it's a southern thing," he said.

He gave me the name of the shop and then hung up. I called information, got the phone number and called. Mike answered on the first ring.

"Hep ya?" he said.

I went through it all again, describing the tattoo.

"Wait a sec," he said.

I did and after about five minutes he came back.

"Where'd ya say you saw this, mister?" he said.

"Saw it at a biker's rally I was at," I lied.

"Well, it must be a biker's tat then," he said. "Go find yourself a biker, and ask him." And with that, he hung up.

Strike two.

Having no other options that I could think of, I called my brother-in-law again, if only because he actually lived in the south. Maybe he had some contacts who knew a guy who knew a guy who knew a biker. I was really on a stretch here. I got his voicemail yet again and went through it all again, describing the tattoo. Looked like that was strike three and I was out - out of any new leads or info.

I pushed myself up from the chair and walked gingerly into the kitchen. I fixed a ham sandwich, grabbed a piece of fruit and a Diet Coke, and returned to the chair. Even though Moshe had just come back to the U.S. for the

3-Tour Challenge in Nevada, he was planning on returning to Israel after the tournament and staying until he came back to the States for the Farmer's Insurance Open at Torrey Pines in January.

I'd be joining Moshe in Las Vegas in a week so I needed to refresh myself about the course. It was being held at the Rio Secco Golf Club, widely considered to be the finest golf venue in Las Vegas. Designed by Rees Jones, it meanders over gentle hills and across shaded natural washes that are typical of that corner of Nevada. From the course, you can see the rugged Black Mountain Range.

With the wide open vistas and clear lines of sight, it would be much easier to trail Moshe than on a wooded course. Besides that, you couldn't beat a trip to Las Vegas at that time of year. So it'd be another job of scouting the course perimeter and trailing Moshe with the gallery to keep anyone from making another attempt at him. I also planned to test out a new pair of FootJoy golf shoes and write a short review in the next monthly column. Nothing like a walk through the desert in a new pair of FootJoys.

I finished reading up on Rio Secco and then shuffled into the bathroom to change the dressing on my leg. It was healing nicely. I'd be up and running again in no time. I went and sat down on the couch with my leg up, taking stock of the situation. On the one hand, the Masters article had been going really well, including the pieces on Gann and SCC, the other directors, Moshe, and Augusta National. And, Moshe was still alive. On the other hand, I still didn't know what group was targeting Moshe or why, and who was after me now or why. I had no new info from Ben on pending Hezbollah hits. I had no evidence to substantiate the allegations about Gann or any of the other directors. I couldn't identify the tattoo. And I didn't know how to fix my slice. On balance, I had squat.

Chapter 36

It was the first part of November and I was feeling good. My leg had healed well and I could run with barely a limp. And very soon I'd be headed for the desert and warmer weather.

I sat at my desk and looked out the window at a cold front pushing in from the west, the wind blowing the trees from side to side. The sky was cloudless and deep blue. The sun shone with no real warmth.

I was finishing packing for the trip out west the next day to join Moshe in Las Vegas. In the meantime, I had to try and find out more about Nathan Levin, the former Israeli golf pro, where he lived and why he left the tour so quickly. All I knew was what Mrs. Frisch had told me. He lived in Phoenix.

I went online and for the next hour worked through Google to see if I could find any hits on him in Phoenix. There were countless Nathans and plenty of Levins, but no Nathan Levin other than a few hits about his fairly brief career as a golf pro on the tour back in the late 90s.

I checked several of the people finder sites. The same name appeared in a lot of cities, but none in Phoenix. I then checked the property records for Maricopa County, seeing if they had any records for him owning anything, but no property was owned by Nathan Levin. There was nothing on him. It was as if he didn't exist in Phoenix. Surely the Israeli embassy couldn't be wrong.

Thinking that he might still be active in golf, I looked up the major country clubs in Phoenix, and worked my way through each one, calling their main offices to see if Nathan was either a member or a teaching pro. None of them had any Nathan or any Levin listed, or had even heard of a Nathan Levin.

I needed some help, so I picked up the phone and called Ben. I asked him if he could run a driver's license and NCIC check on Nathan Levin or any vehicle he owned. He was hesitant but did it anyway. After a few moments he came back to the phone, only to say there was no indication that Nathan had a license, ever owned a vehicle, or had any interactions with the law enforcement community.

What the hell, I thought to myself. Where is this guy? The Israeli Embassy told me he was in Phoenix and if anyone had a reputation for keeping close tabs on its citizens, it was the Israelis. Not to mention the fact that it was Mrs. Frisch herself who told me he was there, and I seriously doubted that woman ever got anything wrong.

I thought of some of the hits I'd seen earlier of businesses in Phoenix with the name Levin in them. There were about a dozen, including a dry cleaner, a bar, a car dealership, and a funeral home. I'd have to take the time to go through each one.

With a sigh, and needing some liquid refreshment, I went into the kitchen and grabbed a Michelob. Then I strolled down the stairs and outside to feel the wind blowing hard across my face, cleansing my mind and chilling me to the bone. Dead leaves rustled along the sidewalk, ushered along at top speed by the wind. I turned my face to the sun, feeling its faint glow, and sucked in a few deep breaths of cool autumn air. Then draining the bottle, I reluctantly returned to my desk and the list of businesses to call.

I started at the top and went down the list, asking whoever answered if they knew a Nathan Levin who had once been on the tour. Twenty minutes later, I was on my tenth call. This one was for a car dealership in Phoenix called Levin Motors. I made the call.

Chapter 37

"Levin Motors, this is Alice and we have the car for you," a voice answered.

"Hi Alice," I said. "I'm Drew James, a writer from Golfer's Journal, and I'm writing an article on the Masters. I'm trying to locate Nathan Levin who used to be a golfer on the PGA tour. I was told he lived in Phoenix, but I haven't been able to locate him. Just checking to see if you've ever heard of anyone with that name?"

"I'm sorry, Sir," Alice said. "I haven't heard of anyone by that name who works here. But I've only been here at Levin Motors for nine months or so. By the way, do you need a new car, or perhaps a quality previously owned car?"

"No thanks, Alice. I think I'm good in the car situation. But can you tell me if there's anyone in your dealership who's been there for a while?" I asked.

"I don't really know, Mr. James. Perhaps the manager of the dealership can answer your question. If you'll hold a moment I'll be happy to see if I can find him."

I waited for about five minutes and then another voice came on the phone.

"This is Mitch, how can I help you?"

I repeated my introduction. "So, have you ever heard of anyone in Phoenix named Nathan Levin?"

"As a matter of fact, I have. Never met him myself, but Nathan Levin used to own this company. He died 20 or so years ago, about ten years before I started my job here. After he passed, one of the other valley dealerships bought this place and decided to keep the name Levin Motors since it had such a good reputation around Phoenix."

"Wait, Nathan Levin the golf pro?" I asked. "The former owner was a golfer with the PGA Tour?"

"Oh no," he said. "Nathan was the father. He was the owner. Never knew the son either, but it was Nathan's son who was a golf pro. Nathan, Jr. I heard that Nathan, Sr. didn't have time for golf. He was always here at the dealership."

"I'm trying to track down Nathan the son, the golf pro. Do you have any idea where he might live in Phoenix?"

"Sorry. I'm afraid I can't help you there," he said. "I have no idea."

"Fair enough," I said. "Can you tell me if there's anyone there now who was there when Mr. Levin owned the dealership?"

After a brief pause, Mitch said, "You know, I think Marvin down in Parts was here then. Pretty sure he started here when it was still owned by Mr. Levin. Hang on a sec. I'll see if I can get him on the phone."

I waited another five minutes.

"This is Marvin," a low quiet voice said.

Again, I went through my spiel.

"Mr. Levin? Yeah, I remember him," he said. "Great man, great boss. I thought the world of him. Came over from Israel in the sixties with next to nothing and after a time had saved enough to start this dealership. I'd gotten into some trouble when I was young, but he gave me a chance to start over. I worked for him for near ten years before he passed."

"What about his son Nathan? He's the one I'm trying to find. Do you know anything about him? Where he might live in Phoenix?"

"No. No, can't say that I do," he said.

"Any chance you know where Mr. Levin used to live?" I asked.

"Now that you mention it, I think I do," he said. "But it was quite a while ago. As I recall, I was working late one evening, you know catching up on work from the day, and Mr. Levin called the dealership. I was the only one still here so I answered it. He needed some papers from his office and asked if I could drive them over to his place. So I took them on over to his house. As I remember it, he lived in a place just south of Northern Avenue and east of 12th Street. At that time, it was the northern limit of the city. Nothing but desert beyond. I'm thinking it was called Hayfield or Haydon, or maybe Haywood. Something like that. No idea what number the house was."

"Anything you can remember about the place, what it looked like? Anything so I could try and locate it?" I asked.

Marvin thought a minute. "Bout the only thing I can remember was the palm trees. There was two tall palm trees growing up right on either side of the front door of the house. Best I can recall, at least."

"I really do appreciate your help Marvin," I said.

Chapter 38

I hung up and with a feeling of anticipation went to my computer and pulled up Google maps. Looking east of 12th street and south of Northern Avenue, I searched the neighborhood for a street with a name that sounded close to what he'd given me. I pulled in as close as I could and went row by row down the gridline of streets. And there it was, Hayward Avenue.

The street itself wasn't very long. Maybe I could find the actual house and address. I hit the button for street level and starting at one end, went down the street doing a 360 and looking at each house. I hit 1235. It was a nice looking house with two towering palm trees situated perfectly on either side of the front door.

That's gotta be it, I thought to myself. At least I hoped so. Not having any other choice at this point, I took a chance that Nathan lived in his parent's former house. So I wrote a quick letter to the address introducing myself, stating what I was doing with Moshe, and telling him that I was hoping to talk with him about his tour experience and his sudden departure. I wrote down my phone number and asked, if it was really Nathan reading it, for him to give me a call or write me back. Hoping for the best, I put it in the mail box and finished packing for Las Vegas.

When I was done, I closed my suitcase and picked up my phone to head out for some dinner. Glancing at the screen, I saw that I had a voicemail. The call must have come through when I stepped outside earlier. It was from John, my brother-in-law.

"Hey Drew. Got your message," he said. "I checked with a local tattoo guy I sometimes help with investments," he said. "He's seen a tattoo like that around once or twice. So here's a quick history lesson he gave me. Back in the 50s, in parts of the deep South, a new branch of the KKK formed up. Hard to believe, but it seems this new branch didn't think the Klan was aggressive enough in accomplishing their agenda. They called themselves Knights of the White Camellia. They wore a tat with a white cross in the middle of a red circle. But during the 60s, with the rise of the civil rights movement and all the new laws that when into effect, their orbit waned and, as an organization, they pretty much fell apart. So fast forward to the early 80s and, amid the discontent of the South in how things had worked out for them on a national scale, yet another spin off emerged, this one rising from the ashes of the old Knights of the White Camellia. They call themselves the SS Brotherhood of the Red Camellia.

"I've heard bits and pieces about them over the years, but no one really knows where or how they started. I'm told the tattoo you saw is one of theirs. It's a twist on the old White Camellia tattoo. It's a black Circle with a red Nazi Iron Cross in the middle, with two SS lightning bolts criss-crossing through the Iron Cross. These guys think of the Brotherhood as the new storm troopers of the KKK, even though they don't really associate with normal Klan members. They're supposed to be pretty hardcore. They fashion themselves after the Nazi SS. You should think twice before you mess around with them, Drew. And heaven forbid if you're thinking of getting that tattoo. I don't expect they'd like you wearing it if you're not one of them. Anyway, bro, you better take care of yourself. I really don't think you should mess with these guys."

The message ended and I took a deep breath. SS Brotherhood of the Red Camellia? What in the world was this all about and why were these lunatics following me on a golf course in Virginia trying to kill me? This thing was getting weirder by the day.

Chapter 39

If Nat King Cole was correct, and the amount of airtime he had on the local radios sure made it seem so, you'd find roasting chestnuts and open fires on every street corner. Christmas had arrived, and shoppers were hitting the malls in droves to find that perfect gift and exceed their limit on every piece of plastic they owned. I was sitting on the train winging my way back to D.C. from New York and sipping a cup of Sumatra blend after meeting with Nick Rosenberg, Moshe's agent, and discussing Moshe's travel plans in the spring when he returned from Israel.

Another weather front was passing through, bringing with it a day that was cold and blustery. Thin dirty white clouds edged with black jetted across the gray sky. The bare tree limbs shook and swayed, buffeted by the wind. Ah, my favorite time of year, full of laughter and cheer and throngs of crazy people scrounging for Christmas sales.

I was in a funk. I couldn't think of any new things to write since I'd penned a column in November on Moshe's performance in Henderson at the 3-Tour Challenge, the review of the FootJoys, and the latest on J. J. Gann and SCC. Moshe had done well. His team of three PGA players had won. He'd fired a three-under par 69 on Sunday to lead his team and clinch the win.

The wind had been warm and gusty in the desert, whipping the golfers' pant legs and causing a whole lot of white-knuckle putts on the open greens. On the par-4 18th hole on Sunday, Moshe hit his approach shot into a greenside bunker. He rolled an amazing chip shot to within four feet of the hole. Despite a 25-mph crosswind, he calmly rolled his ball into the bottom of the cup and his team had the win.

The FootJoy golf shoes were awesome. You wouldn't think that it would be a good idea to basically walk ten miles in a pair of dress shoes with plastic spikes but these were amazing. Then again, it was hard to make any comparisons if they were better than Army jungle boots, which they certainly were.

As for the part on the potential bribery payoff between SCC and the technical evaluation panel, I laid it on Gann pretty good. I didn't much care for the man, or his upstart daughter for that matter, even though she was very easy on the eyes. I pretty much set out what I'd learned about Maybree's conclusions on his part of the panel, where SCC ranked in the best value analysis, the decision by Girard and, absent another motivating factor, how SCC shouldn't have been awarded the contract. Girard's new Mercedes provided a perfect example of another motivating factor. Drew James, investigative reporter, reports. My editor wasn't necessarily thrilled with the piece, saying something under his breath about libel lawsuits and asking why I didn't just stick with equipment reviews, but the attorneys had signed off on it anyway.

My leg had healed completely and I had enjoyed my walk around the desert course trailing Moshe. As for any Hezbollah hit teams, nary a trace could be found. Moshe's biggest concern was fending off the Jewish matrons from Sun City who wanted to hug him and take him home to their daughters. I know I was there to protect him, but I'd clearly met my match when it came to overzealous match-making mothers. He was on his own with them.

So Moshe had headed for Israel and I had gone home to continue writing my Masters column and keeping an ear out for any new threats against Moshe. There had been nothing else to do but ponder why the other kids hadn't liked Charlie Brown's Christmas tree and what Christmas was really about.

Moshe had called the week before to tell me that things were going well in Israel and he hoped I could travel up to New York to meet with Nick and coordinate the schedule for the New Year. I had made arrangements to meet with Nick and bring him up to date on things. I didn't have any answers but I thought it important for him to know what I knew.

The train ride up was uneventful. Nick and I met at a small Italian restaurant on the upper East Side. We'd shared a pizza.

I'd told him of Ben Cooper's suspicions about the Hezbollah splinter group, the unsuccessful raid by the Israeli strike team, and the continuing indication that the group was planning something big in the U.S. I told him about the van leaving the package at Moshe's house and the attack on me. We talked at length about Moshe's success on the tour, how close he was to qualifying for the Masters, and my concerns that if he did qualify, he'd be that much more visible and, consequently, in greater danger. I recommended that he consider urging Moshe to go over to the European tour for a while but he told me it was no use. Moshe was adamant about not giving up his quest for the Masters. As was typical with Moshe, he had refused to even consider any suggestion that he not go to the Masters if he qualified to do so. On that point, there was simply no budging him.

Since Moshe's tour year had just ended, he'd know very shortly if he had qualified for the Masters. Nick assured me that he would let me know as soon as he heard. The money earnings list was due out soon and that would be a critical bit of information.

We'd parted with handshakes and an agreement that I would meet Moshe next at the Farmer's Insurance Open at Torrey Pines. It used to be called the Buick Invitational until the economy and Tiger Woods' meltdown put an end to that.

From what I knew, the course's fairways were pretty generous, although the strategically placed fairway bunkers could quickly change an offline drive into a scramble for bogey. I certainly knew about offline drives and scrambles for bogey. From my last visit there, I recalled that the greens were large with a fair amount of undulation, and they typically sat perched above deep bunkers and grass collection areas.

In January, Moshe would fly back from Israel and go immediately to the Lodge at Torrey Pines to play some practice rounds and prepare for the tournament and the start of the tour. So there I sat, on the train ride home, finishing my cup of Joe and thinking deep thoughts.

Chapter 40

The train rattled and shook as it rolled towards DC, the bare branches of the trees lining the rail bed blurring past like a smear of bar code lines. I got up and walked slowly down the aisle toward the restroom at the end of the coach car, carrying my empty coffee cup and holding the tops of the cushioned chairs for support as I went. Several rows behind mine, a man wearing sunglasses glanced away as I went by him.

For some reason, when I saw him my internal alarm system started jangling. Maybe it was the recent ambush against me at the golf course. Maybe it was the spy movies with train scenes I'd seen. Then again, maybe it was seeing someone wearing sunglasses on a train when the weather outside was cold, cloudy and windswept. In any event, my senses were on full alert by the time I got to the restroom and pulled on the handle only to find that it was in use and locked.

Turning to the connecting doors, I pushed obediently on the appropriate spot that said "PUSH TO OPEN" and, as promised, the door opened. Moving a bit more quickly because of the signals being emitted from my bladder, I went down the nearly deserted next car to the restroom at its far end. To my chagrin, it too was in use. Figuring I needed to go back to the car in front of mine, I abruptly turned to retrace my steps and saw the sunglass man looking at me through the connecting doors I'd just gone through. Seeing me, he quickly moved back out of sight, but not before I could see a silenced automatic in his hand.

That did it. I'd had enough. I'd been winged once already by some thug. My Big Bertha driver was broken beyond repair. My golf bag had a pair of holes shot through it. And now I was being followed by some hood in sunglasses. Worse for him, he was standing between me and the restroom and my vision was beginning to turn yellow.

I sat down quickly in an empty seat and took stock of what I had. I felt each of my pockets and found car keys, a pen, my IPhone, a good amount of loose change, a small pocket knife, and a roll of breath mints. Quickly taking off my shoe and then sock, I took off my watch and military academy ring and put them with the other items into the still warm sock. I compressed the items tightly into the toe of the sock and tied it off just above them. Slipping my shoe back on, I wrapped the length of sock around my hand, leaving a fairly hefty ball swinging at the end of the sock.

I looked around the seatback in front of me and, seeing no sign of the guy, I held my homemade sap low against my right leg and moved quickly toward the connecting doors. Standing to the side of the connecting door, I took a deep breath and punched the door opener. I paused as the door opened, waited a few seconds, and then a few more. Then I went through fast and low spinning my sock in a fast counter-clockwise overhand circle.

As I had hoped, my target had moved his head slightly around the edge of the wall connecting the space between the two cars to try and see who had opened the door and why they weren't coming through. Without hesitation, I stepped quickly with my left leg slinging the full sock hard towards his head. With a satisfying thunk, the sock hit solidly square on the top of his head. He grunted and dropped to his knees, gun and sunglasses clattering and skidding away on the metal train platform.

Tired of being on the receiving end, I wanted to make sure this clown stayed down. Turning sideways to him, I placed my feet shoulder width apart, let the sock hang down between my legs, addressed the spot of his chin as his head hung down slowly shaking from side to side, and swung the sock clockwise several times in a circle like I was making an approach shot with my pitching wedge. I got the sock swinging well and then, with a beautiful follow-through, hips turning to face the direction of my swing, the sock end caught him full under the chin, clicking his teeth together and causing his eyes to roll up in his head. No slice this time. "Fore," I said to myself, as he toppled over onto his face.

I moved quickly towards him, scooping up the gun and the sunglasses. I bent down and pulled him to a sitting position, replaced his sunglasses, and deadlifted him up by holding him under his arms. Seeing through the glass of the connecting door that the bathroom was now empty and the back half of the train vacant, I punched the door opener with my elbow, slid through with my companion, and ducked into the empty bathroom, dumping him on the floor.

I put the items back in my pockets and then used his belt to tie his wrists together in cross position under his thighs. As he made noises and his eyes started to flicker open, I bent, braced myself well, and picked him up. I walked two strides with him, and dropped him butt first down onto the open toilet. He chunked down, tilted slightly back, feet free, knees up, lashed wrists pressed under him against the toilet rim, holding him hunched and about as helpless as a man can be. He shook his head slowly, the movement showing the same KKK tattoo on the side of his neck.

Holding the silenced gun in my hand, I stood close and reached to him grabbing his face in one hand and squeezing like you would a small boy who got himself into trouble. I patted his cheek three times with the barrel of the gun and on the fourth pat I gave it a little more steam, skewing the sunglasses on his face and cutting the skin. It was a sharp demand for attention. He was staring up at me with an uncomprehending look, blood appearing from the cut on his face, trying to figure out how he'd lost the total advantage that he'd had.

"So here's the deal," I said. "You and your buddies have taken one too many shots at me. There's obviously something going on here I need to find out about. I don't know who you're working for, but you're gonna have to give me some clues. Can you understand that, little buddy?"

"I don't know what you…"

"I'm very, very annoyed with you and your colleagues. You've been acting very stupid and you've made some really dumb choices. I don't know what you're up to or why you want to give me a hard time. You should've realized it would backfire sooner or later, scumbag."

"You're making a big mistake…."

"Not a mistake and don't play dumb. It's too late for that. You've had your fun and now I've got no other choice. At the very least, good buddy, I have to break you up a little. Or maybe put a round in each knee cap, pry out an eye, or slice off a finger or two. And if really necessary,

I take you to the door and throw you out headfirst into a passing tree."

The bulge of his eyes tipped me, so when the mouth opened wide for a roar of anger, defiance and protest, I packed it swiftly by shoving paper towels from the dispenser deep down his throat. After he had gagged and coughed, I removed them and hit him again with the barrel of the gun.

"You're dead," he muttered quietly.

"Come again? What'd you say? Speak up so I can hear you," I said with another tap on his cheek with the gun barrel.

"Dead man," he said through clenched teeth. "You're a dead man walking, you bastard."

"So who's your boss, who are you working for? Come on, you can tell me," I said, tapping him a little harder on the head. He winced, then with a sudden strained look on his face, bent over to the side to vomit and then passed out, slumping against the wall of the bathroom.

The entire episode had been so quick and soundless that it had gone unnoticed by the few riders at the other end of the car. As he sat there, hunched over to the side, I removed his wallet, the gun clip on his belt, and the contents of his pockets, and then placed him back in a sitting position, sunglasses still in place.

At the same time, the train loudspeaker announced that we were pulling into New Carrolton, a Maryland suburb north of DC. I'd gotten as much as I was going to get from him in this place. Time to leave the train. With a sense of anticipation, I pulled his shirt collar away from his neck and saw the same tattoo. I wiped down all of the surfaces I had touched, eased the bathroom door open, slipped out, and moved casually to the exit. I left the train and boarded a Metro subway car two tracks over. Forty minutes later I exited in Alexandria, got my car, and headed for home, none the worse for wear and laden with the items from the thug's pockets.

Chapter 41

I drove home, parked on the street, and walked quickly up the stairs, noting again with a twinge of dismay that Anne's place seemed dark and empty. I sank down on the couch and spread the items before me. Maybe now, I thought, I'd have some decent evidence that might actually lead me somewhere.

The first item was a wallet. I flipped through it and found the driver's license. The picture staring at me was definitely the chump in the sunglasses, but the name said Jimmy Hoffa and since Jimmy's current address was alleged to be somewhere in the vicinity of a Meadowlands swamp in New Jersey, I was just a bit skeptical that was his true name. I pulled over my laptop and googled the listed address. Wouldn't you know, the website for the Sherry-Netherland Hotel in New York City came up. Other than a few credit cards with Jimmy Hoffa on them, the wallet contained $160 in cash and nothing else. Nada. Squat.

The next item was a soft pack of Marlboros with a book of matches shoved into the plastic wrapper. The matches were from Holiday Inn Express. Great, I thought. Now I can pinpoint him down to over a thousand hotels spread out in all fifty states. Hardly what you'd call a real clue.

Next was a small leather pouch that contained all U.S. change, nothing foreign. Next, a set of keys that looked like several door keys, a small key probably for a desk drawer, and an older car key with a black plastic cover that was rubbed and scratched. The word BAY in all caps was barely legible. What'd you know, I thought. At long last a clue.

I googled "Bay" and "automobiles" and came up with six hits. A Bay Mercedes in San Diego, California; a Bay Saab in Norfolk, Virginia; a Bay Chevy in Sturgeon Bay, Wisconsin; a Bay Volvo in Portland, Maine; a Bay Chevy in Pascagoula, Mississippi; and a Bay GMC in Savannah, Georgia. Of the six, only three were located in southern states, and calling Norfolk, Virginia a southern city with a possible KKK influence in it was a real stretch. But at least I had a connection between my KKK assailants and two deep-South states.

I got up, stretched, and wandered into the kitchen. I made a quick sandwich, grabbed a bottle of beer and headed back to the couch thinking of Moshe and the upcoming tournament at Torrey Pines. This would be an important tournament for him as he attempted to prepare for April and the Masters, assuming that he got in. I thought about his chances of actually qualifying.

There are thirteen established methods by which players can qualify for the Masters. Moshe had the added advantage of being an international player and Augusta National could exercise its discretion and invite him even if he didn't otherwise qualify. But that wasn't Moshe. If he didn't qualify on his own, I doubted he'd accept an invitation, but maybe he'd surprise me. He wasn't a past Masters champion, or any winner of a major for that matter. He wasn't an amateur, a U.S. Public Links or Mid-Amateur champion, or the winner of a PGA Tour co-sponsored event deemed worthy by the Masters committee. So his only choice was being one of the thirty leaders on the final official PGA Tour Money List for the past tour year. He'd had an up and down year, but he was currently number thirty-one on the money list, before his win in the 3-Tour Challenge. So he was close, but we would see what happened.

As I was contemplating these things, the phone rang. I answered it. It was Nick, Moshe's agent. "Hope your trip back was good, Drew," he said.

"It was excellent," I said, thinking of the satisfaction of slamming that full sock into the chin of the guy on the train.

"Hey, I know we were just talkin about Moshe and the money earnings list," he said. "But you won't believe it. I just got an email from the Tour office. Moshe came out number twenty-nine on the tour earnings list for last year. So whaddya know, he's gonna qualify for the Masters!"

I was happy for Moshe, and for what it would mean for my column since I'd been tracking him the past six months. But at the same time, I was dreading what the new publicity would mean to the Hezbollah group that wanted to take him out, and how they would react.

Chapter 42

I read about Torrey Pines golf course. It was something else. The course was in beautiful La Jolla and set atop cliffs that overlooked the Pacific Ocean. You don't have to be a golfer to appreciate the magnificent views. One just needs to stand on the veranda in front of the pro shop to get a sample of what you'll see from the course, which meanders along the coastline, bordered by deep canyons with thick vegetation and abundant wildlife. High cliffs overlooking the Pacific Ocean provide breathtaking views.

The course was originally designed by Bill Bell in 1953 and built over land that a few years earlier, during WWII, had been used as a training camp. The course was named after the Torrey Pine Tree, a tree indigenous to that area.

Torrey South, the course they'd be playing this year, stretches 7,600 yards. When the sea breeze picks up by mid-morning, or rain or fog sweeps the coastal areas, playing the South course is a challenge even for the pros. I knew Moshe would have to drive the ball long and straight to score well.

I looked out the window and saw snow flurries coming down. Feeling a bit cooped up and needing some air, I quickly changed and went out for a run. The air was refreshingly cold and the snowflakes brushed my face as I ran. I came back invigorated but my timing wasn't good. When I returned, I found that Ben had called and left me a voicemail. He told me that they had captured a mid-level Hezbollah chief and were working him for information. He'd just revealed that they were planning a significant operation against a high value Jewish target in the United States. Ben thought this was the intelligence we'd been looking for. Expressing his concern for Moshe, he cautioned me that this was a first-class hit team and told me to be very careful.

While I'd planned on being with Moshe at Torrey Pines to keep an eye on him, Golfer's Journal had other plans for me. There was a meeting in New York with the board. My editor told me they were a bit concerned with the aggressive nature of my articles and they wanted to discuss it with me in person. I suspected that they'd gotten an unpleasant call from one of the Augusta National Directors demanding them to order me to back off from writing any more articles.

There was no getting out of the trip to New York. Moshe would be a sitting duck at Torrey Pines, unless I could get some quality back-up help. I knew just the person. Eddie Knowles had been a friend of mine since we were teenagers together in middle school. We met at a youth summer camp and by the end of the week we were fast friends and pretty much running the place. He'd gone on to join the elite Navy Seal Team Six, while I'd made my mark in Army Special Ops. He had skin as dark as a moonless night, a smile that made everyone a friend, and an ambling walk that made it seem as if he had nowhere to go fast. But Eddie Knowles was as swift and lethal a killer as they come, in the water and on land. There was simply no one better. He'd retired from the service and was now doing security work in Texas. We'd lost touch with each other over the past few years. I gave him a call.

"Eddie, how you doing my friend, it's Drew," I said when he answered the phone.

"Drew James!" he exclaimed. "Where the hell are you and what have you been up to?" he asked. "It's been too long since we talked. How are you doing and how's Marie?"

I told him all about Marie, her fight for life and eventual defeat, and what I was doing now. I filled him in on my current project with Moshe and the Masters, told him about the attacks on Moshe, and of the current Hezbollah threat that Ben had called me about. I explained why I needed to be in New York and asked him if he was available to help me out.

"Of course I am," he said. "You simply say the word and I'm there. I'd be happy to keep an eye on Moshe at Torrey Pines. It'd be like a vacation for me. And don't worry Drew. He'll be in safe hands."

I knew he was telling the truth. Moshe would indeed be in good hands. Moshe would never see Eddie, but he'd be under his close watch constantly. And anyone trying to get to Moshe would be incapacitated without ever knowing how, or by whom. Eddie was like a shadow in the night, finding a way of blending into his surroundings in a perfectly natural way.

"It's so great to hear your voice again, Eddie. You've always been like a brother to me - like twin sons from different mothers. I'll never forget back at that camp. The guys in the other dorm wanted to take us on in football. With you throwing the ball and me running it, we kicked their ass all over the field. They didn't stand a chance."

"Seems like life was so simple then, Drew. Remember how we'd hang out during the day playing poker, and then sneak into the girls' room at night?" he asked.

"And when the head counselor banged on their door, we'd go out the window and hang on to the gutter five stories up until he left," I said.

"Oh yeah, what a blast," he said. "That must've been the start of our love for special ops."

"Must've been. The start of one lifelong adrenaline rush," I said, reflecting back on the memories. "I really appreciate you being willing to watch over Moshe. I'll let him know you'll be out there and he has nothing to fear. Will you tell me how it goes?" I asked.

"Of course, and don't worry. There won't be any problems for your friend Moshe. You take care of yourself and knock 'em dead in New York."

We talked more about times gone by and agreed that we needed to do a much better job of trying to stay in touch. I promised him a dinner at his favorite steak restaurant when we were together again.

I stood up and stretched, then walked down to my mailbox in the foyer. Flipping through the bills and advertisements I saw an actual personal letter. The return address read Nathan Levin, 1235 Hayward Avenue, in Phoenix.

Chapter 43

Fifty miles out, the plane started its long, slow approach into Phoenix. It was early in January. In the letter he'd sent me, Nathan Levin wrote that he was willing to correspond with me and tell me about his experiences on the tour as a PGA golfer. He seemed interested in hearing more about the articles I was writing on Moshe. He gave me his phone number and asked me to give him a call some time. I knew I was taking a chance visting him in Phoenix without calling first. It was very possible he'd tell me to buzz off. But the stakes were high enough that I thought it worth the trip.

So there I was, gliding over the Superstition Mountains headed for Sky Harbor airport. The sprawl of the city was laid out beneath me in neat squares, occasionally interrupted by various rock outcroppings or mountain preserves. Stretching from one end to another, curved and bent like a rattlesnake side-winding across the valley, the Arizona canal flowed smoothly with life-giving water. As the plane descended through the smog layer that lay like a cap over the bowl of mountains ringing the city, the air became hazy, then all at once crystal clear as we passed below it.

Phoenix had experienced explosive growth since the 1960's. What was once a small city catering to retirees and those disabled looking for the curative effects of a dry and warm climate, had blossomed into a sprawled-out major metropolitan area. Where the city limits used to end and the desert begin, were suburbs stretching all the way up north to Carefree. And as if 120 degree heat in the summer wasn't bad enough, the trees, hedges, flowers, plants and grass cultivated on virtually every square block of the city now produced enough moisture in the summer to result in humidity levels that rivaled D.C. The hard jolt of the landing and scream of engine reversal slowing us on the runway brought me out of my reverie. I'd landed in Phoenix.

I picked up my rental, a convertible, and headed north towards Lincoln Avenue with the top down, the wind blowing away the cobwebs of a five-hour plane flight. I got settled in at the Pointe at Squaw Peak, and then headed for my meeting with Nathan Levin.

I drove towards Nathan's address, going west on Northern Avenue. The air was crisp and clear with the contrails of LA flights headed to the east coast high up in the sky. I turned left and headed south on 12th Street and then left on Hayward looking for the right address. The neighborhoods were composed of neat single story ranch homes with well-maintained desert terrain yards framed by palm trees and Saguaro cactus.

The address looked just as it did on google maps, sitting below the great bulk of Squaw Peak Mountain that was now lit up by the sun as it descended in the west. I pulled into the driveway and turned the motor off. Just as he'd said, there were two large palm trees in the front yard outlined in the early dusk. All was quiet except for a lone dog bark across the alley in the back of the homes and the coo of turtle doves sounding in the distance. I walked up to the front door and knocked, not knowing what or who to expect in the person of Nathan Levin.

<u>Chapter 44</u>

The door opened. Nathan Levin was a neat, well-dressed man who looked to be in his late forties. He looked at me without speaking, a good-humored face under brown hair that had begun to thin on top, quiet brown eyes gazing at me through rectangular rimless glasses.

"Mr. Levin?" I said. "I'm Drew James. I was the one who wrote you about possibly talking with you about your experience on the Tour and your reasons for leaving it after you'd qualified for the Masters. I probably should've called first but it's really important that I talk with you and I thought if I'd called you'd simply blow me off."

"Yes," he answered. "I'm really sorry you flew all the way out here, but I'm really not interested in speaking with you," he said in a very guarded tone.

"Well, as I told you on the phone," I said, "I write a column in Golfer's Journal and in preparation for the Masters golf tournament in April, I'm writing a column on Moshe Goldman, one of your fellow countrymen, and his efforts to play at Augusta National Golf Club at the Masters."

"Yes, I understood that," he said. "But help me understand how exactly you think I can help you. My days of playing golf professionally are well behind me now," he said.

"Maybe you could start by telling me why you dropped off the Tour when you were headed for the Masters. And why you left the Tour altogether," I said. "I'm puzzled that there've been no other Jewish golfers from Israel on the Tour, and besides Moshe Goldman, you're the only one I've been able to find. I just want to talk with you about your experiences."

He moved to close the door, saying "I regret your expenses in coming but I have nothing to say, Mr. James."

I quickly shoved my foot into the gap of the open door before he could close it all the way. With fear in his eyes and his lower lip trembling, he pushed hard on the door, but with my foot wedged solidly in the opening, it wouldn't budge.

"Mr. Levin," I spoke calmly. "Please. You have nothing to fear from me. I'm only trying to get information that will help me with my article on Moshe Goldman. He's a great guy and a good friend and as the only other Israeli golfer on the Tour, I just want to find out how your experience matches his. I'm helping Moshe with some issues he has. Someone is threatening him, and I thought that maybe your experiences and information could help him somehow. If it means anything, the Israeli embassy in D.C. told me you were here in Phoenix."

He looked at me, blinked twice, and, at the mention of his embassy, I saw him relax slightly. He glanced away and when he looked back there was a new look of determination and a glimmer of hope in his eyes.

"Let's start over. Welcome to Phoenix, Mr. James," he said. "Won't you please come in?"

"Please call me Drew," I said with a smile and stepped inside.

"Would you like a beer, coffee, some water perhaps?" he asked.

"Actually a nice cold beer would be great," I said.

"Yes, I think that's a great idea," he said. He left me in the living room and walked into the adjacent kitchen, returning with two bottles of Dos Equis and two tall glasses.

"You may not be able to tell from my actions but you don't know what a relief this is, Drew. For some reason, I feel I can trust you. I'm finally able to tell somebody about my experience and what happened to cause me to leave the tour. My only request is that you have to agree not to publish it. It's for your information and background only. I think you'll see that I'm not in any position to have my story out in the public."

Chapter 45

He paused and reached for his beer, taking a long swallow before settling back in his chair, eyes focused in the distance on another place and time. The fading day outside had caused the room to darken. He reached up and turned on a lamp on the table next to his chair. The light spilled into the far corners of the room. I could see it was a living room from yesteryear with stuffed furniture, the arms covered with lace doilies. Paisley curtains hanging on either side of a picture window. An old console television in the corner with faded photos of children in graduation cap and gown, the faces looking forward to a bright and happy future. A side table with stacks of well-worn photo albums. Everything clean and neat and well-maintained.

His voice brought me back to the present. "I was born in Israel. My family and I came to the United States in the late sixties and we settled here in Phoenix. It was a wonderful place to grow up. The weather was always great and we'd practically live at either the golf course or the swimming pool. That's how I got to be pretty good at playing the game. I was lucky.

"But I know it was probably more than just luck. My father worked so hard to build a successful business and take care of us. I know you heard of Levin Motors. That's how you found me here, I suspect. Well, it was a car dealership he started in the central part of the valley. He was very successful and it was his financial support that allowed me to survive during those tough years when I was trying to get my player's card."

"He sounds like a good father," I said.

"True enough," he said. "But you know how that generation was. They lived to work and to raise a good family. I know he loved me, but he was never real close to me and, after I joined the tour, I don't think he ever came to watch me play in a tournament. I strove for years to be successful as a golfer so he would say how proud he was of me. He never did," he said with a slight tremor in his voice.

"I'm sorry to hear that," I said. "I bet that really hurt."

"Yeah, well the worst of it was, in 1995 I'd won enough on the tour to qualify for one of the at-large spots at the Masters. I thought that might do the trick to find my father's favor. So I planned a trip to visit him back here in Phoenix, let him know about the Masters, and ask him to join me."

From somewhere in the back of the house I heard someone begin to cough. It was persistent and hacking and went on for several minutes. Levin excused himself and left the room. When he returned, he said, "I apologize for the interruption. That's my mother. She's been quite ill for many years. I've been supporting her as best I can."

He sat down. "Well, let's see. Where were we," he said.

"How'd your trip back here to see your father work out?" I asked.

"It didn't," he said with a grimace. "A week before I was flying out here from the east coast to see him, I got a letter in the mail. I opened it and it looked like one of those kidnapping notes you see in the crime shows on television, with letters cut out of a newspaper and pasted to the page. It said that if I didn't turn down the Master's invitation and leave the tour, someone close to me would die. Of course my first thought was it was some kind of practical joke. You know, maybe from one of the other tour pros with whom I was friends. It was really hard to take something like that seriously," he said.

"Was there a return address on the envelope?" I asked.

"No, just my address hand printed in strange block letters. And no signature or anything else on the letter, other than the message. So just the one sheet of paper with nothing else."

"How about the police?" I asked. "Did you contact them?"

"No. I really didn't take it that seriously. In fact, without thinking about it, I tore the letter up and threw it in the trash. I didn't go to the police because I didn't want to cause any embarrassment by sounding alarmist."

"That sounds very familiar," I said. "Moshe Goldman said the very same thing to me. So did anything happen?"

"Not at first. I ignored them. I completed my Master's paperwork and continued on the tour. I was still set to fly out here to see my father and give him the good news about the Masters. Then I got the call," he said, and looked down at his lap, brushing his eyes with the back of his hand.

"What call?" I asked.

"Two days before my trip, the Sheriff's department out here called me. They'd found my father dead. They told me it was a terrible accident, probably a suicide. They said a typed note left at the scene stated he had been under severe financial pressure because of the recession, but I never knew him to have any problems with money. They found him under a car motor that had been hoisted up in one of the car repair bays. They said he'd rigged a wire to the hoist release and after lying down under it, pulled the wire. The motor fell and crushed his chest."

As he said this, he bent forward with his face falling into his hands and sat still as a stone, rocking back and forth a few times.

"Nathan, I'm sorry," I said. "That's terrible."

He looked up at me with dead eyes. "Even with the relationship we had, I always believed in him. He would never, ever, have committed suicide. Never. I'm as certain of that as anything I've ever known. I'll tell you straight up, he was killed. I just wish I could prove it, even after all these years."

I looked at him and dreaded what I was about to say. Drew James, protector of Israeli golf pros.

"I may have some people I know who could look into this. Do you have anything from the police investigation?" I asked.

He looked at me like one of the passengers on the Titanic looking at a nearby floating lifeboat.

"Yes, as a matter of fact I do," he said. "I still have a copy of the autopsy report and photos, if you think that will help. Oh, and I also found the envelope the letter came in. It had fallen behind the dresser and I found it just last year."

Chapter 46

I got back to DC, tired from the long trip back. When I'd returned, I'd sent the autopsy photos and records to Dr. Scott Kimmett, an old friend who had been with me on one of my special ops teams. He was an expert in combat wounds and now was Chief of Pathology at the new Walter Reed Medical Center.

The envelope Nathan had found didn't have much on it. Just his address on the front, written in the style of a right-hander writing with their left hand. The postmark was very faint, having faded over the years. I got out a magnifying glass and studied it but the listed post office address was just too faded. I couldn't make out the city. I moved over to the window with the sun streaming through and looked at the mark in the bright light. It had been mailed from Alabama.

About a week later, Kimmett called me and asked me to come by and see him. I drove into DC to his office near the new medical center. There'd been a certain charm to the old Walter Reed that had been built in the 60s right next to the original version built in 1909. This new one had none of that.

Scott took me into a small office and closed the door, and took a folder out of the locked file. He was thin, wiry, and totally intent on finding out why people die.

"Drew, when I looked at the autopsy photos, my first impression was that there's just too much damage. It doesn't seem to square with the description of suicide. I found so much damage in the chest area that actually trying to locate any specific tissue damage or bone damage not caused by the impact of that weight dropping on him was pretty much impossible. From your phone call, I understand you'd like me to rule out a suicide if I can do that."

"But if you can't------"

"So listen up and take a look at these." He put three prints of the autopsy photos on the desk top. He pointed to the first one. "This is a blowup of the bottom of the car motor hoisted all the way up to the top of the chain lift. See this single bolt sticking out of the bottom of the motor block? It's not clear why it's the only thing protruding from an otherwise smooth underside of the engine, but there it is. Now this next print is a full photo of the chest area of the subject showing a puncture wound in the skin caused by the lone bolt on the engine bottom. I've marked it with a red circle. This third print is actually an enlargement of the chest area. It shows the same clear hole in the chest cavity caused by the bolt impacting the chest area. I've also circled that in red. The circle marked in blue shows another smaller puncture wound about four inches from the red circle, in a lateral direction across the crushed chest, from right to left. Now, here's a third circle marked with yellow and, as you can see from the print of the whole chest area, it's yet another wound an inch and a quarter or inch and a half further, going from right to left, from the blue circle. But as shown in the yellow circle, as the bolt struck, or would seem to have struck a previously damaged area, it's a very faint impression. However, looking at it closely, I think you will see that it is reasonable to suppose that impact area marked by the yellow circle represents the same lone bolt sticking out from the bottom of the engine."

"You're talking way too fast for me, Scott. Can you put this in simple straight language that I can understand?" I asked. "It sounds like you're telling me that you believe that the engine block was dropped onto him twice, and it's even possible that it could have been dropped, cranked up, dropped again, cranked up, and dropped a third time."

"Yes," he said. "To me, after viewing all of the photos, it is quite clear that it isn't consistent with suicide. In my opinion, it's clear he was murdered. There is simply no possible way imaginable this man could have dropped the engine on himself, then cranked it up to drop even a second time, much less a third time as these photos indicate."

"This is amazing work, Scott," I said. "This will be a great comfort to the family to know it wasn't suicide. Tell me straight though. With what you've seen, do you think we have enough here to take to the DA for a possible murder prosecution?"

"What could you do with it, especially this many years later? Assuming you could even find anybody who did it, they'd just say that the police got real clumsy. They found him crushed under that thing and so they cranked it up off of him and it slipped and fell on him again and they cranked it up again and locked it. He was obviously dead, so why make a big deal about the crank slipping after he'd died? We can't prove the third drop, even though I feel certain it happened. In a court of law you'd never be able to get anywhere near, much less beyond, a reasonable doubt."

"You are damn good, Kimmett," I said.

"Better believe it," he said. "The best, actually. My pleasure to help. Keep in touch."

All I could tell Nathan, or wanted to tell Nathan, was that any faint possibility of his father's suicide was obliterated. I called him that afternoon and told him. He didn't say a thing for a long time. Finally, in a strained voice, he spoke. "You have no idea how much this means to me and my mother, Drew. It confirms what we felt in our hearts for these past many years. It's the most priceless information I've ever received. Thank you."

I told him I'd let him know if I learned anything more and we hung up. I thought of the implications of Moshe's current situation and this confirmation that the only other PGA tour player from Israel was forced to leave the tour through the death of his father. For whatever reason, someone was doing their best to keep Israeli Jewish golfers from going to the Masters and they were using any means available to do so.

Chapter 47

The weather was abysmal. Mid-February in DC was what I affectionately called "the Gloom Period" in honor of my rockbound Hudson highlands alma mater. The wind was steady out of the north, with gusts up to 25 mph. Snow squalls scuttled through, alternating between heavy sheets of snow and fine ice that at 25 mph felt like buckshot out of an Avenger combat shotgun. It was truly time to skip town for somewhere warm, and the Northern Trust Open (formerly the Nissan Open) at Riviera Country Club in Pacific Palisades, California, was just the ticket.

Moshe had done well at Torrey Pines. I'd been skewered by my board of directors in New York, but at the end of our meeting, they were all satisfied that the column was actually pretty good and it was a fair piece of journalism.

During that time, I'd been a pest with Eddie, constantly calling and texting him on my cell phone to check on Moshe. Of course there was no need to do so. Every time, Eddie would simply chuckle and tell me nothing was happening that he couldn't handle. I knew that was right, but not being with Moshe still made me nervous.

Now Moshe was focused on the Northern Trust and so was I. The tournament has produced a glittering assortment of champions over the years, in no small part because Riviera is the sort of course that demands accurate shot making and ball striking. The greens are small and beautifully bunkered and the fairways are narrow and lined with thick rough. And since the course sits in a canyon, the winds that come off of the nearby Pacific tend to gust and swirl. All things considered, I figured Moshe would have a pretty stressful time in L.A. And of course the Hezbollah hit team was still operating somewhere. It seemed the timing was right for the operation Ben had warned me about. But this time, it'd be on me to take care of Moshe.

Riviera opened in 1927, and a year later Douglas Fairbanks, the great actor, put up $1000 of his own money to lure the game's top professionals to L.A. for a tournament that would help put Riviera on the map. In 2007, the Northern Trust Corporation out of Chicago became the tournament's sponsor.

The course is closely associated with Ben Hogan, and became known as "Hogan's Alley" after he won the 1947 and 1948 L.A. Opens and the 1948 U.S. Open there. As good as Arnold Palmer was, he never won at Riviera, in part because his attacking style of play wasn't a good fit for such a narrow, demanding course. On one occasion, he hit his drive deep in the underbrush, into what was virtually an unplayable lie. As he studied his options, he asked a local L.A. Times sports columnist, "You're always writing about Hogan. What would Hogan do in a spot like this?" Much to the gallery's delight, and Palmer's dismay the columnist quipped, "Hogan wouldn't get in a spot like this."

We flew out on Monday. I flew with Moshe in first class and we talked about the tournament the whole way. It was good to see the excitement in his face as he talked about golf, and not the look of unpleasantness caused by his other troubles. Whether right or wrong, I'd chosen not to tell Moshe about the pending attack. No need to get him overly worried and I was always cautioning him to be careful anyway.

"This is the type of course where length is not a huge factor," he said. "That's good for me since I'm not one of the tournament's big hitters."

I laughed to myself thinking, for Moshe, this meant drives of merely 300 yards. Of course 300 yards was not unusual for me. Except that usually meant 150 yards straight ahead and 150 more at a right angle into the woods.

"I'm really going to have to work my ball around here, play smart, and hit my approaches on the correct side of the hole. I love the little rolls and gentle slopes and the nice little dog-legs that make me have to carefully shape my shots. In my mind, that's the way golf should be played."

We landed at the airport and took a limo to the Ritz Carlton in Marina del Rey. Moshe took the Executive Suite and I took an adjoining room. We rode together to the Riviera; he went to the driving range and I did my usual recon of the course. Surrounded by neighborhoods and a high fence, I couldn't see this being a place where a Hezbollah hit squad would attempt to take out Moshe, and my recon confirmed no areas of concern.

When Moshe was finished with his practice round, we ate dinner and then went back to the hotel by way of a different route, my eyes looking ahead and behind for any trailers. With the time change, we were both tired and ready for bed. I gave Moshe the usual instructions. Keep your cell phone close by your bed. If you hear anything, call me. I'm right next door. I patted his shoulder, told him to sleep well and lock and bolt the door, and then went next door to my room. I was asleep as soon as my head hit the pillow.

<u>Chapter 48</u>

I was dreaming that I was being chased by a bee and couldn't get away from it. It was incessant and I kept swatting at it, but it wouldn't quit. With a start I pulled out of the dream and realized it was my cell phone buzzing on the night stand. It was 3:24 in the morning. I grabbed the phone and answered it.

"Drew," a whisper said, "it's me Moshe. I'm out on my balcony. I think I hear someone in the other room of my suite." The tremor in his voice reflected the sense of sheer terror he was feeling.

"Stay right where you are Moshe," I said as calmly as I could. "Don't move and be as quiet as you can, I'll be right there."

I threw on a pair of running shorts, putting my room key in the pocket. I reached for my 9mm handgun but thought that might not be so smart in a confined area in the dark. So I grabbed my two-foot long telescopic steel baton I'd thrown in my bag at the last minute. The rubber grip felt comforting in my hand. I ran to the double doors of my balcony, jerked them open and stepped out. Moshe's balcony was to my right extending the length of his suite. I could see him huddled at the far end just outside of his bedroom. The air was cool with a slight breeze blowing in from the water. From below, the fronds of a palm tree clacked in the breeze. I estimated the length between our

186

balconies at about five feet. Not a far distance to jump if it was five feet off the ground, but we were up on the 15th floor. I climbed over the railing and stood on the edge of my balcony, my heels wedged back between the railings. I took a deep breath and jumped, reaching with my right hand and holding the baton and my cell phone tightly in my left. I grabbed the top bar of the balcony, my body swinging in towards it. With a jolt, my midsection slammed down into the edge of the balcony floor. The cell phone popped loose from my hand and fell clattering off of the balcony below Moshe's and down into the night. At least I'd held on to the baton.

Straining from the effort, I pulled myself up enough to get my toes on the surface of the balcony floor, then stood up and vaulted over the railing. I signaled to Moshe for silence as I landed in a crouch. I tried to peer inside the French doors to the living area of Moshe's suite. Muttering under my breath Caesar's fateful words as he crossed the Rubicon, "the die is cast," I flicked the baton out to full length with a flick of my wrist and opened the right hand French door as quietly as I could.

There was no light inside the room. As I slipped in through the cracked door, the faint light from the glow of nighttime LA shone weakly into the living area of the suite. No one was there. I glided in a crouch towards the door that separated Moshe's bedroom from the living area. There was a two-foot opening between the door and the frame. As I stepped to the gap and peered around the edge, I saw a black clad figure step up to the edge of Moshe's now vacant bed and swing a glittering arc through the air down into the place where Moshe would have been. As he straightened with surprise at the bed being empty, I was on him in two quick strides, swinging the baton as I moved.

I struck him hard across the back of his neck, and then followed with a quick slash to the back of his right knee driving him to his knees. He yelped with pain, rolled to his right and came up unsteadily with the knife pointed towards me. As I moved towards him to strike his knife arm, Moshe chose that moment to open the balcony door right behind me, tripping my leg and pushing me off balance towards the man.

I saw the knife blade coming towards me and moved the baton just enough to deflect the knife away from my stomach. I felt a flash of pain as it sliced the outside of my left arm, the blow knocking me backwards onto the floor. As he moved towards me and planted his left foot to stab down at me, I hooked my foot behind his ankle, holding his foot and leg steady and at the same time kicked as hard as I could with my heel towards his kneecap. With a snap, his leg bent backwards and he collapsed in a still heap on his stomach.

My arm burned with pain as I stood over him waiting to snap him with the baton if he moved, but he didn't budge. I used the baton to roll him over and saw the handle of the knife protruding from just below his chest where it stuck when he fell. He was obviously dead. The air quickly filled with the strong copper scent of blood as it pooled dark black on the carpet. He had a ninja style hood on and was dressed in black. Hard to tell who he was or where he was from, but he definitely wanted Moshe dead. I turned and called for Moshe.

As he entered the room from the balcony I said, "I'm afraid there's no holding off any more Moshe. The hotel will see this so we have to call the police and bring them in. They'll have to work this with the intelligence agencies to identify the terrorist group that's after you."

"Drew, you know what that will mean for me, don't you?" he asked.

"Yes," I said softly. "But with this mess there's no avoiding it any longer. And we got lucky here tonight, really lucky. We've got to make the call."

With an air of complete hopelessness, he looked down dejectedly. "OK," he said. "If there's no other way then." We went into the living area together to get away from the body. He turned on a light and reached for the hotel phone. He looked at me oddly and handed the phone to me. It was dead.

Chapter 49

I grabbed him and hustled him towards the front door. Looking out the security peephole, I saw no sign of anyone. Yanking the door open, we hustled to my room, locking and bolting the door behind us. I secured the balcony doors and turned towards Moshe. He was sitting on the bed shivering and looking nearly catatonic. The stress had been too much and the shock of the attack had caused him to retreat inside himself. I grabbed a small bottle of Crown Royal from the mini-bar, forced him to drink it, and laid him back on my bed, covering him with the blanket.

"You rest now Moshe," I said gently. "You did well tonight. We'll work this all out tomorrow morning."

Moshe's eyes flickered and with one last effort he said, "Thank you so much for helping me Drew." And then he was fast asleep from the trauma. I checked the security chain and deadbolt on the door and pulled a chair over in front of the balcony doors. I checked my room phone and it was dead also. It looked like someone had cut off the connection to our rooms. With my cell phone gone and the phone in the room dead, I'd have to get Moshe's from his balcony when he woke up in the morning.

I took out my first aid kit, stripped my shirt off and looked at the cut on my arm. It was a fairly deep cut but nothing serious, thankfully. I dressed it and cleaned up, putting on a fresh shirt. Then, making myself as comfortable as I could, and placing my gun in my lap, I settled in, watching over Moshe. The body and cops would have to wait.

At seven a.m., the watch on Moshe's wrist beeped, waking him and startling me from my reverie. I got up and walked over to him.

"How are you feeling?" I asked.

"Groggy, but OK, I guess," he said. "I have to get to the course for my practice round."

"You really think that's a good idea? Is your head on straight enough now to play golf?"

"Honestly," he said, "probably not. But it is my job and I do not want to let these terrorists believe they are defeating me."

"I'm really not worried about them defeating you Moshe. I'm worried about them killing you. I really think you should consider withdrawing this week."

"No," he said stubbornly. "I will play."

Exhaling slowly, I shook my head and marveled at his obstinacy. "Well if that's the way it is, I'll go next door and do my best to take care of things. Is your phone still out on your balcony?" I asked. "I'll need to call the front desk and then the police."

"Yes," he said. "I dropped it there when I heard you fighting inside and came in to try and help."

"I'll go get it and be right back. You stay here and get cleaned up," I said. "Lock the door behind me when I leave."

"I will. Be careful," he said.

I checked the peephole again, and again no one was there. I slipped out to the corridor and pulled the door behind me, holding the gun ready. I walked to Moshe's room and slid the plastic key card into the lock. The bolt clicked and I pushed the door open and went in.

The first thing that hit me was the smell. Not the one I was expecting from the coagulated blood and dead body in Moshe's bed room, but the strong smell of disinfectant and air freshener. The living area looked and smelled like it had just been prepared for the next guest. Walking in disbelief towards the bedroom where the attacker's body was, I opened the door wide and saw......nothing. No mess, no blood, no knife, and no body. It was as if the events of the early morning were merely a gossamer memory of fading fragments of nightmare.

It was clear to me now, if it hadn't been already, that we were dealing with a serious group. Any organization that was capable of doing this type of cleanup this quickly was one to be feared. There was no way we could call the police now. With no body, no blood, and no crime scene, the police would think of Moshe exactly how he feared, as a paranoid nutcase. Moshe was right. He needed to go practice and play as well as he could.

I went out on the balcony and picked up Moshe's cell phone, still wedged over to one side under the railing. I went inside and packed up all of Moshe's stuff and brought them to my room. He was still in the bathroom so I called from his cell phone to the front desk and got him placed in a different room under my name. He came out of the bathroom toweling off his hair, while I filled him in on what had happened next door. He was as surprised as I had been.

"You were right, Moshe," I said. "We can't call the police right now. You're just going to have to play and I'll be watching you the whole time. This thing is getting weirder and weirder."

"Thank you for understanding. I will try and put this out of my mind and do the best I can. As long as you are nearby, I feel safe enough to concentrate properly on my game."

Moshe moved to his new room and then we headed for the course. I followed him closely during each round and he did his usual amazing thing. Even after a vicious attack in the middle of the night, he opened with scores of 68-67-69 and had a two-stroke lead going into the final round. Then things got interesting when his playing partner put on a surge that would eventually see him shoot a 67 while Moshe struggled to an even-par 72. Moshe had been one up at the turn but his lead slipped and, after 16 holes, he was tied for the lead. The 18th hole, a demanding par-4, proved to be the turning point. Moshe hit a drive into the thick, wet rough guarding the ride side of the hole. He couldn't reach the green in two and his third shot went to the back of the green, leaving him a difficult, downhill 12-footer to save par. His partner hit an indifferent second shot and had to play his third shot from the rough, but after playing an aggressive chip, he holed out with a birdie. Moments later, Moshe missed his par putt and his partner had the victory.

Chapter 50

He exploded with rage, screaming expletives and threats at the three men gathered in the room and slamming his fists on the desktop, causing the picture frames to topple over onto the floor. Spittle flew from his lips as his face turned bright red. His eyes were a singularly pale clear cold blue and they were as merciless as a guillotine blade.

In a voice seething with anger and barely controlled, he leaned forward in his chair and spoke in a husky whisper. "Y'all are supposed to be my most capable planners. The ones I've hand selected and trained to execute every operation we develop. I've paid you very, very well boys and I expect you to do just exactly what I order you to do. Yet time after time, over the course of these past months, you and your men have consistently failed me. And you're tellin me now that this one man is the problem? One man has caused all of these screw-ups?

"Boss," one of the men said, "take it easy. You gotta understand. We had good plans, they just didn't work out exactly right. We just had bad luck."

In one smooth and continuous motion he pulled open the right-hand desk drawer, pulled out the silenced hand gun, pointed and pulled the trigger. A dark hole appeared on the man's forehead and the back of his head exploded in a red shower of flesh, brains, and bone that dripped down the wall behind as the man's body slumped down onto the floor.

"That's what I'd call bad luck," he said staring angrily at the two remaining men looking at him with open mouths and *unbelieving eyes. "No more damn excuses. You understand me? You get this done. You make it happen. That Jew can't get to the Masters."*

Chapter 51

Back home from California, Moshe was gearing up for a succession of tournaments leading up to the Masters. I called Ben to tell him about the hit on Moshe. Before he could say anything, I detailed all that had happened. I described how the attacker was dressed, and the quick cleaning action someone had performed. I then paused and asked him what they'd seen in the wires on the hit and if the group they were looking at had claimed responsibility yet.

After I finished, Ben said, "sorry to hear about that buddy. Of course I knew you'd handle it well like you always do. But haven't you heard the latest news?"

"No," I said. "What news?"

"It looks like your hit was by a different team. Just about an hour ago, the Israeli Prime Minister was attacked. He was at a conference in downtown Los Angeles. It was just like Hinckley's attack on Reagan back in '81. He was exiting his hotel through the kitchen and out the back door, under tight security. Don't know how, but the hit team must have known he'd be leaving at that time and location. A cab driver pulled in front of the limo, while the morons on duty were waving him on, not seeing him as a threat. In the meantime, the guy in the back seat of the cab starts spraying rounds with an AK-47 out the back window. Security naturally pushed the prime minister away from the cab and over towards the hotel entrance, where surprise, surprise a third guy was waiting in the crowd. As the prime minister gets close, the third guy pulls out a handgun and shoots him in the chest at point blank range."

"Is he dead?" I asked.

"You would've thought so," he said. "It knocked him the hell over backwards. But the Israelis always have their VIPs wear the new light weight concealed body armor undervest. So he had the breath knocked out of him pretty good, but all things considered, he's fine."

"How about the hit team?" I asked. "Did they get anybody to question?"

"No chance," he said. "I would've loved to have spent some time with the attackers, find out about other planned missions and maybe about other teams in the U.S. like the one that went after your boy. But you can imagine those Israelis couldn't have cared less. All three of the bad guys ended up with double gunshots to the forehead. So for now, at least, it looks like the intel I passed on to you wasn't about Moshe."

"Sounds like good news and bad news Ben. He wasn't the target of this mission, but on the other hand, he sure as hell was someone's target and we don't know whose."

"Hey, hang tight. I'll keep looking. Whoever it is, these guys are showing themselves more and more. And as we both know, that just means more opportunity for them to screw up and allow us to latch on to them," he said. "For now, you keep watching him and working it from your end. I'd suggest you think about getting him some of that body armor like the prime minister wore, but I'm figuring there's no way your guy will wear it. It's kinda hard to golf 72 holes wearing that stuff."

"Yeah, you're right," I said. "Absolutely no chance of that. I'll just have to stick with him the whole time."

"Do that," he said. "And watch your back. I mean real carefully."

"I will, Ben. Thanks for everything," I said. And then remembering his mistake with Clive Perkins and the National Criminal Information system, I asked him to run his name again. He said he would.

We hung up and I took stock of the situation. Moshe was still being targeted. It wasn't the Hezbollah team Ben had heard about, but perhaps it was a different one. For some reason, I was still being targeted by a hit team with KKK symbols on their necks. And as time passed, things were getting more violent.

I called the number for the Virginia Commonwealth's Acquisition Office and asked for Mark Girard, the head of the technical evaluation panel for the Wilson Bridge Project. When I gave the secretary my name, he told me that Girard was in a meeting and was booked for meetings for the rest of the week. Kinda like being told by a girl you ask on a date that she had to stay home and wash her hair – for the next three months.

I wasn't buying it, but there was nothing else I could do. I asked for, and got, Girard's voicemail, then left a detailed message asking him about the panel, Casey Brady, the ratings he had changed, SCC having the best value, and what I now called the Wilson Bridge Conspiracy. Catchy name, but not likely one to endear him to me, nor to cause him to open up to me with any information. But with the brush-off his secretary gave me, I figured maybe it would make all those meetings a little more tedious for him. Have a nice life, pal.

Finally I called my favorite gal pal, Michelle Gann and amazingly, same drill and same voicemail message. As a nice touch, for her benefit, I even threw in the Virginia Commonwealth criminal code section for bribery.

Later, thinking back on it, maybe I shouldn't have stuck such a big stick in those hornet nests, much less used such vigor in stirring it around.

Chapter 52

It was towards the end of March, and it felt like Spring was on the way. Moshe and I had been to Florida for the World Golf Championship at Doral in Miami and then to the Transitions Championship at Palm Harbor, Florida. Beautiful places to visit if you could sit by a pool drinking Pina Coladas. But I was spending my days moving along miles of wood line and marsh and shadowing Moshe through practice rounds and 72 holes of tournament golf at each stop.

I guess I should've been happy that it seemed to have paid off, since there were no other attacks on Moshe and his game was peaking for the Masters the next month. Nevertheless, my feet were sore, my face and arms were burned dark red, and my bosses at Golfer's Journal were wondering if somehow I'd lost my mind and was living in a world of hallucinations.

The day had been bright with clear blue skies, white puffy clouds, and a light breeze. I'd taken the opportunity to hit the driving range to work with my driver. I knew that my pre-shot routine on the range should be the same as if I was on the golf course. So I'd hit a shot then step off to the side, change targets and clubs, and go through my routine again.

I spent the first half of my time working on the shortest full-swing distance. I hit into a green, using my wedge with a full swing. It was supposed to improve the tempo of my swing by taking my emphasis away from distance. I worked my way through the bag hitting a slight draw with my irons. I pulled my driver out of the bag remembering I should not hold the club too tightly. But true to form, something about that beast of a head and the length of the shaft made me grip it tighter, so, like usual, the club face was open at impact and, presto, a left-to-right ball flight. So much for practice.

It was now around nine in the evening. I got off the phone with Moshe after calling to check and see how he was doing. I'd given Anne a call, and for the first time, she seemed happy to talk to me. We made arrangements to grab lunch the next day.

I put Diana Krall on the CD player and shuffled into the kitchen, trying to piece all of this big mess together. There were too many gaps and holes in the pattern of facts, like a jigsaw puzzle of blue sky missing most of the pieces. Because of their timing, I'd tried to connect the Hezbollah attacks on Moshe with those against me by my assailants with the KKK tattoos, but couldn't come up with anything. My instincts told me that my articles on Augusta National were seriously hitting a nerve and causing the attacks against me, but I had no proof to connect them. And there were too many seeming coincidences that pointed to some connection between me, Moshe, and J. J. Gann, but I just couldn't nail it down. Somehow I had to knock my head around and shake something loose --- little did I know. Be careful what you ask for.

I made a grilled chicken Caesar salad, grabbed a wineglass, and a bottle of Cabernet and headed for the dining room. Fine wine, good music and a date on tap for the next day made me a happy camper. But isn't that always the way it works? There ought to be a warning bell on the happy meter, so that every time it creeps high enough you get that ringing alert. Be very careful. That happy glow makes you too visible. One of them is out there in the boonies, adjusting the windage, getting you lined up in the cross hairs of the scope. When it happens so often, wouldn't you think I'd be more ready for it?

As I was savoring the wine and thinking of lunch the next day, there was a knock on the door. With a sigh of exasperation and thoughts of how little I wanted to buy anything from the Boy Scout, Girl Scout, or whoever was interrupting my dinner and my thoughts, I walked over and yanked the door open.

I felt more than saw the hand holding the silenced gun pointed at my face and jerked to the right just as the gun spit with a flame of fire. A searing pain exploded high above my left ear and flashes of light blossomed behind my left eye. With the blackness starting to close in, I shot my right hand up, slamming the heel of my palm into the base of my attacker's nose. He cried out sharply and I heard with satisfaction the crack of his nose as it bent to the side. Then grabbing his outstretched arm and turning into him, I elbowed him with my left arm in the throat as hard as I could. He gasped and pushed me hard away from him.

I turned and started backpedaling to try and create some space, but he'd recovered enough to be on me, hitting me in the head with what felt like a Titleist alloy pitching wedge but really must have been the gun he'd just fired. My left arm was numb and swung uselessly by my side. My right forearm took most of the force of the remaining blows as I tried to cover my head and keep it from being turned into ground beef.

I lashed out with my right fist when I could, jabbing it into his body and face as hard as possible. I ducked and bobbed at the blows, catching glimpses of the familiar small tattoo on the left side of his neck. As I was forced backward, I realized I'd backed all the way into the bathroom and felt my foot slip on the throw rug. Flailing my right arm for balance, I grabbed at his shirt, tearing his front pocket off in the process. Turning as I fell backward, I heard another shot fired and was propelled towards the tub. Tumbling inside as if it were my own cozy porcelain coffin, the lights went out.

Chapter 53

The mind does funny things when trying to avoid the realization of great pain. Generally, it devolves into either nothingness or some complex dream state. I was pleased to note that mine involved the latter in the form of a rather elaborate and pleasurable fantasy. I was on the 16th tee at Augusta National, a gentle breeze sighing through the pines and ruffling the surface of the pond that stood between me and the green. The azaleas shone in the warm Georgia sun like a sequined scarlet curtain, alive and moving in the breeze.

As I stood in the tee box and lined up my eight-iron, I turned to the gorgeous creature caddying for me, and saw that it was my wife Marie. Dark blonde hair, blue eyes, a smile to light up the heavens, and a figure that could stop time, she held out a glistening bottle of Bass Ale with the ice slipping down its side. She was the essence of perfection, whispering exaggerated compliments about my character, shot-selection and short-game. All was right – the sun, the water, the flawless grass, the liquid refreshment, and the love of my life.

Unfortunately, dreams have a way of changing just when you begin to enjoy them. As I stood there reaching for the bottle from Marie, raindrops began hitting on my face out of the clear blue southern sky. As if that wasn't enough to ruin my cozy little dream, Marie suddenly transformed and became rock hard, like some ancient former inhabitant of Pompeii or the newly discovered remains of Lot's wife. Beautiful to look at, to the touch she was a cool and smooth porcelain doll. And she kept moving closer to my face, ruining my view of the green and making me feel cold all over.

Slowly my consciousness rose to the surface, bringing with it the realization that small drops of water were rhythmically tapping the side of my face and running down my neck. And then the pain hit like the shock of a 30-ton locomotive hitting a stalled vehicle at a crossing and I fell back into darkness.

Minutes later, my eyes cleared and I woke again to reality. I found I was holding the gun, no longer with the silencer. Taking stock of which parts of my body didn't hurt, I was happy to note that my toes felt just fine. My head felt like I'd received a deep tissue massage with a crow bar. Rolling over as best I could, I looked up at the spout and saw my favorite leak ready to spill yet another drop. I grimaced and wondered how much longer I'd have been out cold if I'd ever made the mistake of playing handyman and fixed the damn thing.

I reached up and grabbed the inset soap holder and grunting with the strain, pulled myself up to a sitting position while the room spun and twirled around me like so many childhood merry-go-rounds. The gun slipped from my hands and fell into the small trash can next to the tub. When the house stopped moving and the bile retreated back down my throat, I slowly rolled over the edge of the tub, paused to catch my breath and slowly pushed myself to a kneeling position. After waiting for another wave of blackness and nausea to pass, I touched the top part of my head where I'd been shot and felt the shallow groove. Another lightning flash of pain shot through me. But I realized that another millimeter more and I'd have been gone. I slowly stood up and braced both hands on the bathroom door opening.

As I stepped out of the bathroom, I felt my foot kick something that skittered across the bedroom floor and under my bed. I took baby steps towards the kitchen for some ice and any pain medication I could lay my hands on, preferably in great quantities.

As if the physical shock I was feeling wasn't enough, as I stepped into the bedroom I glanced at the bed and reeled from the mental shock that slammed into my brain. There, sprawled across my bed with a swollen blue face and splayed out arms and legs, was a woman with her clothes hanging off of her.

Chapter 54

I could tell from the swollen, discolored face, the unseeing half-open eyes, and the curious slackness of body that only the dead display, that she hadn't had a good day. I was also pretty positive she hadn't been there when I sat down to eat my dinner, which seemed like an eternity ago, but was in reality only fifteen minutes earlier. It was obvious from her cheap and skimpy clothing, as well as the remains of copious makeup, that she was, or at least had been, a prostitute. It was also obvious that whoever had killed her and placed her on my bed thought I was dead or still out cold in the tub if I was lucky enough to still be alive.

Moving as quickly as my wobbly legs would allow, I went to my front door and eased it open. The stairwell was empty and brightly lit. I stepped down to the switches by the entrance door and flicked them off, killing the lights on the stairs and outside the entrance. Shuffling back up the stairs, I gingerly wobbled back into the bedroom. Scooping up the woman in my arms, along with my bedspread, I groaned out loud with the pain and headed back through the darkness out the front door. Pausing in the darkness outside, my heart pounding and my head still ringing, I heard a distant sound of police sirens.

I gulped in a few deep breaths and, staggering slightly with the awkward load of the dead woman, moved as quietly as I could across the front of the building to the far corner. Peering around it, I repeated my moves to the parking lot located in the rear of the building. In the back corner of the lot was a trash dumpster, conveniently situated in the shadows. I stumbled forward and, seeing that the top lids were open, strained with effort and heaved the body up and into the dumpster. I opened the small door on the side, reached in, and covered the body with the bedspread, whispering an apology to whoever she was as I did so.

On still-gimpy legs, I moved as quickly as I could back to my place, flicking on the lights in the apartment foyer as I shuffled back inside. The sounds of the sirens grew louder. I went into the bathroom, grabbed a handful of toilet paper and shoved it on top of the gun in the trash can. Then I frantically straightened out the remaining bedclothes and searched around the bedroom for any signs of my recent houseguest. On hands and knees, I saw a crumpled ball of a sweater under the bed and what looked to be a pocket memo book. I grabbed them and moved as fast as I could into the kitchen, shoving them both together into the freezer compartment of the refrigerator under some bags of frozen vegetables.

As I took in air and tried to calm my breathing, I heard a knock on the door and someone called out "police!" I croaked back, "Just a minute!" Grabbing a mouthful of Caesar salad and carrying my plate with me, I pulled on a DC Nationals ball cap to cover my bloody head, wincing from the sting, and a jacket to cover my now bloody shirt. Then I opened the door, chewing my food as casually as if I'd just been seated at dinner.

The two uniformed cops were in their mid-twenties, one tall and stocky, the other slight and wiry. Both had military haircuts. Looking stern and officious they introduced themselves as Officers Angelo and Garvin and asked if they could come in and look around.

Angelo, the stocky one, said "Sorry to disturb you this evening, Sir. We received a report that a woman was in trouble in your apartment."

"I certainly don't know what the problem is Officer," I said. "I haven't heard a thing all night. I was just sitting here eating my dinner."

"Well, if you don't mind Sir, we'll just take a quick look around," he said.

"Help yourselves," I said.

As they moved through my place looking into rooms, I noticed through my open front door that Anne, my neighbor, was looking at me through her cracked open front door. "Perfect," I said to myself. "Now she'll think I'm some kind of degenerate serial murderer."

Angelo walked back to my front door. "Everything appears to be in order," he said. "Sorry to disturb you. You sure you haven't seen any people you don't recognize or heard anything in the last hour? Any odd noises?"

"No, nothing unusual," I lied.

"Ok then, have a good evening. Please call us if you hear or see anything out of the ordinary," he said and then with Garvin trailing behind him, he left.

Chapter 55

I closed the door, not wanting to explain myself to Anne, and slumped back against it, taking several deep breaths while my head swam. Oh you bet I'll call you, I thought to myself. Nothing out of the ordinary here Officer. I frequently get shot in the head and it's not unusual at all to have dead hookers dumped on my bed. Then looking down at the carpet, I noticed several spots of blood. Good thing I'd just happened to be standing on them when the cops were there. Guess it's truly better to be lucky than good.

Not wanting my luck to run out, I sucked in air, gathered my strength and headed back outside to try and figure out what to do with my uninvited houseguest. I'd have to figure something out. It'd be too easy for the police to make the connection between the body and my bedspread in the dumpster and the call they'd received. I limped around the corner of the building and pulled up short. With loud bangs and engine noise, a trash truck was in the process of lifting the dumpster up with its dual tines, and dumping the contents inside its bowels. As I watched, I saw the flash of familiar color of my bedspread as the contents of the dumpster spilled down inside the truck. The engine revved as the dumpster was lowered back to the ground with a loud thud and with a grinding of the gears and a strident beeping of the backup horn, the truck backed up and then sped away from the lot. And just like that, the body was gone. Guess my luck was still holding out.

I wobbled back to my apartment using the walls to brace myself as I went and, as I climbed up the stairs, saw Anne's door open again and she looked out at me. Obviously fresh from the shower, her hair was wet and combed back and she was wearing a pink silk bathrobe.

"Hey Anne. Everything OK?" I slurred.

"Hi Drew. You tell me. I thought I heard gunshots. What's going on? What were the police doing here?" she said.

I opened my mouth to answer, but before I could do so, the world got fuzzy and I fell against the door of my apartment, sinking to my knees. With the rush of adrenaline no longer fueling me, my body was shutting down as a result of the injuries I'd received.

With a shriek, Anne opened her door wide and stepped out towards me. Grabbing my arm, she struggled to help me on my feet and together we stumbled into my apartment towards the couch, my arm around her shoulder and hers around my back. As she turned me, I backed up, hit the edge of the couch, and fell backwards, my hat flying off, revealing my blood-covered scalp. Anne gasped loudly and lunged to grab me, her robe spilling open and revealing her beautiful naked body. Even in my weakened state, it was the best thing I'd seen all day. All year for that matter. And it was the last thing I saw as I blacked out.

<u>Chapter 56</u>

When I awoke thirty minutes later she was sitting next to me on the edge of the couch gently dabbing the wound on the side of my head with a wet cloth, now stained dark pink. Blushing from her unintended exposure, her robe was wrapped tightly around her with the belt double-knotted.

"What happened to you?" she said stiffly, speaking quickly.

"It's a long story. Suffice it to say for now, I got waylaid," I said.

"You've got a nasty wound on your head. I think I've about got the bleeding stopped," she said. "What's going on Drew?"

The tension between us was palpable. About what you'd expect under the circumstances. Here she'd tried to help me, a virtual stranger, and in the process embarrassed herself by accidentally exposing her whole body to me.

"Thank you for helping me," I said slowly sitting up towards her. "I'm sorry to bother you like this and bring you into my problems," I said quickly. "And the thing with the wardrobe malfunction and all? I mean, I'm sorry about that too. But don't worry, I really didn't see anything," I said, then stammered hurriedly, "not that I didn't want to...I mean. What I did see was ... I mean, you look fantastic, it's just that...," I stuttered and then stopped short. "What

I really mean, is, you don't have anything to be embarrassed about. And, you were really sweet to help me."

I leaned back on the couch, shut up, and looked at her. Notwithstanding my normal propensity to say the wrong thing, I'd managed to say exactly what was needed and in the process, slain the three-hundred-pound gorilla in the room.

She smiled gently with apparent relief, the color again momentarily brightening her cheeks as she visibly relaxed. Then, with a wider grin, she said "You could've at least thrown some dollar bills my way, like you would for any good stripper.

"But I appreciate you not jumping to any conclusions, although I couldn't really blame you if you did. I mean, I cart you into your apartment, lay you out on your couch and then almost drop my robe on the floor," she said. "And I barely know you," she finished, looking at me with a smile and a sideways glance.

I was amazed at how well she handled such an awkward situation. I figured this was as good a time as any to try and bring some clarity to all that had happened and she certainly seemed level-headed enough to listen and give me advice. So for the next hour I talked and she listened. I told her the whole story from beginning to end.

The more I spoke, talking about the group or groups targeting Moshe and me, the angrier it made me until it seemed that what I was saying came from a strange direction, as if I were standing several feet behind myself. This had finally come to a head and I'd had enough. I told Anne, "I'm gonna keep at this, looking everywhere I can for these guys. Eventually I'll catch on and find out who they are and where they live. And when I do, I'll take them down one by one. They'll be looking for a way out but I'll box each one of them in their place, nail them shut, and cut their throats in the process."

At this last part, she stiffened and looked shocked and sad. Then looking up at me, she reached to hold my hand and said softly, "Please just smile at me with your eyes like kindly Drew James, my new neighbor, to kind of erase that other.... look."

She paused and took a deep breath. "This is too bizarre to be making it up," she said. "It sounds like Moshe's in real trouble. And it looks like somebody's out to put you away as well. Can you imagine if that guy hadn't missed, or if you'd been unconscious a little longer, or if the police had showed up sooner? I'd have really pegged you as a wacko then," she said with another smile, trying to lighten the mood. Then with a hint of tease in her voice she said, "of course I might have been able to avoid my little strip tease act if that'd been the way it went down."

She stood up and looked down at me, pushing a strand of hair back behind her ear and crossing her arms. "It's really late," she said. "I need to get back to my place and you need to get to bed. If you want, we can talk more tomorrow, not that I have a clue how to help you or Moshe. You'll probably want to take some Advil and then just sleep; feel free to call me if you feel sick. I bet you've got a concussion and you should see a doctor tomorrow," she said. "And don't take this the wrong way, but maybe you should give me a spare key so I can check in on you later tonight and see if you're still alive."

I gave her a key. "I'll think about seeing someone tomorrow, but I don't want them to look at a gunshot wound on my head and be suspicious. And thank you for everything."

She left to walk back across the hall. I swallowed down four Advil and then crashed into a deep and dreamless sleep. But the night was not over.

What I told her had had a real rough effect on her. In the middle of the night I woke to hear a sound at my front door. In the faint light from the window, I saw her push open my bedroom door and walk with light steps to the side of my bed. With a whisper of soft silk, she slid in beside me, her skin warm and velvety to the touch. She spoke softly, "This is totally crazy. Please don't take this the wrong way. What you told me is just way too much for me to bear. I'm just not used to all this violence and death. Won't you please just hold me. It seemed like such a dark, dark night to be alone."

She turned her back to me, her head on my arm, her hand holding mine, shaking and sobbing softly. I could smell the fresh scent of her hair. I put my hand on her shoulder and held her without saying a word, not wanting to spoil any part of the moment. Then she shuddered, took a deep breath and was quiet. After about twenty minutes, she turned, whispered "thank you" to me and went back to her apartment. I laid there and thought for a while about Anne forty feet away, across the night in her own sadness and turmoil, doubtless covered, also, by a thin layer of sheet.

Chapter 57

I woke up with my head throbbing. I imagined it was the same way driving range mats would feel like after a beginner's golf lesson. Pummeled and flattened. Anne's scent lingered on the sheets and a note that had been slid under my door said simply "thank you." I rolled to the side of the bed and sat up slowly, swinging my legs down to the floor very gently. I had to figure out soon what was going on with all of this and put a stop to these attacks.

After several minutes sitting with my head in my hands, elbows braced on my knees, I pushed up off the bed, steadied myself on the wall, and shuffled like an octogenarian into the kitchen. Moving at glacial speed, I made coffee, took a bagel and yogurt, and grabbing my laptop sat down heavily at the kitchen table and looked through all the local news sites I could find. The light from the screen made my eyes hurt. The sound of the clock in the kitchen sounded like a loud thumping on my skull. Even chewing the bagel made my teeth hurt. Some action figure I was.

I made my way slowly through the news sites. As I had hoped, there was no mention yet of a dead body or missing person, or the comings and goings from the previous night. As I scrolled through the pages, the events of last night slowly seeped back to full consciousness. And as I was thinking again about the awkward, yet pleasing, encounter with Anne, and then holding her while we fell asleep, I suddenly remembered the sweater and memo book I'd shoved into my freezer the night before.

The sweater was cheap and almost threadbare, with no identifying information. The memo book was small with a black cover and a rubber band holding it closed. Thinking back to last night, I realized it was the object I'd kicked from the bathroom entrance under my bed. It'd probably fallen out of my attacker's pocket when I'd ripped it while falling backwards into the tub. Just thinking about it again brought back a momentary wave of pain and nausea.

It was full of information, written in small, tight, cryptic shorthand. It looked like a planning notebook. I started from the back, thinking that might reflect the most recent attack on me, but if I was reading the dates right, it was for something in April. I paged back, looking for yesterday's date. Two pages back I found it – a single page with yesterday's date written at the top. Underneath the date were several lines of code with letters and numbers. The more I looked at it, the more confusing it appeared.

All I could see were letters and numbers that made no sense. So I stopped, got up, and walked to my bathroom to take more Advil. I went out on my balcony and looked up at the sky. It was blue as a Robin's egg. The limbs on the trees were still bare, with just a hint of new buds. The pine at the corner of my building sighed slightly in the stiffening breeze. I inhaled deeply, smelling the aroma of needles and bark suffused with pine tar. If I closed my eyes, in my mind I could picture a day just like this on the land navigation course out near Harmony Church during Ranger training at Fort Benning, Georgia. Smells always evoked such sharp memories for me of past places and times.

And then it hit me. What an idiot I was. What I was looking at in the notebook were topographical map grid coordinates with two letters followed by six numbers. And below those were apparently airline schedules with a flight number, followed by the time written in military fashion and then airport codes.

I walked quickly back to the couch and looked at the page for yesterday's date. I felt certain the grid coordinate was for that part of Alexandria where my apartment was. The flight schedules followed. It looked like the arrival flight left yesterday morning from MOB, went through IAH, and landed at DCA and then repeated the process back to MOB late last night. I should've recognized that DCA was the airport code for Reagan National Airport here in DC. I looked all of the other ones up on-line. MOB was the airport code for Mobile/Pascagoula and IAH the code for Houston. So the clown who waylaid me yesterday had flown from the border of Alabama and Mississippi, through Houston, to DC. He'd known where I was, scouted me out and likely grabbed the girl during the day, then shot me and beat the hell out of me, and then dumped the girl on my bed before heading back to Mobile.

I thumbed through the other pages, seeing similar notations on most of them. I pulled up topographic maps on line and was able to identify some of them. The one dated in October was the grid coordinate for my golf club and one in December appeared to be the coordinate for Penn Station in New York City. Pretty slick using military times and grid coordinates for locations. If I hadn't lived with them for years, I wouldn't have had a clue what they meant.

On another page was a rough drawing of something long and metallic. Had to be a weapon but not like any I'd seen. I scoured the rest of the book and buried in numbers on the third page was the connection I'd hoped to find. It had to be. In several places the initials JJG appeared.

Then, remembering the first attacks on Moshe at his house in Florida, I went to the front of the notebook to see if there were any codes or dates that correlated. As I was paging through and thinking of the attacks, a picture flashed in my mind of the blurry video of the man in the white van in the security tapes for Moshe's community. Now, the more I thought about it the more it hit me that there might have been a tattoo on the man with the ball cap, the guy with his arm out the window.

I ran and pulled the tapes out and looked at the first tape again. As the second white van came into view again, I played it on slow motion and studied the view of the left side of the driver's neck. It was hard to identify anything clearly, but it did look like there was something on his neck. As I stopped the first tape, it struck me that I had stopped watching when I saw the first van with the Hispanic housebreakers. With a sense of urgency, I pulled out the rest of the tapes. I watched the second one all the way through, but there was nothing on that tape after the first white van went through. I put in the third tape that started with midnight of the same night and pressed play on fast forward.

I watched the empty gateway illuminated by the gatehouse lights, the time rolling through with each minute. Then something flashed by in the fast forwarding. I stopped and rewound, then pressed play on normal speed. There it was. Right at 4 am, darkest part of the night, a white van came slowly through the entrance. It was the same one from the first tape. A white van with no markings or signs and the same bent license plate. The driver had his window down and the same hat on his head, although his elbow was inside the van this time. I could see some marking on the left side of his neck in the light from the gatehouse. I paused the tape and zoomed in on the driver. Knowing what I was looking for this time, I could tell it was the same mark. A black circle with a red SS Iron Cross. I swore at myself under my breath for not having finished the tapes, but realized that finally, I had confirmation that the guys with the tattoos who were after me were the same ones after Moshe.

It all came together. There was no doubt in my mind that Gann was the one behind all of this. "Now I'm pissed," I said out loud. "I'm gonna nail Gann, bring his company down along with his bratty daughter, and destroy his punk KKK comrades."

Chapter 58

So I finally had it. The guy in the train with the sunglasses had a key that was likely from the Pascagoula area, which was right next to Mobile. The guy who shot me and made mincemeat out of my head was also from the Mobile area. And my good friend J. J. Gann was from Mobile. All of my attackers had the same tattoo on their necks for a KKK group that had started in the deep south, and Alabama was definitely in the deep south. Label me a conspiracy theorist, but I didn't think coincidences came in fours.

The attacks to scare me off, the notebook I'd found, and all my research led undeniably to Gann. I was certain of it. My curiosity at the complexity and massive size of the construction of the Wilson Bridge construction site had led to my discovery of a possible murder and the probable bribe that allowed SCC to get the contract. The article about J. J. Gann that had started off as a human interest piece was now turning into some actual investigative journalism. Imagine that. And now, finding the same tattoo on the goon who attacked Moshe at his home in Florida made it clear that it was somehow all connected.

But if I was really going to blow Gann, the construction bribe, his redneck hit teams, and his vendetta against Moshe out of the water, I needed to get better evidence. It was time to visit the dragon in his lair.

I needed to take some covert action and take a trip to see him. Gann had originally come from Mobile, SCC was headquartered in Mobile, so it only made sense that Gann lived there now as well. March was rapidly coming to a close and with the Masters right around the corner, it was time to find some hard evidence on Gann and then concentrate on protecting Moshe at Augusta.

First thing I needed to do was find out where Gann lived and if he'd be home this coming week. The Masters was starting the following week, so I was pretty certain he would be in Augusta with the rest of the board. But I needed to make sure.

I called SCC headquarters and asked for Gann's secretary.

"Mr. Gann's office, this is Helen speaking, how may I help you?" she said.

"Hello Helen. This is Harold," I said, trying to sound a bit snotty. "From the Ritz Carlton in Atlanta calling to confirm Mr. J. J. Gann's reservation with us on Saturday."

"Oh, no sir," she said. "There must be some mistake. He won't be there."

"What do you mean he won't be here?" I said. "We have a suite reserved for him."

"I'm so sorry sir," she said. "He'll be in Augusta starting on Friday. He won't be in Atlanta."

"Well that is rather inconvenient," I said, with a faint sneer. "It is our Peachtree Suite and we've turned down several other customers already. In the future, please be kind enough to call and cancel a reservation as soon as it is no longer necessary, or we will have to charge Mr. Gann for the room."

"I assure you, sir, that we do call in any cancellations," she said, with a huff in her voice. "I don't know who made that reservation but it certainly wasn't me. Good day, sir."

So the coast for Saturday was clear. As I suspected, Gann would be in Augusta. So now to find his address.

I went online again to find the tax records for Mobile. Like most states, in Alabama you could find the county property tax records, which listed property in the county by name and address. Naturally, Mobile was in Mobile County, so I found the county website and put in Gann's name. My computer did its thing and a hit came up on the screen. With a groan I saw that the address was blanked out. Of course Gann would have his contacts in the county office, and of course he'd pay well to stay as private as he could.

With that door closed I had to come up with something else. It'd do me no good to show up in Mobile without an address for Gann. As I was thinking how I could possibly get personal information on Gann, my mind kept thinking back to something I'd seen or read in the Commonwealth's contract files. If I could get at least the last four of his social security number, I had an idea for using one of my old time-tested approaches.

I went over to the boxes on the floor that contained the Wilson Bridge contract proposals and found the one from SCC. For the next hour, I poured over it. Finally, there it was. On one of the pages for the SCC management team, someone at SCC had mistakenly put Gann's name in the taxpayer identification block, instead of SCC. Next to it was a number, whited out except for four numbers. Hoping that it was the last four of Gann's social security number, I called Direct TV and Cablevision, but struck out.

They had no records for a J. J. Gann. I crossed my fingers and called Dish TV.

"Welcome to Dish TV, my name is Tammy. May I help you please?" the nasal voice said.

"Yes ma'am," I said, using my best South Alabama drawl. "This is J. J. Gann. I'm callin' to try and get someone to repair my satellite dish. My wife back at the Mobile house tells me it's out. She thinks lightning hit it."

"Well I'll be happy to help you with that, Mr. Gann. What's your account number please?"

"Well shoot. That's the thing," I said. "I wish I had it, but I'm away on business and callin from the road and don't rightly know what the number is. I don't have it with me."

"That's no problem, sir," she said. "If you can just give me the last four digits of your social security number and your home address zip code, I'll be happy to assist."

I held my breath and gave her the four numbers printed on the form in the solicitation packet, as well as the zip code for Mobile. There was a pause while she looked up the records. "Yes, sir," she said. "I have it right here, let's see what the problem is."

I realized I'd been holding my breath waiting for her response. Finally exhaling and taking a deep breath I said quickly, "and by the way, Tammy, what street address do you show for my home in Mobile? Your fellas have gone to the wrong house before and I don't want em doing that this time" I said, holding my breath again.

"Sir, I'm showing an address of 1525 Canal Drive."

"Yeah, that's it," I said. "That's the correct address. So you mind havin' someone come on Monday?"

"Don't mind at all, sir. One of our technicians will be there between nine and noon in the morning. Please have someone over the age of eighteen there to let them in.

Enjoy your day and thank you for calling Dish TV. Is there anything else I may assist you with, sir?"

"No, thanks hon," I said, smiling to myself. "I surely do appreciate it."

Chapter 59

It was the last week of March. Moshe was playing at the Shell Houston Open, the last tournament before the Masters. As much as I wanted to be there with him and root for him while watching his back, the time had come for more direct action. I had called Eddie again, since he lived in Texas, to see if he could shadow Moshe around one more time. For the cost of a free ticket to the Open he had been more than happy to oblige. Besides, he'd told me, he was happy for the diversion. I was out a dinner and the cost of a ticket, but it was worth it. Moshe was in very good hands.

I had Gann's home address and he wouldn't be there. With Shelley living in Washington, his home in Mobile would be free and clear for me to check out. If I could get into his home office, perhaps I could find some hard evidence of the crap he and his men had been doing. If I was caught, I knew it would be illegal breaking and entering, but from all that had happened, I felt it was worth the risk. First, though, I needed to arrange for some special equipment with which I could mount my attack. I called my old Ranger platoon sergeant, Steve England, who now lived in Fort Walton Beach, Florida. England looked like a Wall Street investment broker - suave, polished, and as smart as any Ivy League grad. He could've worked for any

Fortune 500 company but instead, he'd opted to serve a full career in Army special ops.

"Top, how you doing? This is Drew James!" I said with genuine excitement to hear his voice again and using the nickname for senior non-commissioned officers.

"Is that you Lieutenant?" he queried. "I thought you'd dropped off the face of the earth. I haven't heard a word from you in years. What have you been up to? How's life treated you?"

"I'm doing alright. A few ups and downs but nothing I can't handle. Right now, I'd say things are going well and life is good." I said. I then brought him up to speed on all that had happened with me, including Marie's illness and death, some of my last ops, my leaving the service, and the blessing of my new job. "How about you?" I asked. "You still kicking butt and taking names?"

He told me all that he'd done since we last saw each other, informing me that he'd been promoted to Sergeant Major for the 7th Special Forces Group. We traded stories about people we both knew. I told him about my work on the Masters and all that had happened with Moshe.

"You've certainly been through some rough patches, Drew. I'm sorry to hear about Marie and what you had to go through with her. What a terrible time. I can understand why you left service with that situation, but I'll tell you this. With the world going to hell in a handbasket, we can't afford to lose the services of a man as good as you," he said.

"You sound just the same, Steve. Hearing those words from you means the world to me. Wish I could've stayed in, fighting the bad guys and keeping the Nation safe, but life goes on and we all have to find our place in it. How do you like your latest gig with 7th Group?" I asked.

"Hard to believe how much fun it is. Along with my real work, they let me go on some of the patrols at the swamp phase of Ranger School at Eglin Air Force Base. What a hoot. I get such a kick watching these Ranger students on patrol, asleep on their feet, and running into each other in the dark. I should film it one of these days and send it to one of those TV reality shows. But I have a lot of excellent operators who work with me. Not as good as the ones we used to have, but they still do the job pretty well. So tell me Drew, what can I do for you? Any way I can help with Moshe's situation? Anything at all?"

"Actually there is. I could use your help with some supplies," I said.

"Just name it and I've either got it or can get it," he said. "Are you settled on the notion that you don't need a wing man? I'd love to come along."

"Thanks Top, you're the best. I've always said that. But you've still got a great career and retirement to think about and, if something goes wrong, this little escapade could end it all for you. But here's what I need, if you can get it for me." I gave him a list that included a combat outfit set, binoculars, a commando knife, bolt cutters, an air pistol tranquilizer gun, night vision goggles, and a folding grappling hook with rope.

"Just let me know what it comes to and I'll send you a check," I told him.

"That's no trouble at all. And I know you're good for it. You always have been. Where and when are you flying in?" he asked.

"Probably Pensacola on Friday noontime, so I'll rent a car and meet you wherever you'd like," I said.

"There's a park south of Hurlburt Field, just off Route 98. We used to launch rubber patrol boats from there into Santa Rosa Sound. Do you remember it?" he asked.

"Of course I do. I remember it well. Meet you there Friday afternoon at 4. And thanks so much for doing all of this. I owe you as usual," I said.

"Forget about it," he said. "We've been through too much together to start keeping track. Whatever it is you're doing, you play it safe. And if it goes south on you, you know where I am. Just call."

"Thanks, Top. See you Friday," I said, and hung up.

Chapter 60

Friday, the first day of April, dawned bright and clear. I had a name, an address, and a lot to get even for. I was headed for Reagan National. It was calm and sunny with a touch of warmth in the air. The Potomac looked smooth and placid, with the trees showing the first sign of real buds on their branches.

I carried a black leather briefcase with my laptop and a dozen of my business cards. I am Andrew James, Assistant Director of NTSA, Inc. It is not a lie. I incorporated the company a few years ago, and keep it active by paying the nominal annual fee. NTSA means nothing at all. I picked the letters because they could mean anything and sound as if they mean something - National Transportation Safety Agency, Network Triage System Association, or whatever works for the moment. And in poking around, the card often gives me access I might otherwise not have.

Because it was a Friday, the usual massive volume of commuting traffic heading into DC through Old Town, Alexandria, was much less, and the drive was pleasant enough. As I drove past Daingerfield Island, I could see the sailboats rocking gently in the slight swell, the pennants on the masts fluttering in the air. Spring and Autumn were definitely the best seasons in DC.

I flew through Atlanta to Pensacola Regional Airport and rented a Ford Crown Vic. It was a little more expensive than most of the other cars that were available, but it was big, powerful, and gave the impression of officialdom. Putting a small, cheap CB radio antennae on the back would make it look even more like an unmarked government car, and hopefully allow me to be left alone.

I drove to the Gulf Breeze Parkway, crossing the bridge over Pensacola Bay. An hour later, I turned into the park near Hurlburt Field. I was a little early, so I pulled into a spot facing the beach, got out and leaned against the front hood of the car, looking out towards the water. The turquoise waters of the gulf lapped gently against the white sands of the beach. An offshore wind ruffled the waves as they rolled gently onto the sand.

As I stood and watched, I thought about the nights I'd spent there preparing to cross the sound to Santa Rosa Island, usually in cold weather, often in rain. Small boat ops were no fun in those conditions. The thought of straddling the side of a 12-man rubber boat, and paddling with the outside leg literally dragging down in freezing water, brought back memories of being soaked, frozen and exhausted. I gazed out at the island far out in the sound and pictured our practice assault, the parachute flares arcing through the heavy night sky and slowly descending with a bright illuminating light, the rhythmic sound of heavy caliber machine guns off to one side providing supporting fire and overwatch, teams of Rangers advancing low and fast in alternating groups across the sand of the island towards the objective with the bright muzzle flash of automatic weapons, and the concussive blasts of grenade simulators shattering the stillness of the night, the air thick with cordite and smoke from smoke grenades used to mark the objective.

A chatter of voices brought me back from my memories, and as my eyes came back into focus, I saw two gorgeous twenty-somethings walking towards me from the beach. The words from the Girl from Ipanema, that classic song by Stan Getz and Astrud Gilberto, rushed into my head as I watched their own Samba sway of ripe, tanned bodies. And just like in the song, I smiled at them, said "ahhh" to myself, and they walked right by without even seeing me. With a sigh, I turned to watch them and saw Steve England drive up in his pickup truck, turning his head to look at them as well.

"Hey Top," I said, as he got out of his truck. "No need to look. You're well over 30 and you drive a beat up old pickup truck. They didn't even see you drive in."

"Now, Lieutenant," he said, a big grin on his face. "That's the difference between officer types and real soldiers like me. You didn't see them give me the once over?"

"Man, you haven't changed a bit. It's so great to see you," I said, as we gripped each other's shoulders.

"Same here. You look like you haven't lost a step. I miss those days working together. I miss all the guys on our old team. It's a pleasure doing this with you now, though. You can't imagine how much I wish I could tag along for the action." As he handed me a black canvas pack he said, "here's what you ordered. I got it all."

I took it from him and looked through the items. "Trust me. I'd like nothing more than to have you with me Steve. It'd be a blast. Unfortunately I have to do it alone. Besides I couldn't live with myself if something went wrong and you got busted. I hope you can understand. So, is the gun air or CO_2?" I asked.

"CO_2," he said. "That's more reliable and much more powerful. I don't know what you're planning on shooting with this, but this baby will put down a charging Rhino."

"Perfect," I said. "There shouldn't be any Rhinos involved but no doubt this should do the trick. I don't want to put anyone down for good, just take them out of the action for a while. When everything's done and finished, we have to get together. I'll tell you all about it over steaks and fine Bourbon."

"You got it, my friend," he said. "Please just take care of yourself. Stay safe, Drew."

We shook hands and then bear hugged each other. I climbed in my car and started it. "You do the same Top. Take care of yourself and call me if you ever need anything. It was really great seeing you again." I said, and pulled away.

Chapter 61

I drove out of Pensacola, crossing Perdido Bay at Paradise Beach. The road then ran straight as an arrow for miles, with nothing but scrub oak, pine, and the occasional double-wide trailer. I stopped at the light in Foley and turned left onto Route 59, accelerating straight south to Gulf Shores. The Crown Vic felt powerful and solid in my hands. Driving with my window down, the sun on my face and the smell of salt air brought back memories of long forgotten family trips to the beach when I was a child, listening to songs played loudly on the car radio and stopping for ice cream.

Under a fake name, and paying cash in advance for two nights, I checked into an end unit of a Mom and Pop motel on Gulf Shores Parkway and brought all my equipment inside. I checked it all out, disassembling and then reassembling the CO_2 gun, checking my high speed digital camera to ensure it was fully charged, and putting fresh batteries in the night vision goggles. Everything was ready to go. Grabbing the binoculars, I locked the room up, and went to scout out Gann's home. It was located at the end of Canal Drive, just south of a canal lined with large, beautiful residences. I drove down his street, found the house with his number on it and went slowly past, looking north on either side of his property towards the houses on the other side of the canal. There was a six-foot high stone wall all the way around the property and not much to see of the house through the closed iron-spiked gate.

I went to the end of Canal, turned around and returned past Gann's house, taking note of the mileage out to the main road. I turned to the North on the main road and then drove west on Oyster Bay Road, which paralleled Gann's street on the other side of the canal. When I was roughly even with where Gann's lot should be, I pulled over to the curb and shut the car off. I grabbed a notebook and the binoculars and started down the side of one of the houses towards the canal in back hoping to do a recon and take notes of the back of Gann's house.

I rounded a large Camellia bush and saw a tall, thin woman facing away from me and watering a bed of flowers. She wore fawn-colored stretch shorts, and a faded green blouse. She had a deep tan. I noticed that she moved swiftly and to good effect, limber as a dancer when she bent and turned to water the entire bed. She was sweaty with sun and effort, her back glossy, accenting the play of small hard muscles under her skin as she moved. As she turned, she saw me standing there and looked at me with curiosity.

I moved into the shade of the camellia and stood within comfortable conversation range. She finally stopped, placed the hose on the grass and turned to me, tossing her black hair back.

"Hello," she said. "May I help you with something?"

"Certainly ma'am," I said, trying to sound as official as I could. I pointed back at the Crown Victoria and took out my NTSA card out of the notebook. "My name is Mr. James, and I'm with the National Transportation Safety Agency. We're doing a survey of canal depth here and I need to spend some time along the canal back there to see if it requires dredging by the Corps of Engineers."

She looked at me with a mixture of worry and disbelief, and then waved her hand in the vague direction of the canal. With a trace of suspicion she asked, "why hasn't anyone told us of any problem? We've got a 23-foot Bayliner we dock back there and now I'm worried we could have hit something. Why now?"

Why? It was a very flat and very abrupt question, and there was something about the flavor of it that made me wary. So I reached into the old bag of tricks and pulled out the one labeled Real Nice.

"Well, Ma'am. We sent out notices to your street about two weeks ago. Didn't you receive it?"

"No," she said. Then with an expression of disgust, she said "that new mailman. Of course. He's been putting mail from the Forsythes next door in our mailbox. I'll bet he put ours in theirs and, since they've been away this past month, it's probably just sitting there. Go on ahead then."

I thanked her, put the card back in the portfolio, and walked down the lot-line towards the canal. It was lined with open sandy areas and patches of scrub oak and palmetto plants. Each property had a length of dock reaching into the canal and most had a boat tethered to the dock. I walked twenty yards along the canal to the west, behind what the woman had described as the Forsythe's house, and found a small copse of scrub oak trees on a slightly elevated stretch. I went in among the leaves and turned to look back at the woman's house. She was gone and other than the croaking of frogs in the canal, all was quiet. The Forsythes had a 35-foot sailboat tethered to their dock with a ten-foot inflatable dinghy tied up to the stern.

I was directly opposite the rear of Gann's residence. The spot gave me a perfect view of the house sitting within its stone walls on the other side of the canal, which was roughly twenty-yards wide. I pushed dead leaves and pine straw together in a pile and settled in the shade with my back against a tree while I studied Gann's house and yard.

I waited. It stirred old instincts, old training. Terrain, cover and concealment, field of fire. The brown pine needles underneath me had a faded aromatic scent. Skirr of insects. Piercingly sweet call of meadowlark. Swamp-smell of the canal water nearby. Sway and dip of the grasses in the breeze. A motor sound in the distance became audible, grew, and then as a boat moved slowly past, died away.

The main part of the complex was a large three-story plantation style house set in the middle of the property. I was looking at the back of the house with the yard, plantings and pool surrounded by a pebbled concrete apron. The sun glinted off of the aluminum lawn furniture and pool water. I could see the heat waves radiating up off of the concrete in the pool area. A balcony ran the length of the second floor on the rear of the house, the windows and doors looking out onto the pool area and canal.

There were two other wood-sided buildings on the perimeter of the compound. One was clearly an offset multi-car garage and the other was likely a storage shed for yard equipment. There was a single car parked on the left side of the house where the driveway snaked in from the front street. The yard was landscaped with plenty of Palm trees, flowering pear trees, and manicured bushes. Most of it was covered thickly with grass. In one corner near the edge of the canal, there was a small putting green. Placed around the pool area were various chairs, tables, umbrellas and lounges. I could see the breeze ruffle the pool water, moving an inflatable raft in slow circles. The stone wall down the sides of the property was made of plaster and stucco with little glints of embedded pieces of glass along the top. The back of the property ended at the canal in a gently sloping grass covered bank. On the bank was a small dock house with an adjoining dock and several power boats sitting still in the heat, fenders bumping gently against the wood pilings.

Through the rear windows I could see occasional movement on the ground floor in the living area that fronted off of the pool. All in all, the complex had a drowsy, warm weather feel to it. A wind chime tinkled softly in the light breeze. I scanned from left to right with my binoculars, noting the plantings at the base of the walls on the sides of the house and the way the balcony was fashioned. Nothing unusual, but of course this was the middle of a business day. Hard to tell what the lighting would be like tonight.

I studied the entire layout with approximate distances until I had it memorized and could close my eyes and visualize it all in my mind, then eased back out of the trees and returned to my car. The woman was still nowhere to be seen. I noticed the Forsythe's house next door did indeed appear to be deserted and closed up. Tonight when I returned I'd go through the Forsythe's yard.

With the sun starting its slow descent towards the horizon, I headed back to the motel. I took a shower, went to the restaurant for dinner, and then back to my room for a quick nap.

Chapter 62

As I lay back against the pillow, I thought through my plans for the evening. Calm and relaxed, I thought of the great golfer Harry Vardon, who won the Open Championship six times at the turn of the 20th Century and had a run of fourteen straight PGA wins – a record that still stands today. Harry said, "to play well you must feel tranquil and at peace. I have never been troubled by nerves because I felt I had nothing to lose and everything to gain."

Now that I was finally entering my element, and taking action, I too felt tranquil and at peace. Not that I had nothing to lose. Getting shoved by an Alabama Deputy Sheriff into a south Alabama jail cell for breaking and entering was not anybody's idea of fun. But I'd do my best to keep that from happening.

The alarm went off at 2 am. I got up, splashed water in my face and got dressed in the combat outfit Steve had brought me. I packed my equipment in a small backpack, had a cup of coffee from the in-room coffee maker, and was ready to go. Taking all my gear with me, I went to my car and drove well within the speed limit to Oyster Bay Road. On the way, I drove past a deputy sheriff's cruiser, idling at the side of the road. Last thing I wanted was to be pulled over in this get up, with this equipment, but the Crown Victoria and my limited speed did the trick and I didn't even get a second glance.

I drove further down along Oyster Bay past the Forsythe's house and parked in front of an undeveloped lot on the north side of the street. I waited before getting out, looking up and down the street for any movement or any signs of life. Everything was quiet and still. I put on a leg holster with the tranquilizer gun, then black skintight gloves. I got out, put the backpack on and closed the door gently with no noise. I turned and walked back towards the Forsythe's, walking close to the front of the houses to prevent being silhouetted on the street or sidewalks.

Just as I was approaching the house next to the Forsythe's, the front door opened and a square of light splashed out into the front yard. I froze five feet from the front walk then jumped back and hit the ground, rolling as I did to land up next to the bushes that lined the front of the house. I held my breath then slowly released it as I heard two teenaged voices whispering sweet farewells followed by a breathless silence, which I could only assume was a long passionate kiss. The door closed gently, the light went off, and the boy walked out to his truck, whistling as he went. As the truck took off, the noise receding in the distance, I stood up again and moved quietly on until I reached the Forsythe's house.

Moving quickly now, I ran down the lot-line to the edge of the canal and then walked along the canal bank to the Forsythe's boat dock. I stepped as quietly as I could down the dock and, grabbing the rope attached to the front of the small inflatable dinghy from the back of the sailboat, I pulled the dinghy over to the edge of the dock. I climbed in, untied it from the sailboat and paddled slowly across the canal, constantly scanning all around for any light or any movement.

With a gentle bump, I hit the dock on Gann's side. I climbed out, secured the dinghy, and started walking towards the back of the house. At the same time I started thinking this was turning out to be a piece of cake, I heard a strange sound, like crabs scrabbling across hard packed sand. I'd heard that sound before and just as I thought "dog," I heard the guttural sound of a low growl and saw a dark shape sprinting through the plantings around the pool straight towards me.

It looked and sounded like a Doberman. I watched the blur of dog approach me and then jump, and at the same time I took several quick backwards steps and reached out towards the leaping dog's front paws. I grabbed one and, rolling over backwards, kicked my feet up into the underside of the dog, did a backwards somersault while extending my arm behind my head, slammed the dog to the ground behind me, and rolled up onto my knees. As it scurried to its feet with another growl, I snatched the tranquilizer gun from the holster. I took a deep breath and, as the dog sprang towards me again, I squeezed the trigger and shot it in the chest. The dog's mouth fastened on my forearm and then, with a loud sigh, collapsed to the ground fast asleep.

I was breathing hard and my forearm hurt. I shoved my gun back in the holster and pulled my backpack off. There was a gash in my arm, with blood seeping out. I took out the first aid kit and wrapped a dark colored bandage around my arm. I moved over to the dog, checked that it was still breathing and pulled out the tranquilizer dart. As the National Park Service always insists, I had to take with me everything that I brought in.

With the dog out of the picture, I ran over to the base of the house on the left side. Figuring that Gann's bedroom suite was at the back of the house opening onto the second floor balcony, I took out the grappling hook and rope. Holding the coiled knotted rope in one hand, I swung the grappling-hook with the other hand up and over the edge of the balcony. I pulled on it gently but firmly to make sure that it held. Hand over hand, I climbed up quickly to the edge of the balcony and vaulted over the top. Drawing in a deep breath, I said to myself, "I'm in."

Chapter 63

As I stood on the balcony, I looked down the row of windows and French doors to see if any of them showed any light, but they were all dark. I pulled on the handle of the door nearest me. It moved easily. When it was open enough to fit through, I listened and, hearing no sound, moved very slowly through the split in the partially drawn curtain, gently pulling the door closed behind me as I went.

I put on the night vision goggles and looked around. In the middle of the room was a large pool table, the balls neatly racked together at one end. Two pool cues lay flat on the surface next to the rack. Around the walls were an assortment of leather chairs and couches and on the left wall was a giant flat screen TV. Amazing man cave, I thought to myself. There was a door at the far end, obviously leading in from a hallway in the middle of the house. On my right side was another door. I hoped it led to Gann's office.

I walked over to the connecting door, put my ear against it, and listened intently. I heard nothing. I pulled the door gently towards me. Moving my head very slowly through the opening, I looked into the next room, still wearing my night vision goggles. In front of the French doors leading to the balcony was an immense and ornate desk. With a slow exhale, my body relaxed. I was in Gann's office.

I moved slowly around the room, looking behind the pictures on the walls for any hiding places. Nothing. There were several large bookcases filled with books. I pulled random books out and rifled through them and looked to see if there were any hidden compartments. Still nothing. If he did indeed have any papers hidden in the books, it'd take me forever to find them.

On a credenza on one side were a number of formal pictures sitting in frames. One was of Gann surrounded by what looked to be a number of fraternity brothers. Looking at it more closely, I could swear that the man standing next to a much younger Gann looked just like the picture I'd seen of Clive Perkins in the materials I'd received from Augusta National. Another picture looked to be Gann standing with his parents.

I moved over to the desk to see what I could find there. As quietly as I could I pulled open each drawer, looking for anything that might tell me more about Gann. There were pads of paper, pens and pencils, and desk ornaments, but nothing else of interest. Closing the bottom drawer as quietly as I could, I stood up and leaned back against the desk to think.

I put my hands out behind me on the edge of the desk and felt my right hand brush a large glass paper weight. Spinning quickly around I tried to catch it, but it fell to the floor with a loud thump and rolled just under the desk. I froze and looked at the bottom of the entrance door to see any signs of lights coming on out in the hallway. As I started to relax, the light came on in the outer hallway and shone through the crack below the door, blossoming into clouds of light in the night vision goggles. I dove under the desk, pulling the desk chair behind me as I slid all the way back under the desk.

Staying as still as I could, I heard the door open and footsteps walk slowly into the room. Whoever it was looked around, walked to the side of the desk, paused, and then turned around and walked back out the door, pulling it shut behind them. I let out my breath and crawled out from under the desk, pausing to pick up the paper weight, which was resting against one side of the bottom of the desk. Something looked odd. I studied the bottom of the desk. It hit me that there was a lot more desk below the drawers than there should've been. With a smile, I knew that the desk had to have a false bottom underneath each bottom drawer.

<u>Chapter 64</u>

I took off the night vision goggles, pulled a small pen light out of my pack, and bent down to examine the bottom of the desk. There was no obvious way to open the compartment at the front of the desk. I pulled out the lower drawer on one side and looked in the opening but it seemed solid with no handles, lid or latches to open it up. Then realizing that Gann probably wouldn't want to have to pull the drawer out each time, I replaced the drawer and looked carefully at the inside base of the desk in the area below each drawer. Pulling and pushing different ways, a section of the facing moved slightly and then slid noiselessly towards the rear of the desk. Behind it was an open space about the size of a large shoe box.

I shone my light into the open space. There were two hand guns and a hefty packet of cash but nothing else. I slid the section of facing back in place and turned to look at the inside base on the other side of the desk. It had a similar facing section that slid under my touch, revealing another opening, this one with a single leather bound journal book, fastened with a rubber band.

I picked it up and opened it. It was filled with densely written pages. I pulled out my digital camera and started taking shots of each page.

Then I heard it. A faint sound out in the hallway of someone quietly opening and closing doors. I could hear the sounds approaching Gann's office. The number of pages left to photograph was too large. I'd never make it. With no time to spare, I shoved my penlight, night vision goggles and the notebook into my pack, slid the facing section closed, and moved quickly towards the door. As I moved, I could see in the crack of light beneath the door a shadow stop just on the other side.

I pressed up against the wall on the hinge side of the door just as the door handle rotated quietly. With a burst of speed and noise, the door was flung open and a man moved quickly into the room in a crouch, holding a handgun out in front of him with both hands and turning left and right to survey the room. I stepped up behind and to the side of him and swung my tranquilizer gun at the side of his head, hitting him cleanly just above his right ear. He dropped like a stone, out cold.

I breathed out slowly to calm myself. He hadn't seen me, but now Gann would know someone had been in the room and likely think to look in the hidden compartment. So with his man face first on the carpet, I laid out the book on the desk and quickly photographed each page.

I put the journal back in the compartment, put the paper weight back on the desk then looked around the room to see if I missed anything. I then eased out of the office into the entertainment room next door. Retracing my steps to the balcony, I freed the hook, draped the rope over the rail, and slid down to the ground. I pulled the rope free and sprinted back to the Forsythe's dinghy.

I paddled quickly across the canal, retied the dinghy to the back of the sailboat, and jogged back to my car. Standing still next to the car, I listened intently for any noise that was out of place and looked all around for any movement. Not a sound and all was still, so I got in the car, started it up, and headed back to Pensacola and home.

Chapter 65

I was home enjoying the beautiful spring weather, packing my bags for joining Moshe at the Masters, and pondering all that I'd read in the journal book. When I'd gotten home, I'd read it cover to cover.

The first forty or so pages described typical days for a young man at college. From what I could tell, this must have been during Gann's second or third year at Alabama. It described in terse shorthand notes about his classes, sporting events, fraternity and sorority mixers, school work, and the emotions inside him that came with the new love of his life, a girl named Heather. Half-way in, the tone of the writings suddenly and dramatically changed.

On November 3rd something had happened. Gann wrote about some kind of tragic accident or event that had happened at the fraternity house where he was living. In cryptic short sentences with no names or full descriptions of what had actually happened, he wrote that she was gone forever, he never meant it to happen, and it was his fault. The agonizing pain that he felt oozed out from the pages. The plaintive hurt in the words were heartbreaking.

Then the writing became angry and violent, filled with threats and promises of retribution against someone, a "he," who had been there with Gann when the incident occurred and was apparently causing him some trouble over it. After another page or two filled with rage and anger and mixed with expressions of hopelessness, the writings ceased altogether.

I'd then gone on-line and done a quick search of the newspaper archives for the Tuscaloosa News for the November 3rd date mentioned in the journal. It had been big news at the University. The article mentioned the tragic death of an unnamed girl in the Phi Delta Theta house that had led to a temporary suspension of the fraternity and its activities. There was little detail to the story but it listed the names of the two fraternity brothers who reported the death. One was J. J. Gann. The other was Clive Perkins. It was hard to imagine a connection between the two, but thinking back to the picture I'd seen at Gann's house, it was clear that they had been fraternity brothers at Alabama.

Surprised to find this previous connection between Gann and Perkins, I had to find out more. So I looked at the Gulf Coast News archives to find any stories that mentioned Gann or his family. The first thing l read was that Gann's father had grown up in Gulf Shores before going to college at the University of Alabama on a football scholarship. It looked like he'd been Gulf Shores' favorite son back then. As a sophomore, he'd started the Phi Delta Theta fraternity at Alabama and in three short years, turned it into one of the top fraternities at the university. He'd been the student body president his last two years and dated Shelley Keegan, the captain of the Alabama cheerleading squad.

Gann, Jr. followed in his father's footsteps. He also played football before a serious knee injury in his senior year of high school apparently ended any hopes of his playing in college. But he still went to Alabama and was a Phi Delta Theta like his father. The rest of the articles were very small pieces about Gann's company, SCC. Many of them looked like the same press releases I'd been able to dig up online. There was no mention of the November event at the Phi Delta house, how he'd started SCC or of his later years and no other information of any kind.

I had been sitting trying to make sense of it when the phone rang. It was Ben Cooper.

"Hey Ben, you got something for me?" I asked.

"You bet I do, Drew," he said. "Listen to this. I went back like you told me and put Clive Perkins in the NCIC instead of Clyde Perkins. You got yourself a live wire with that boy, Drew."

"What do you mean?" I asked.

"This guy's a real thug," he said. Then continuing, he explained that the records showed that in 1981, Perkins had been arrested for disorderly conduct for spray painting graffiti on a local storefront window. In 1982, he was arrested for public intoxication and destruction of private property. Based on the brief information in the NCIC, it seemed that Perkins and two other teens had gotten drunk and taken baseball bats to a Lincoln Continental belonging to a local businessman causing over $5,000 in damage. In 1983, Perkins had been brought in for questioning about a boating accident involving a local Jewish businessman. The report stated that a witness heard screaming from the boat anchored in Bon Sucour Bay next to Mobile and saw it sink. Minutes later, the same witness had seen Perkins loading scuba equipment into his truck near the place where the boat had sunk.

Ben read from the report that stated when the boat was pulled out of the water there was a bar securing the aft hatchway, locking the man inside. Holes had been drilled into the bottom of the boat causing it to sink. The police released Perkins because they could not find any underwater drill in the equipment in his truck and had no other evidence of his connection to the crime.

Over the course of the next 30 years, there was a succession of crimes Perkins was suspected of committing, including blackmail, bribery, and murder. There was a suspicion that he was behind the murder of a prominent Jewish lawyer in New York. But in each instance, the evidence was always lacking.

Ben paused and concluded by saying, "here's an interesting tidbit I picked up from our organized crime task force section."

"Wait, organized crime?" I asked, with surprise.

"Yeah," he said. "Catch a load of this. Perkins is rumored to be the head of a KKK off shoot that runs drugs and illegal weapons through his chain of restaurants. They're perfect stopping off points along all the major interstates. They've got an open investigation into it, but nothing they can confirm yet."

"You're kidding me," I said softly. "The SS Brotherhood of the Red Camellia."

"Hey, how'd you know that?" Ben asked. "Our folks didn't even know that much."

"Long story," I said. "I'll tell you all about it sometime over a drink. Suffice it to say, you just nailed it Ben. No question now that Perkins' guys have been the ones behind all these attacks on Moshe and me."

"Hope you're right, Drew. And here's the kicker. Gives us a motive for this piece of garbage. After reading these reports, I did a search of Perkins and his family and found out that Perkins' father had been a big wig in the Foreign Service in the '60s. He'd been assigned to the embassy in Beirut, Lebanon. Both his parents died when Israeli fighter jets did a bombing run at the start of the first major engagement there. Perkins had been with them at the time so he saw them die, but he was miraculously spared from any injury."

And suddenly all the basic patterns emerged, the way a design will appear after the etcher has made his ten thousand tiny engravings on the copper plate. Seeing his parent's death must have been the event that triggered Perkins' hatred of Israeli Jews. If that was true, then he was indeed the driving force behind keeping Moshe from playing in the Masters, and he was also the one behind the multiple attacks against me. I realized he must have been the one behind the murder of Nathan Levin's father to keep Nathan from the Masters. And I'd be willing to bet that each of the suspected crimes and murders with which he'd been associated involved a Jewish person. He had to be planning to do something against Moshe at the Masters.

"That's it Ben. That's exactly it. This guy's been demented since he saw his parents die. Now I need to get my ass down to Augusta as quickly as I can to try and find these guys, put a crimp in their ops, and watch over Moshe. I can't thank you enough Ben. You solved this whole mess for me."

"I'm not certain I did Drew, but if you think so, you're welcome. Go get em but keep your head down."

Chapter 66

I was outside getting into my Land Rover for the ride to Reagan when it hit me. The cobwebs all melted away and the picture became crystal clear. Thinking of all that I'd just learned, and what I already knew about Gann and Perkins, it was clear that they were tied together somehow from the November 3rd event. And if I could read it right, it must be a connection that lasted to this day. I had to find out what the connection was and I knew exactly who to call. I pulled out my cell phone and dialed Shelley Gann.

"Why hello, Drew," she said, in a smooth and sultry voice. "It's so wonderful to hear from you. It's been a while. How may I be of assistance?"

"No BS anymore Shelley," I responded quickly and sternly. "It's time to stop all this crap and help me out. Time to help me keep Moshe Goldman safe. I know what's going on, or at least most of it. I know who Clive Perkins is, I know about his little army of KKK thugs, I know something happened with him and your Father back at Alabama, and I have some pretty good guesses at the evil he's done through the years. He's a very bad man and I'm thinking you know that already. So stop screwing around and come clean with me. Let's try and put an end to this. Tell me what you know. Please."

There was silence on the other end at first, and then with a sharp intake of breath and a surprising tremor in her voice, she responded softly and emotionally, "oh, my God, my God, Drew. For years, I hoped this day would come but never dreamed that it actually would."

I paused then said, "I want to help. Just talk to me. Why don't you start by telling me how this all started back at the frat house on that November 3rd?"

Everything crumbled for her in that instant. I heard her sudden sob through the phone and after several minutes of hearing her weeping, she finally spoke.

"You're right. There was and is a terrible connection between Daddy and Perkins. From the very beginning, there seemed to be no way out for him. He and Perkins went to school together at Alabama. They were roommates in the same fraternity. My Dad did something really stupid. He was head over heels in love with a girl and he got her pregnant, or at least she claims it was him."

"Was that Heather?" I asked.

"Goodness, I don't know how you know that, but yes. It was," she said.

She continued, "he was never really certain about that, although he continued to love her. One night she came to his room and demanded money from him, threatening to go to the University President if he didn't pay her. In those days in the South, that would likely have led to his expulsion from school. Daddy got angry, because he so wanted her to love him like he did her, and because she was blackmailing him. Out of frustration, he pushed her away. She tripped over one of his shoes, fell, and broke her neck when her head hit the edge of his desk. She died instantly. It was just a freak accident, Drew, but my Dad panicked. He spilled beer on the floor to make it look like she slipped on the liquid coming into his room. That's what he told the police when they arrived. He could kick himself, especially now, for not telling the truth about what happened.

"What he didn't realize is that Clive Perkins had been coming up the staircase to their room and saw the whole thing. From that point on, he told my Dad that he saw him kill the girl, but he wouldn't say anything about it to anyone as long as Daddy worked with him and did what he asked in the future. At first it was little things that didn't amount to anything – buying him beer, giving him his tickets for a home football game. But after time it got worse, much worse. After Perkins stole some land from a developer named Harry Michaels down in Mobile, he forced my Dad to build the shopping center at a cut rate price. After that, when SCC got bigger and was able to win larger road construction projects, Perkins was always nearby, forcing Daddy to give him contracts for his restaurants. He got rich off of my Dad. And the more my Dad did what he asked, the more Perkins had to hold over him. And to answer your questions about the Wilson Bridge project, yes, Perkins did something to get the contract for Father. Somehow he pulled strings with the Commonwealth to get the contract. Throughout all the years, Perkins was not only threatening to kill me if my Dad didn't do what he said, he was also claiming he was ready to go to the FBI.

"Drew, you just have to believe me. My Father would be mortified if he knew I was telling you all of this. But it has to end. It just breaks my heart to see what he's going through and I'll do anything I can at this point to try and help him. You might not have seen it when we met in D.C., but I was really impressed by you. You struck me as a guy who can handle himself, who can stand up to people and get things done. Will you help us?"

"Of course. I'll do what I can. The most immediate need now though is keeping Moshe from any harm. I'm sure that Perkins is out to kill him at the Masters. Thank you for coming clean and telling me all of this," I said. "It's a step in the right direction. I'm sorry to hear what Perkins has been doing to your Father and sorry it's lasted all these years. It is time to bring Perkins down."

"Thank you Drew. I thank you with all my heart. Daddy is a very fine man. He really is. He hadn't heard anything from Perkins for a good while and thought he might finally be in the clear, but of course no such luck. He called my Dad yesterday, just as my Dad was getting ready to go to Augusta, and told him he needed Daddy to do something for him next week. But he didn't say what. My Father really thought it might all be over with the completion of the Wilson Bridge Project and the amount of money he paid to Perkins for it, but when he heard from him again, he realized it would never end. It's just killing both of us and I want it to end."

"What does Perkins want from him this time?" I asked.

"Well, Perkins has told my dad that he hates Jews, always has and always will. He told my dad that he has to join him in a closed door session with the board and vote with him to ban Israeli Jews from the course and the Masters."

"How did your Dad react?" I asked.

"He thinks Perkins is certifiably crazy, a sick man. First, you need to know that my Father's grandmother was Jewish. She went into Dachau as a young girl and came out old beyond her years. But she survived. I just feel terrible for Daddy. That's absolutely the last thing he would ever want or agree to do. I suppose in some way it was a good thing because it was literally the last straw. It made him so mad. It made him realize he had to find a way to end this, to get free from Perkins once and for all. Now finally, with your help it might happen. What do we do now?"

"Just hold tight and don't tell your Dad anything. I don't want him alerting Perkins in any way. I'm headed for Augusta tonight to keep an eye on Moshe and do what I can to find Perkins and try and take him and some of his goons out of action," I said.

"Is there anything I can do to help?" she asked.

"Any chance you'd happen to know where Perkins is staying in Augusta this week?"

"Actually, I do," she said, and then after a moment's pause, she read the address to me. "He's staying in a private house in Augusta. Thank you from the bottom of my heart for your help, Drew. I hope you save Moshe, and I hope you get that bastard."

"I'll do my best," I said and hung up.

Chapter 67

Moshe was in my sights. He was on the second hole stroking his putt into the bottom of the cup. It was Tuesday, the second day of practice rounds. I was breathing a lot easier now than I had been two days earlier as I hurried to Augusta to catch up with Moshe.

The second hole, named Pink Dogwood, was spectacular. As I watched Moshe putt, the tall pines on either side of the fairway glistened in the sun, their needles looking like splinters of shining silver light. The dogwoods in full bloom surrounded their trunks, the white crosses and golden crowns in their blossoms waving gently in the breeze. The sky was blue and cloudless. The grass was a deep green color with a perfectly smooth surface and not a weed in sight.

Moshe had known to avoid the trees left of Pink Dogwood's fairway because they were a disaster waiting to happen. There was an old joke about an airline ticket counter being located over there – for a quick trip out of town after you miss the cut. But Moshe had driven the ball as close as he could to the right fairway bunker to set up a favorable angle to the green for his second shot. It was a par five, but because of his perfect drive, Moshe had hit the green in two. He'd hit the same approach shot that Louis Oosthuizen had hit for a par–two double eagle in the 2012 Masters, but with the pin placed differently, Moshe had ended up fifteen feet from the hole. A two-putt gave him a birdie. I hoped he could hit as well when the real deal started on Thursday.

I thought back to the last few chaotic days. My time back home had been a blur. I'd packed another suitcase, complete with collapsible baton and light-weight body armor under-vest, just in case I could convince Moshe to wear it. I also packed my .45 automatic and an Ithaca semi-automatic combat shotgun with shortened barrel and pistol grip. It was an exact replica of the version used by the tunnel rats in Viet Nam and it was perfect in close quarters. I had gotten a concealed carry permit for the handgun and all the requisite paperwork filled out for TSA so that I could send both weapons in my luggage through security. Moshe had carried it into the course inside his golf bag to avoid the metal detectors that I and all the other patrons had to go through. So I now had the .45 in a holster in the small of my back under my golf shirt and the shotgun in a backpack on my back. I was ready for anything.

I'd called Eddie and asked for his help one more time. Covering Moshe with just one man at a normal PGA event was hard enough but with the swirling, tight crowds at the Masters, it'd be near impossible. Eddie would circle the course constantly, moving in and through the ever-shifting gallery crowds and looking for anyone or anything that looked suspicious. As dangerous as he was, Eddie could still put on khakis and a polo shirt, looking like an Auburn frat boy, and blend into any crowd as easily as a chameleon on a fresh green leaf.

I would shadow Moshe, elbowing my way through the gallery of watchers to be as near to him as I could. With my height and build, people tended to shift away from me and let me pass when I stood right next to them, so hopefully I could stay close to him.

I'd made it clear to Moshe that after what I'd found out about Perkins, we just couldn't keep it to ourselves. I would have to contact the authorities. So my last call had been to the local FBI office. I'd gotten affidavits from Maybree, Nathan Levin, Scott Kimmett, and Michelle and written down all I'd learned and suspected and placed them in a large envelope. I asked to speak with the Special Agent-in-Charge, gave him a quick rundown of all that had happened, and told him where he could pick up the envelope that I'd left with my secretary at my office. He told me he'd take a look and call me if he thought they could do anything with the material. I left out any mention of my trip to Gann's house. Telling the FBI about breaking and entering into someone's house didn't seem like a particularly good idea.

Finally, on my way out the door, I'd seen Anne across the hall. Had that actually been a smile on her face? Without a trace of awkwardness, she said, "Hi Drew. How's your head feeling? I haven't seen you around at all since you were attacked and I was afraid you'd had some complications. I've been worried about you."

"Thanks Anne," I said with a smile. "No reason at all to be worried. As you've already seen, I'm pretty thick headed, so it's healed up nicely, and thank you again for all you did to help me."

"It was my pleasure. By the way, any progress on trying to find out who's after you and Moshe?" she asked, looking up at me with a smile in her eyes.

From what I'd put her through, I thought it only fair to keep her up to date. I filled her in on my trip to Gulf Shores, cringing slightly when she'd said with wide eyes, "Isn't that illegal?"

"Yes. It would certainly come under the heading of illegal activities," I said with a smirk. "But under the circumstances I just thought it was a risk I had to take. And look at the outcome. After my talk with Michelle Gann, I've got everything I need to know that Perkins is behind this. Puts me in a much better place to protect Moshe and to try and bring some heat down on Perkins."

"I'm glad then. I guess sometimes the end does justify the means," she said, with a firmness in her conclusions. Then she looked up at me with a hopeful look. "Drew, I was just wondering. I have an extra ticket to the National Symphony Orchestra at the Kennedy Center this Wednesday. I've no idea whether you like that sort of thing, but I'd love it if you could go with me."

With a groan that prompted a quick fading of her beautiful smile, I told her that I was already late getting down to Augusta for the Masters and taking care of Moshe and was leaving that day. Trying to make up for the disappointment that I felt, I asked her if I could take her to dinner when I got back, perhaps to my favorite Italian trattoria that was close by. Just as quickly, her smile came out, more radiant than before.

"That'd be great. I'd really like that. And of course how could I forget?" she'd said. "I knew you'd be there with Moshe. I love watching the Masters every year. There's just nothing like the sound of that music and the voices of the television announcers on a weekend afternoon. Hope this is as good as last year's. Have fun but take care of yourself. And of course take good care of Moshe."

"Thanks. I promise I will. And thanks for the offer to the Kennedy Center. Maybe we can do that another time."

"Yeah, that sounds like a perfect plan. Just give me a call when you're back, and we can set a date and time for that dinner. Actually it's probably the least you could do, given what you've put me through," she'd said, her green eyes gazing openly into mine. Or at least, that's how I imagined it.

And with that, with a little flutter in my chest, it looked like I'd been able to pull my plane up out of the tailspin it'd been in since I met her the first time. Maybe I could actually land this sucker without nose diving it into the rocks.

Chapter 68

So here I was watching Moshe. I trailed him for the rest of his round, moving in and out of the crowds that flowed next to him like shifting sand. Eddie was somewhere out there. I expected I'd never lay eyes on him, but I knew he was there.

I looked around at the different people on the course. The pros were certainly recognizable with their tailored and matching golf shirts and slacks and golf caps or visors emblazoned with the names of endorsers. Most walked with an air of contentment and appreciation for the crowds who applauded them.

Every golfer had a caddie with him carrying the heavy golf bag. They wore white one-piece coveralls with the golfer's name on an embroidered patch across the top of their backs and green Masters hats. The caddies rarely strayed far from their pro.

The crowds were typical for a classic PGA golf tournament. The throngs of people were dressed in every color and style of golf shirt, many with the prominent Masters logo that showed an outline of the U.S. with a yellow flag stuck right where Augusta is. These patrons, as they were called at Augusta National, wore Khaki shorts or slacks and running shoes or golf shoes. Most of them wore caps with the Masters emblem or the symbol of some southern university or golf company on the front.

At the crossing points located on many of the holes there were three crossing guards who would let people cross after the golfers passed by. They looked like they were mostly in their fifties or sixties and I figured if the crowd pushed hard to cross, the guards wouldn't really be able to stop them. But then again, with the politeness of the patrons at the Masters, I felt certain the crossing guards had nothing to fear.

The Masters was a very efficiently and well-run event. The course was meticulously maintained and supported by an army of workers, all of whom were very friendly. Along every hole, there were men collecting trash from the ground with trash tongs and emptying the trash receptacles that were spread around the course. They wore khaki slacks, green Masters polo shirts, and blue hats with the Masters symbol on the front and the word "grounds" on the right side. There were valets in the restrooms, directing people to empty stalls and picking up after the crowds. They were dressed like the trash collectors, but without the trash tongs and blue hats.

The concession stands did a booming business selling pimento cheese sandwiches and beer without any brand names labeled regular, light, and import and served in a plastic souvenir Masters cup. Surprisingly, despite the copious flow of beer, there was no sign of any inebriated patrons. All in all, it was a very respectful and quiet crowd.

There was a constant swirl of motion and shifting kaleidoscope of colors and shapes as the crowds swelled and blossomed around the superstars and popular players. As Moshe moved throughout the course, I concentrated on the patrons closest to him, scanning quickly from one to the next for any sign of danger or threat.

Despite the number of people in a small area, the silence around the course dominated everything. It seemed that everyone whispered while they watched or walked around the course, resulting in a low murmur of indistinct words and sounds. For every swing or putt, there was a noticeable pause in conversation when I could hear nothing but the pines sighing in the breeze and the birds singing. Throughout the day, I would hear occasional brief surging roars in the distance when a player made a great shot.

As Moshe continued his way through the course, he was putting together a fine round, prompting the increasingly larger crowd that accompanied him to frequently call out "get in the hole" after he stroked a putt, or encourage him with "good job Moshe." He putted for par at the 18th to end his round and I exhaled deeply as he strolled towards the clubhouse. Two days down, five to go.

Chapter 69

While Moshe headed for the driving range, I met up with Eddie. We talked about the chokepoints on the course and where we would stage an attack if it were us doing it. We figured it would be where the patrons are right next to a tee box and close to the boundary of the course. A quick shot or assault, and then over the fence and gone. We both decided that either the 5th or the 9th tee would present the best opportunity. We would shadow Moshe around the course and then on those two tees, move in as close as we could to him while he was driving.

As we were standing talking near the parking lot at the front of the clubhouse, a small group of men came out of the clubhouse and walked towards a black Cadillac Escalade waiting by the front door. We paid them scant attention until I heard one of them address another as Mr. Perkins. My ears perked up and as I looked at Eddie, it was clear he'd heard the same thing.

We casually glanced in their direction, and wouldn't you know, there was Clive Perkins looking just like the picture I'd gotten from Augusta National all those many months ago, and a lot older than the picture in Gann's office. It was clear by the way the men were standing around him who the important person in the group was. Up close, I got a much better view of him then the picture from Augusta National had revealed. He was a large man with tan hair and a big, sun-reddened, flakey face, a barrel of belly, a network of smile wrinkles and weather wrinkles, big red hands like ball gloves, and eyes that seemed to have the same size and expression as a pair of blueberries. A face that might have been handsome if it didn't have a certain irregularity about his features. His voice was surprisingly deep, rich, and resonant. He had exceptional presence. It is a rare attribute. It is not so much the product of strength and drive as it is a kind of quality of attention and awareness.

It has always puzzled and intrigued me. People who without any self-conscious posturing, any training, are immediately aware of you, and curious about you, and genuinely anxious to learn your opinions have this special quality of being able to somehow dominate a room. It was clear from this particular conversation that he was dominating the discussion within the group. With a final murmuring of good byes, he got into the back of the Escalade and it pulled out of the lot.

After Moshe was done with his evening practice on the range, we discussed our thoughts with him and cautioned him that we'd always be near him throughout the day, but particularly close to him on the 5th or the 9th tees. I didn't want him to be distracted from his game by us, but I also wanted to know that he understood and recognized the potential threat in those areas.

I had Moshe stashed under a fake name in a hotel across the Savannah River in North Augusta, South Carolina. We got him settled in after eating dinner and checked that he'd locked himself in. Eddie and I were staying nearby in an old fashioned motor court, like the one I'd stayed in at Gulf Shores. It was the best we could do with the short notice travel for the Masters. I'd purposely signed in with my own name. If Perkins' goons were going to try and track us down, I wanted to make it easy on them. But Eddie and I had a little bit of a surprise in store for them.

It was dark as we drove back to our motel because Moshe had used every last bit of sunlight on the driving range. We'd called for a pizza delivery, paying for it over the phone so the driver could leave it, and on the way to our motel, swung into a convenience store for beer, water, and other essentials. It felt just like the old days when Eddie and I had to blend into the community during an extended reconnaissance operation. We got to the motel, picked up our pizza, and went in to eat, talking about our plans for the evening.

Michelle had given me the address of the home where Perkins and his men were staying. Each year during the Masters Tournament, local Augustans rented out their houses to golf pros, corporations, and tournament pass holders. It was big business, given the large influx of visitors each April.

Eddie and I had decided it was time to take the fight to the enemy, which in this case was certainly Perkins. After eating, we dressed in dark clothing and drove to I-20, heading west back to Augusta. We took the exit for Stevens Creek Road and headed north into the prime residential neighborhoods of Augusta.

We turned left off of Stevens Creek onto a street named Pebble Beach Drive. As Eddie and I drove slowly down the road, we saw the number come up for the house Perkins was in. There was a long winding driveway bordered by tall pines that led up to a large plantation style house, its front windows glowing with lights in the dark.

We continued past the house and parked in a side street a couple hundred yards from the driveway. I turned off the car and as the engine ticked in the silence said,

"Don't know about you Eddie, but I'm thinking it's high time we had us some fun. Put a little pucker factor into these meatheads. Let's go take a little look-see and see what we got?"

"Let's do it," he said. "I feel like lighting me up some night. These guys would really be dangerous if they weren't so stupid."

We got out of the car quietly and moved back down the street to the beginning of the lot-line of the house where Perkins was staying. Or at least where Shelley Gann said he'd be staying. I hoped her information was accurate. Together, Eddie and I stepped carefully into the wood line, avoiding any dead fall and spread out, moving quietly while keeping each other in sight.

As we moved closer to the house, we could see movement in the front windows through the banisters of the wrap-around porch. A porch swing hung down, secured by two lengths of chain bolted to the ceiling. It moved slowly in the breeze, causing a flickering shadow from the lights inside. There were several pickup trucks parked in the drive way in front of the closed garage, but no sign at all of Perkins's Escalade.

We made our way to the side of the house and rolled over the top railing of the wrap around porch, landing lightly on hands and knees and moved one after the other up against the side wall of the house. Looking around the corner to the front of the house, two small windows on either side of the large picture window were open, their curtains moving in and out of view in the cool evening breeze. I slowly moved around the corner and then Eddie and I went to each side of the front windows to listen and look. Through the front curtains I could see six or seven different men sitting in the front room watching a widescreen TV, one or more of them occasionally getting up and moving into another room.

I recognized one of the voices as Perkins's. He was sitting in a large leather chair, a heavy tumbler of brown liquid in his hand. One of the other men said something and Perkins laughed out loud.

"You're right about that," I heard Perkins say. "Can't wait to see that Jew boy's face when he sees you coming at him and he realizes his luck has finally run out. Been a long haul getting to him, but I'm thinking it's probably pretty good to do it right here, this week. A fitting end to this load of crap with him thinking he could win at my course. And then we'll take care of his little friend. Thinks he's hot stuff but we got something for him too."

Perkins laughed after he finished and the other men in the room laughed with him. Then looking around the room he said, "you know boys, when we're finished with that sucker there won't be enough left of him to be proper road kill."

As Eddie and I continued to listen, Perkins voiced his frustration that Moshe was able to play at the Masters at all and he made it clear to his men that with their target in sight, they'd better not let him win the Masters. Then he motioned to one of his men for a refill, and sat back in the chair. I signaled to Eddie to move back the way we had come.

Chapter 70

We got back to the car and looked at each other.

"You ready?" I asked.

"Born ready," he said, with a grin spreading across his face.

"How many did you count?" I asked.

"Three on the couch, Perkins in the arm chair, two leaning against the wall, one sitting on a stool near the television, and one or two in the back part of the house."

"Yep, that's what I got. What do you think?" I asked.

"Thinking it's not exactly even," he said and winked. "Pretty sure you and I have them outnumbered."

With that, we moved to the back of the car and unlatched the trunk. I took out the Ithaca shotgun and Eddie took out a short barrel assault rifle with a large capacity magazine and a silencer attached to the muzzle. I never knew where he got his equipment, or how he carried it around, but he always had an arsenal of weapons at his disposal when he needed it.

"Hey, just saying we have to be cool here." I said. "We can't afford to have any dead bodies around. I expect the local police are likely to be in Perkins' back pocket. So let's stay unseen, maybe put a leg or two out of action, and set them back on their heels a little bit. Sound good?"

Eddie looked at me with knowing eyes. His was a very tough grin. "Of course that's the way it has to be. Because taking them all out now without any provocation would screw you all up. It would bitch your big romance with your own image of yourself - defender of the weak, protector of the downtrodden. I know you couldn't do that to anybody, at least not in cold blood. But that's ok. That's what makes you you. That's what I need to have rub off on me. It's why I like spending time with you Drew. Your humanity. And I need that. Guess that's what ultimately makes us both incurably small time when it comes to unrestrained violence and mayhem. So what do you say we go holler howdy to these good ole boys in our own special way?"

And with smiles lighting up our faces, we again melted into the woods and drifted smoothly back towards the house. I knew well enough that it was much harder to aim for a leg or have a pellet or two hit one of them in the butt than it was to take out the entire room. But the latter could well land us in a southern jail for the rest of our lives. Not that this half-baked plan wouldn't either. But a guy's gotta have his fun.

With a muttered apology to the owner of the house, we eased our way back onto the front porch. Staying out of sight from the windows, we reached up with our weapons and knocked out the light bulbs hanging from the ceiling, pitching the porch into darkness. With the lights burning brightly inside, we'd be invisible to them, especially when they were falling all over themselves trying to get out of the way.

With Eddie on one side and me on the other, we could clearly hear them laughing about past exploits while they drank and cursed Jews, blacks, Hispanics and any other people group they'd grown up hating. When Perkins spoke, there was immediate silence, followed by murmurs of agreement or approval. It figured he liked to be surrounded by "yes" men.

I looked at Eddie and, holding my fingers up, I counted down from five to zero. Then staying to each side of the small windows, we stood and opened up. The Ithaca worked flawlessly. My first shot took out the screen of the window in front of me, as well as, the curtain that had been hanging on either side of it, and as I pumped the next round into the shotgun, I could see the uncomprehending look of disbelief on the room occupants as they froze in place and looked towards the front windows. And then it was mayhem with people scattering to get behind any cover they could find.

Eddie placed shots all around the room, carefully avoiding any serious hits. I put my second shot into the floor in front of the couch and as its occupants pushed backwards upending it, I shot again, catching two of them in the lower legs. Another was headed for the back door, but Eddie hit his foot and he skidded into the wall and curled into a ball. I pumped another round and blew a hole in the ceiling. Plaster and shredded drywall rained down into the room. Eddie hit full auto and stitched a line of holes in the back wall from one side to the other, ensuring that their heads stayed down. Two quick pumps and shots and I blew out the remaining two table lights, plunging the room into darkness.

Eddie and I looked at each other and then together turned around and jumped over the balcony railing. In seconds, we were back in the car, weapons stowed in the trunk, and driving away at a stately pace. I listened for any sounds of sirens in the distance, but all was quiet. We headed for another hotel next to the one Moshe was in. And this time, Eddie registered us with a fake passport.

I thought it very likely that Perkins would choose not to call the locals, given the arsenal of weapons he likely had in the house. Even someone as important as Perkins was in this town would have some explaining to do. And the house had been just remote enough, the action so quick, that we stood a good chance of no one in the neighborhood even hearing it, much less calling it in. So in our new room, coming down off of a serious adrenaline high, we fist-bumped, drank the rest of the beer we'd bought, and talked about the past, content in the notion that, at the very least, we'd incapacitated three or four of Perkins' goons.

Chapter 71

We'd made it to Saturday without incident. After our events at Perkins' place on Tuesday night we hadn't seen him or anyone else with a tattoo on his neck. Eddie and I had followed through with our plan and walked every step next to Moshe. Where it was possible, I was on one side of him and Eddie on the other.

On Wednesday, Moshe had played in the Par-3 contest. It was played on nine holes that encircle two ponds in the northeast section of the course. The contest has been a Masters tradition since 1960, but since its beginning, no Par-3 winner has ever won the Masters. Ray Floyd and Chip Beck came the closest. Each of them took second place the year they won the contest. Moshe came in tied for fourth, so I hoped that was a good sign for him for the tournament.

As I watched Moshe go around the course on Saturday, I marveled at the beauty of his swing. Just like Ben Hogan's, Moshe's swing created a controlled draw that moved his ball in a gentle right-to-left arc, landing within only a few yards off the desired line. Nothing like my dramatic slice, Moshe's draw allowed him to almost always drop his drive exactly where he wanted.

I watched Moshe's swing carefully and saw how he did it. He would gradually cup his left wrist on the backswing, and then, no matter how much wrist he would put into the downswing, the face of the club could not close fast enough to become absolutely square at impact. Just like Ben Hogan, the result for Moshe was a lovely, long-fading ball.

With his perfect swing and his pressure sand shots, Moshe had made the cut for the weekend. He had started out a little shaky on Saturday. On the 1st hole, Tea Olive, his opening shot faded a little too far to the right and hit the bunker, lodging itself in the sand just under the edge of the front lip. He was able to punch it out, but it ended up on the left side of the fairway, leaving a fairly difficult shot into the green. Then despite the common knowledge of the pros to never, ever mess with the left side of the Tea Olive green, Moshe had put it high and left, leaving a long downhill putt for par. Two putts later, he'd lost his first stroke for the day.

Then on the par 3 4th, Flowering Crab Apple, Moshe's tee shot bounded through the green and ended up on the far side of the mound that's a favorite spot for spectators. He had almost no green to work with. He played a delicate wedge shot over the mound, but unlike Sandy Lyle's shot in 1988, which went into the hole for an amazing birdie, Moshe's shot hit the flag on a bounce and caromed into the front left bunker. He was able to get up and down in two, but he dropped another stroke.

As the day wore on, the sky went from being cloudless to being filled with puffy white clouds, and finally, with sharp gusts of wind, large thunderheads began to roll into the area. The golfers hurried to complete their rounds, resulting in higher scores and a tightening on the leader board. Moshe had steadied himself as he moved through the round and ended up birdieing four of the last five holes, leaving him in a tie for fourth place and only two shots off the lead. On Sunday, he'd be in the third to last pairing.

Chapter 72

Sunday dawned bright and clear and I knew if anything was going to happen, it had to happen today. Eddie and I got up, cleaned our weapons, packed our bags, and then picked up Moshe. He looked rested and refreshed and ready for his final round of the Masters.

"Moshe," I said, "this is it. This is what you've worked so hard for. Try to keep all of this out of your head and just concentrate on doing what you do best. Get into your zone and forget about everything else. We're going to be there with you and doing all that we can to keep you safe. Don't worry about where we are, just stick to your game. You may or may not see us, but don't worry. We're always around. Don't let these creeps get you off your game."

"Thank you. You know how important this is to me. You better believe I'll be giving this my all. And of course I know I wouldn't be here now if it wasn't for you. And for Eddie," he said, as he looked at both of us. "So thank you both." Then he looked at both of us. "Let's do this," he said with a firm set to his mouth and a glint of anger in his eyes.

We stuffed his golf bag with our weapons and had no problem getting him and our equipment, into the course. He hit the driving range again, while Eddie and I took a seat in the stands that faced the range, flanking him on either side. We each took a break for lunch and shortly after, he was called by the starter. We shook hands, and he turned and strode purposefully towards the first tee, with me trailing behind and Eddie somewhere off in the crowd.

The course was buzzing with energy as the patrons watched each of the last pairings tee off to start the round. I was anxious enough as it was, expecting anything to happen, but with the vibe flowing around the course, I felt like a junkie high on a meth hit, hearing all the noises and moving my head quickly from one side to the other as I scanned the crowd. My senses were tingling with the same feelings I had when moving through a crowded slum in Mogadishu, knowing my team was being tracked by insurgents from the darkened inside of mud-covered buildings.

As we walked along in the crowds lining each side of the holes, there was a curious grapevine effect. With the leader boards scattered haphazardly around the course, and a delay in new postings, it was hard for the patrons to know what was happening in other parts of the course with other golfers. So as fans would hear roars erupt in the distance, a countless series of questions and answers would swirl from one hole to another resulting in a flow of information that rivaled the gossip trail in any small town. You could hear who was moving up and who was moving down, but the information gap was such that it was always somewhat dated.

Moshe made it through the 1st hole, hitting the green in two and two-putting for par. When he holed out, the crowd yelled for him, urging him on.

I had to work constantly to elbow my way through the mass of people, seeing flashes of green Masters hats, every color of polo shirt imaginable, crossing guards with their arms spread wide, trash collectors with their trash tongs, business execs holding Masters cups brimming with beer, and couples walking hand in hand with collapsible chairs in bags over their shoulders. It was looking like a quintessential Sunday afternoon at the Masters.

In quick succession, Moshe worked his way through the front nine, making birdies on numbers 3 and 7 and par on the rest. As he putted out for par on the 8th, the crowd swelled as word spread around the course that Moshe was one shot behind Phil Mickelson for the lead.

I moved around behind the bleachers that look out on the 8th green, moving towards the 9th tee. Moshe had gone directly from the green towards the tee box. As I cleared the bleachers and caught sight of him again, I was momentarily distracted by a particularly well-endowed red-headed woman wearing a tight green t-shirt with the words "Master This." Then, as I looked back again towards Moshe as he stepped up on the tee box, I saw out of the corner of my eye the flash of a familiar tattoo on the neck of a man moving towards the far side of the tee.

Then it started.

Chapter 73

I recognized him immediately. It was the same guy who played the bongos on my head with his Glock and tried to make my stay in my bathtub considerably longer. He was dressed like all the other trash collectors and he held a trash tong in his right hand and had a bag slung over his left shoulder for trash.

The area around the tee was densely packed with people. He was a good fifteen yards from me, leaving only about a hundred or so people between me and him. When he turned sideways to push his way through the crowd, I saw him pull back on the top of the trash wand and I knew instantly that it was actually a one-shot gun that he'd just cocked. It was the metallic tool that I'd seen sketched in the notebook that fell from his pocket in my apartment.

He moved closer towards the edge of the gallery surrounding the tee box, as I shoved my way through the crowd, pulling on arms and pushing bodies out of my way. There was a sudden roar of noise that came from the bleachers around the 8th green as the group behind Moshe's hit onto the green. I was getting closer to the gunman but I could see I wasn't going to be able to reach him before he got to Moshe. I pushed harder, throwing people to the side as I raced towards the tee box. Moshe had teed his ball up and was in his pre-swing ritual, looking up the fairway towards the 9th hole.

I stumbled through the last few lines of patrons around the tee box, and watched as the man lifted the trash tong towards Moshe, who was in his stance addressing the ball. At that instant, the crowd noise stopped. It was like a tableau set in a wax museum. Moshe held his driver and began his backswing. The man held out the trash wand, his finger beginning to tighten on the homemade trigger. In the perfect silence of the moment, a bird started singing in the pines surrounding the tee.

"Moshe!" I yelled, bursting through the last line of patrons.

I dove through the air at Moshe, grabbing him around the waist and rolling him under me over to the side of the box. At the same time, there was a loud pop, and an explosion of smoke out of the end of the wand gun. I felt the kiss of the shot sting past my arm, as the bullet dug into the soft turf of the tee box. Moshe grunted with the pain of me landing on top of him.

Out of nowhere, Eddie appeared next to the man, chopping down on his extended right arm. With a loud snap of his bone breaking, the man screamed. But moving as fast as a snake, he reached into his bag with his left hand and slashed backhanded towards Eddie, a double-edged Gerber throwing knife glittering in the sunlight in his hand. The knife entered Eddie's upper triceps, as Eddie swung hard with his other hand towards the man's throat. But Eddie's blow didn't quite find its mark. Just as he swung, one of the tournament marshals stepped in between Eddie and Moshe's assailant saying in a perfect genteel Southern voice, "ya'll break it up now," followed by Eddie's blow hitting him square on the side of his jaw and sending him cartwheeling off the side of the tee box.

Had Eddie's blow found its mark, the man's larynx would have been crushed. But the man acted quickly by grabbing a woman and child who were standing watching with wide eyes and open mouths, and pushing them towards me and Eddie. At the same time, the crowd reacted in panic and with screaming and shouting, people pushed in every direction. Some stumbled over lawn chairs, others over people. Hats and beer cups littered the ground. Eddie was down on one knee, pulling at the knife but it was lodged in the bone of his upper arm. I stayed covering Moshe, my .45 in my hand, but there were too many people around for me to shoot. I saw the man shake his head to clear his pain, then snatching up the wand gun, and cradling his shattered right forearm, he pushed patrons and course workers to the side. He stumbled off into the woods beyond the 9th tee and behind the 1st green.

Chapter 74

When order was finally restored, I got up and helped Moshe to his feet. He was bruised and obviously shaken, but otherwise unharmed. Course security had arrived and set out after the attacker.

Eddie acted no differently than if he'd had a hangnail, but it was hard to ignore the knife sticking out horizontally from his arm and the blood dripping down his arm and off of his fingertips. The course marshals escorted him towards the front entrance of Augusta National for a trip to the emergency room, even while he protested that he was fine.

In characteristic Augusta National fashion, with a smoothness and deftness that defied belief, the players were reorganized, the crowds were reformed around the tee box, and play resumed. Moshe looked a bit unsteady, but his tee shot went down the right side of the 9th hole fairway leaving him in perfect position for a short iron second shot.

While Moshe moved down the fairway, I quickly jogged back to the spot where the attacker had fled, but there was no sign of him. Several security men walked back from the woods towards me.

"Any sign of him?" I asked.

"Nothing," they said in unison with a shake of their heads.

The lead man, tall and thin with bright red hair sticking out from his Masters hat, pointed as he spoke.

"There's an old entrance gate back in the trees over there. He must've come in that way. The chain was cut and the gate's standing open now, but there's no sign of him."

I thanked them for their help and went to rejoin Moshe. He hit his second shot towards the green, causing me to think back to my readings about the course. When the course had first opened, what is now the first nine was the second nine. But by the fall of 1934, morning play on what is now the second nine was often delayed because of frost in the shaded valleys through Amen Corner. So the one-year experiment was reversed and Moshe now swung for the 9th green instead of what used to be the 18th.

The 9th green was elevated and slanted severely from the back towards the front. Moshe needed to stick it just right so the ball wouldn't roll off the green and back down into the fairway. I watched as Moshe lined up his shot, then cool as ice he stepped up and swung. His club hit the ball causing an immediate cheer from the crowds, who now were fully behind Moshe since the attack on him. But the cheer turned into a groan as Moshe's shot hit the green, bounced once, and rolled straight into the bunker off of the left side of the green.

Undeterred, Moshe walked up the hill towards the green next to the gallery, glancing over at me and winking. "Put it exactly where I wanted to," he said. "Watch this."

And true to form, Moshe chipped the ball perfectly to the top part of the green and watched it slow almost to a stop, before it turned, gradually picked up speed and rolled faster and faster in a slow arc straight toward the cup. The 9th green was so slick and fast that Sam Snead once said of putting on it that he'd yell "Whoa!" even before he hit the putt. The gallery's cheers rose with a crescendo into a roar, when the ball sped towards the flag and then dropped into the cup for a birdie and a tie with Mickelson for the lead. Moshe shot his arm up into the air in celebration and I finally exhaled, feeling good about Moshe's chances for the first time in months.

Chapter 75

The sun sparkled on the surface of Rae's Creek as Moshe putted out for par on the 11th hole, White Dogwood. He was in the famed Amen Corner, the 11th, 12th, and 13th holes. The tall pines above me swayed in the wind that was so typical at Amen Corner, sending a fine curtain of needles down among the patrons.

Moshe had gotten a par on the difficult 10th hole, which was a par-4 but long enough to qualify as a par-5. He'd played it in textbook fashion, hitting a right-to-left draw off the tee and catching the down slope on the left side, leaving a medium iron from a flat lie. His second shot landed just onto the putting surface, rolling to the left side of the green. He lagged a long putt within a few feet of the hole, and then tapped it in for par.

Moshe now moved towards the 12th tee. I marveled at the beauty of the scene. The depth of the view was amazing, looking across the gentle slope of green grass with Rae's creek flowing slowly past, crossed by Hogan's Bridge, the shaded 12th green in the distance surrounded by Azaleas, with flowering dogwoods over the Azaleas, and towering pines arching over the entire scene.

Hogan's Bridge, topped with artificial turf, cast a perfect mirror image on the surface of the creek, the three stone arches beckoning golfers to cross. The footbridge was named in honor of Ben Hogan, who won the 1953

Masters with a then-record score of 274. It was dedicated on April 2, 1958, with a plaque placed in the ground at the entrance to the bridge commemorating that record-breaking accomplishment and included a statement that his score "may even stand for all time as the record for The Masters tournament." Of course, Hogan's record didn't stand for all time. Nicklaus first bettered it at the 1965 Masters.

The sun shone brilliantly through the pines to the west as it headed for the horizon. With the shadows lengthening, Moshe hit his tee shot. The 12th is one of the most fearsome par-3 holes ever. It's the shortest hole at Augusta National, but the most dangerous. The wind, which gusted in the tops of the trees, was the toughest to figure. Standing near the tee, it felt to me like I was downwind, but as I looked at the Dogwoods around the green, they were waving in the opposite direction. I recalled Tom Weiskopf stating that he'd shot a thirteen on the 12th in the 1980 Masters and never really hit a bad shot.

Moshe's shot was to the left side of the green, which is a few yards deeper than the right and the safer play. I stood just off the 11th green watching him, looking at the beautiful tableau set before me and thinking he was in perfect position for par, and with a nice putt, maybe even a birdie. Moshe strolled down the slope towards Hogan's Bridge, chatting with his caddie in preparation for his putt.

As Moshe approached the bridge, there were shouts off to my right. I saw the gunman from the 8th hole shove a woman to the side and stagger out of the crowd, his right arm hanging limply at his side. In his left hand, he gripped the trash tong gun. Once in the open, he broke into a stumbling run, crossing the 12th tee box and heading down the slope for Moshe. I started to run towards him, but just as I did, a hand from behind grabbed me by my backpack, pulling it down my back and stopping me short. I felt the .45 fall out of my waistband. I pulled forward out of the straps, spun and saw the same man who had shot at me from the golf cart back in October. The tattoo stood out on his neck. He was as big as ever, but his face looked oddly shrunken. His big hands were shaky. His eyes had a strange look, somewhat like the eyes of people who wear glasses when they have their glasses off.

When I turned, he punched at me with a short left jab that I easily blocked, but there was no time to screw around with this guy. Much to his surprise, I stepped into him and head-butted him full in the face, following up with a fearsome left uppercut right into his solar plexus. As he doubled over, I held the back of his head, and kneed him in the face. He went down like a lead weight.

I spun around and broke for the bridge, watching the gunman sway, then lift the gun and aim it towards Moshe, who strode over the bridge unaware of what was happening behind him. Having lost my weapons, I raced over the 11th green and grabbed the flag stick from the hole that had been placed in the corner of the green nearest me. I saw the smoke from the shot before I heard it. Moshe fell to his right, his body spinning from the impact of the round high on his left shoulder. His caddie dove after him as the gunman stopped on the top of the bridge, awkwardly reloading the gun for a final shot to finish Moshe off. I sprinted towards him, watching him slowly raise the gun.

Still thirty yards from the bridge, I had no other choice. Like a javelin thrower in the modern decathlon, I took three steps, planted my left foot and heaved the flag stick with all of my strength at the gunman. In a perfect arc, the flag stick flew through the air, the yellow Masters flag trailing behind like a kite tail. With a sickening crunch, the sharp end of the flag stick hit the man at the base of his neck, the end holding fast in his vertebrae. As I continued running towards the bridge, the gunman dropped his gun, took several staggering steps, and with hands reaching up behind his head to the flagstick lodged in the back of his neck, he tumbled over the low stone edge of the bridge. As the current caught him, he slowly floated face down in Rae's Creek; the flag stick standing straight up with the yellow Masters flag fluttering in the wind.

<u>Epilogue</u>

It was a beautiful early evening in June. The days had become longer and the evenings were mild and filled with the festive dancing light of fire flies. The sun lit up the tops of the trees as the shadows on the ground began to lengthen.

I had called Anne to ask her out for the promised dinner but getting no answer, left her a voice mail. Not wanting to waste this beautiful evening, I was at a new driving range that had opened near Alexandria trying to work on my drive, while I played around with a new range finder for a future review. I thought through my entire checklist then took a swing and watched my ball take its usual hard turn to the right. Pausing before teeing another one up, I thought back to all that had happened since my appointment with Perkins' lunatics at Amen Corner.

Despite his grit and determination, Moshe couldn't play out the rest of the round at the Masters because of his shoulder wound. As expected, Michelson won another green jacket. But being the guy he is, Phil convinced the Augusta National Board to let Moshe have an asterisk honorable mention and a green jacket as well. In the pictures, Moshe had his arm in a sling when Phil helped drape the jacket around him, Moshe's grin wider than I'd ever seen it. I returned to DC and Moshe had returned to

Israel to heal and to prepare him for next year's PGA season.

On the basis of the information I'd given the FBI Special Agent-in-Charge, they opened a major civil rights investigation into the past murders of Jews and started a nationwide manhunt to find Perkins and the rest of his SS Brotherhood. J. J. Gann had finally come forward to describe what really happened that dreadful night long ago in the fraternity house and provided information on all that he'd been blackmailed into doing for Perkins. The United States Attorney in Washington was working a deal with him because of his helpful cooperation.

Even though Perkins was nowhere to be found, the Augusta National Board of directors announced that he had been removed from the membership rolls of Augusta National. The entire affair was front page national news which quickly faded out of the headlines after Perkins was found in a restroom in one of his Southern Grill restaurants. He'd ended his tormented life by sucking on the barrel of a handgun and blowing the back of his head off all over the bathroom wall.

Eddie was upset that I'd had to finish the matter by myself, but after healing quickly, he'd gotten over it and was off on another grand adventure. More than likely, the fabulous steak dinner with plenty of Woodford Reserve bourbon I bought him, Ben Cooper and Steve England didn't hurt. But having seen him again, we'd promised to stay in better touch.

So on another sparkling evening, I found myself still working on my slice. I waggled my club head, tried to relax, and began another swing. As I started the backswing, I heard a familiar voice behind me.

"Hey, Drew."

I turned around to find Anne, looking beautiful in golf shorts and a sleeveless blouse with a bag of clubs standing next to her. It was the first I'd seen her since all the excitement at Augusta.

"How are you?" she asked. "I didn't know you came here, I thought you belonged to a different golf club."

"Hey, Anne. It's great seeing you again. Looks like we've both been so busy that our paths haven't been able to cross. And you're right, I do belong to another club, but I saw this range had just opened and thought I'd try it out. Still working on that terrible slice I have. Moshe did his best with me, but so far, no luck. I've been feeding balls to the right side of the range pretty steadily," I said.

"So I've seen. I've been watching from back there the past few minutes. Want a quick tip?" she asked.

"Listen, I'm always willing to take any suggestions at this point," I said.

"Your grip looks pretty good, but it seems to me that your swing speed is too slow. You might try increasing it by pulling your driver farther back before you start your down swing. That will help close the club face when it strikes your ball," she said. "Give it a try and I'll watch."

I stood there dumbfounded, staring at her with my mouth hanging open. I was speechless. I'd had no idea at all that she was interested in golf, much less knew the first thing about it. I turned in somewhat of a daze and faced my ball, trying to collect myself. I went through my normal pre-swing routine, not a little nervous with Anne watching behind me. I did my best to keep in my normal stance, while concentrating on swinging the club back farther and increasing the speed when I swung. I turned my shoulders, drawing the club head back smoothly, but farther than normal. Then keeping my arms extended out, I turned back towards the ball, the club head closing fast as it hit the ball. I stood and watched in wonder. The ball flew straight, rising slowly in a powerful climb to its apex and then arching gently down to the grass. It had to be over 250 yards and it'd gone straight as an arrow with just the hint of a draw.

I turned and looked back at Anne, my mouth still open in surprise. "That was awesome," I said. "How'd you learn that?"

"You spend enough time watching the Golf Channel, you're bound to pick up something," she said with a smile on her face and a glint in her eye. "I guess you really do owe me a dinner or something now."

"Are you kidding me?" I said, trying to keep the excitement out of my voice. "It's absolutely the least I could do after all you've done for me. Why don't you finish this bucket of balls with me and then I'll drive us to dinner?"

"Sounds like a perfect plan," she said as she stepped to the range mat next to mine.

Later, after a fabulous dinner, a terrific bottle of wine, and a complete recap of Moshe's appointment at Amen Corner, we walked up the stairs to the foyer between our two doors. Seemed like ages since I'd knocked her down right in that very spot and saw in my mind's eye that smoking plane spiraling down towards a fiery crash landing. Oh what a difference time made.

As cool and natural as the golf swings I'd seen her make earlier, she asked if I wanted to come inside and grab a beer with her. We went into her apartment with its cheery kitchen. Grabbing two beers from the refrigerator and handing me one, she leaned back against the sink, elegant ankles crossed, up tilted the bottle and drank until her eyes watered.

Then she looked at me and smiled almost shyly with a look of challenge in her eyes. And then, I could see how it would be this summer. There'd be music and golf, beach and sunburn, smiles and laughs, wine and cocktails and the sometime kiss, and the sparkling green eye look through curl of lashes.

www.ingramcontent.com/pod-product-compliance
Lightning Source LLC
Chambersburg PA
CBHW030028180626
46810CB00001B/264